400

# THE LAST MAN STANDING

Also by Jim Wright

*The Last Frame*

# THE LAST MAN STANDING

## JIM WRIGHT

Carroll & Graf Publishers, Inc.
New York

All characters and incidents in this book are pure invention. They have no existence outside the imagination of the author and are not related to or based on any persons bearing the same or similar names, or to any actual events.

First Carroll & Graf edition 1991

Carroll & Graf Publishers, Inc.
260 Fifth Avenue
New York, NY 10001

Library of Congress Cataloging-in-Publication Data

Wright, Jim, 1950–
    The last man standing / by Jim Wright. — 1st ed.
        p.    cm.
    ISBN 0-88184-744-5 : $18.95
    I. Title.
    PS3573.R53665L34   1991
    813'.54—dc20                             91-23690
                                                         CIP

Manufactured in the United States of America

For my friends

The author wishes to thank N.J. Assistant Attorney General John C. Holl, Police Chief Frank Corkum of the town of Warwick, N.Y., Don and Gail Sampson of the Mount Peter Ski Area, George E. Knight Sporting Goods of Warwick, Lynne Nilsestuen, and Barbara Hoffman for their assistance.

"I worked for newspapers. I worked for newspapers at a time when I was not competent to do so. I reported inaccurately. I failed to get all the facts. I misspelled names. I garbled figures. I wasted copy paper. I pretended to know things I did not know. I pretended to understand things beyond my understanding. I oversimplified. I was superior to things I was inferior to. I misinterpreted things that took place before me. I over- and under-interpreted things that took place before me. I suppressed news the management wanted suppressed. I invented news the management wanted invented. I faked stories. I failed to discover the truth. I colored truth with fancy. . . ."

—attributed to Donald Barthelme

# PART I

# Chapter One

Stuart Reed got the word at six in the morning, during his routine cop checks. The night before, a teenage couple had been necking in the picnic area off Route 10, and the boy had smelled something fetid when he went to drain his bladder of beer. The boy had figured dead deer; the boy had figured wrong.

Using his chin to cradle the phone against his left shoulder, Reed began to input the particulars into the computer. Female Caucasian. Approximately five-foot-three. No positive ID yet. Brown hair. No determination of her age yet. Fully clothed. Black silk blouse, Guess jeans.

Reed's heart began to race. "What about her eyes—what color were they?"

Reed could barely hear Raf Wilson, the desk sergeant, calling to someone, and Reed cupped the phone hard against his ear in hopes of catching some stray information.

After a few moments came Wilson's reply: "Can't say."

Reed sat bolt upright. "What do you mean—can't say or won't say?"

"Stuart, you don't seem to get the picture. The body was probably in the woods for a couple of days. Varmints, vultures, insects—she was down to her sockets when they put her in the body bag. But if you're guessing what I think you're guessing, forget it. I've never worked homicide, but this MO is completely different. Cause of death looks to be a small-caliber bullet in the base of the skull. Textbook drug-related hit. Go back to sleep, or whatever you do at *The Clarion* at this hour."

"When did you hear about the body?"

Wilson stopped to think. "About midnight, just after the last round of cop checks."

"Why didn't you call me then?"

Reed could sense Wilson's voice growing testier. "Stuart, we find a body, we got a million things to do—call the Bureau of Criminal Investigation, get cops out to secure the area. Besides, you can still get it in today's paper, right?"

Reed looked at the newsroom clock. "No way, Raf. This is a dime-cutting operation. We only stop the presses these days for assassination attempts and World War Three."

"Then why do you insist on calling me at this stupid hour every dingdong day?"

"Because that's what journalists do at real newspapers, and I'd like to pretend *The Clarion* is a real newspaper. When I stop believing it, I'll have to move on, and I don't exactly have a résumé that a managing editor keeps on the top of the pile."

"You're talking about ages ago, Stuart. When will you give it a rest?"

"Actually, since you're counting, it's been almost a year. I guess I've been edgy for a couple weeks now, half expecting . . ."

"But nothing's happened, has it?"

Before Reed could stammer out a reply, Wilson continued his mini-lecture. "So then cut the crap. It's over, got it? Like you said a hundred times yourself, the killing stopped when you confronted Jenkins. He wouldn't dare try again. Can't you get it through your thick skull? The murders are fifty miles and a year away. They're history."

"Raf, if it had been you who had stumbled across that girl, you'd feel the same. And the fact remains that Jenkins got away—"

"Drop it, Stuart."

"If I had any balls, I'd—"

On the other end of the line, silence gave way to a metallic click.

Stuart Reed wrote obituaries on the graveyard shift. His place of employment was *The Bradner County Clarion,* a daily paper in the northwesternmost reaches of the metropolitan area of New York City. The area was far away enough from the city to have horse farms and apple orchards and county fairs, and near enough to have gourmet delis, crack babies, and skinheads.

In addition to obits, Reed handled the cop checks, the crank calls from the local mental hospital, and the subscribers' complaints. He was the only person in the newsroom from midnight to seven A.M., and it suited him fine.

A year ago he had been a promising reporter for a bigger paper in Jersey, but he apparently had investigated a murder with a little too much gusto for the executive editor's liking. The editor killed the story and axed Reed.

Now that Reed finally pulled out of his nosedive, he kept telling himself that he'd put the bad patch behind him. But every time he took a call about a homicide, his stomach churned. Although Reed did his best to think of Diana Diaz only in abstractions, the image of that rainy October morning haunted him—the coldness of the ground, the stark whiteness of the body as it lay sprawled like some discarded mannequin in the underbrush.

Reed had no control over when the memory would surface. He could be driving to work, watching TV, running along a country road, and suddenly the image would taunt him. It was always the same. An indelible grainy black-and-white image, splattered red.

For a while, Reed had tried to suppress the memory, but have you ever tried not to think about something? Friends said to confront it, to deal with it, to rationalize what had happened. If he had failed to nail her killer, it hadn't been for lack of trying, they told him. Maybe he hadn't been cut out to succeed in the first place. Maybe it had been impossible. Life was filled with bum deals—brownnosers get ahead, drug pushers get rich, crooked politicians get re-elected. It was the American way.

And if by the yardsticks that others would measure him—job, money, family—he now came up short, he understood that failure was only as permanent as he allowed it to be, and that defeats were victories as long as they developed one's character.

For that reason, Reed considered himself wise beyond his thirty-six years. Yes, he'd made mistakes, but now he knew better. If he had his marriage to do over, he knew what he'd change. And if he ever had the chance to go after Jenkins again, he knew what he'd do different. But that was yesterday's paper, as the saying went, and yesterday's paper was today's recycling nuisance.

Reed pushed his blue swivel chair from his computer terminal, grabbed his plastic Dunkin Donuts mug, and walked to the staff coffee machine. He was too tired to let the murder eat at him once more.

On the burner sat a Pyrex pot containing half-inch-thick molten goo that had passed for coffee in a previous life. Reed flicked off the switch under the burner and walked away—let the dayside jerks deal with it.

Hungering for caffeine, Reed went to the vending machines by the rear stairwell and deposited sixty cents for his third can of Pepsi. He also bought some off-brand peanut butter and cheese crackers, which tasted enough like dirt to ruin his appetite until he could get home and heat up some decent food.

On the way back to the rim, the copy editors' semicircular work table, Reed paused at the bank of windows facing east. Streetlights glowed wanly in the twilight. Commerce Avenue was empty, the morning rush an hour away. A jogger in a bright red running outfit plodded by the gym right across the street and watched his reflection in the windows. Reed studied the man's herky-jerky gait, guessed his weight, and dismissed him—Reed could take the guy in a race. The *Clarion* parking lot was deserted, save for his battered brown Mazda econo-box and the pickup trucks and Camaros of the pressroom crew.

A layer of dew had settled on the windshields, and for an instant Reed mistook it for frost. His lips went dry. He took a sip of his Pepsi, cold and sweet, and wished it were beer.

Reed studied his reflection in the plate glass window. He couldn't detect any new gray hairs, but he couldn't help but notice the network of dark veins just above his cheekbones. He knew that with his gaunt runner's build and his sunken eyes, he had the look of a prisoner fresh from solitary. And—he shuddered—his self-assessment wasn't too far from the truth. But that would change.

# Chapter Two

At seven-thirty A.M., Stuart Reed started up his Mazda and headed home. The radio was tuned to a rock 'n' roll wake-up show, hosted by a pair of loud-mouthed disk jockeys who specialized in crude jokes.

Although Reed found some of the tunes the musical equivalent of a dentist's drill, he left the dial alone. The music kept him awake, and to tune in an easy-listening station was to surrender to middle age.

In truth, he fought getting older at every turn. Sure, he admitted to himself that the days were over that he could drink till 4 A.M. and bounce back a few hours later, but because of the running he was in his best shape ever. He could outrun guys half his age, and did so at every opportunity. Even more satisfying was the knowledge that the guys who were jocks when he was in high school had turned into lard asses living on yearbook memories.

"Wake up, Marshall County. This is Frick."

"And this is Frack. We're the lords of morning drive time. It's seven forty-five A.M. and fifty degrees. It's gonna rain tonight."

"So wear your rubbers if you're going out."

"And your galoshes, right, Frick?"

"Right. Let's play some new Aerosmith for the folks, Frack. That'll pop the lead out of their pen—"

Reed lunged for the buttons on the car radio. He hopped from station to station in hopes of picking up a news report, but all he heard were commercials for car stereos and singles clubs.

Reed cranked the Mazda in third, pushing seventy miles an hour along Route 71A. Time to wind down. He slid a cassette into the dash, an old album by an on-again, off-again British group called Fine Young Cannibals. He always played the tape at this point on the drive home. The lead singer's voice had the same timbre and inflections as Otis Redding, and there'd occasionally be a dash of moody Miles Davis–style trumpet. The music went with the weather, the season, the time of day. His favorite was coming on now, a cover version of the Elvis oldie, "Suspicious Minds."

By the time the song ended, Reed was in the foothills of the

Ramapo Mountains and almost home. Rounding a sweeping curve about a mile before his turnoff, Reed eased it into fourth and let the speedometer drift down to fifty-five. At least twice a week, a cop was planted on a side road up ahead, looking to nail speeders on their way out of town—while commuters merrily went seventy-five miles an hour in the other direction.

The black-and-white came into view, and Reed cruised by at fifty-four miles an hour. He waved and gave his best law-abiding smile. Around the next bend, Reed cranked it back up to seventy. Ahead, the Ramapos loomed. Reed could see the Iron Hollow Ski Area, with its five downhill runs resembling gigantic claw marks scratched out of the wooded mountainside. Reed lived along Iron Hollow Road, a rutted two-lane affair that ended a quarter mile later at the ski area's parking lot. Aside from the occasional lost tourist, Reed rarely encountered other cars and didn't expect to until ski season.

Reed pulled onto Iron Hollow Road and coasted the final five hundred yards to his home, past the long-neglected stone fences and tree trunks darkened by an overnight rain. Several spots in the road were matted with fallen leaves, and he could feel the Mazda's rear tires go into a slide as he made the turn into his gravel drive.

He pulled alongside his small clapboard house at 8 A.M., grabbed several sticks of firewood he'd left by the front door, and went inside. His white cat, Culp, greeted him at the door with a "feed me" yowl, which Reed ignored. In the living room, he flicked on *The Today Show,* then got a light beer from the refrigerator and dumped dry food in Culp's bowl. The house was damp and cold, so he kept his hat and coat on.

He thought about going for a run, but he'd taken a twelve miler the day before, and his calves were still tight. Better to rest a day. He thought about cleaning the room but decided he'd only mess it up again. He thought about starting a fire in the wood stove but decided it was too much trouble. The chimney didn't extend far enough above the roofline, and unless he got the fire going quickly, the stove back-puffed and the smoke alarm screeched. Besides, with any luck, he'd be asleep soon, and the warmth would be wasted.

Although Reed was cold, he went through his daily ritual, fetching a few ice cubes from the freezer, plunking them in a New York Jets mug that he'd gotten with a fill-up at the gas station in Warfield, then opened the light beer.

He filled the mug and opened the freezer. He grabbed the first packaged dinner, removed the foil, and slid the tray into the microwave. He set the dial for eight minutes, then placed the empty box on top of a pile of others on the kitchen counter—a dozen in all. He did some quick arithmetic. Since he averaged two a day, that meant tomorrow was trash pickup.

Reed wondered what Caroline was doing. She had been on a business trip for four days now, and he felt like he'd been out of commission for three times that. What was worse, he wasn't sure how much longer she'd be gone. She wasn't big on communications.

He wondered if Caroline was seeing anybody else on her trip, and wondered if he'd be wise to get started looking around himself, just in case she decided to dump him. Like the old Off-Track Betting ad said, you had to be in it to win it, and aside from responding to Caroline's overtures, he'd become an introvert heading toward recluse status. He'd lost most of his friends when he'd gotten the axe at *The Riverton Transcript*—hell, most of his co-workers had acted like he'd been caught plagiarizing *The National Enquirer*—and working nights and living in the sticks didn't afford him much opportunity to make many acquaintances.

Reed's place was more cabin than house. It had been the family summer home since his great uncle had purchased it in the twenties. The one-story white-clapboard structure was modest—living room, kitchen, bedroom, bath. It did have a nice view of the woods, though, and Reed figured he might do some fishing in the stream behind the house come spring.

Reed had inherited the place after his mother had died last summer, and coming on the heels of the divorce, it seemed to beckon him northward. He moved into the place in July and spent two weeks cleaning it, painting it, winterizing it.

He had even repaired the leaking roof on the shed in the backyard, although he had lost interest and left the ladder propped up between the base of the wild rosebush and the shed. He had meant to remove the ladder and prune the bush, but then he had meant to do a lot of things. And so there it sat, reminding him of all his unfinished business.

When Stuart Reed left his old life, he left the drinking as well. During those two weeks he went cold turkey. Whenever he craved alcohol, he put on his Nikes and a pair of shorts and took to the roads.

If his mind turned in the wrong direction, he picked up his pace, concentrated on how his arms swung, how his running shoes struck the pavement, how his chest heaved under the strain. When that failed, he scanned the terrain for the steepest hill and attacked it until he was too bone weary to think. He'd stagger home, pull the comforter over him, and cry himself to sleep.

At first he hated the hills, hated how they made his legs ache and his throat burn. They were his penance and his escape.

After the first month, the hills got easier and he had to run farther to find terrain steep enough to wear himself out. Then one day he ran to the Iron Hollow Ski Area and started running up a slope that the owners had dubbed the Devil's Apron Strings, named after an outcropping of boulders at the top of the hill. According to legend, the devil had been gathering rocks in his apron when the strings broke—depositing the rocks at the top of the ridge.

The ski trail just below the rocks was so steep and hellish that the name was a perfect fit. Reed certainly thought so as he tried to run up it. The slope rose eight hundred feet over eight tenths of a mile.

The first time he attacked the Strings, he got a hundred yards before he had to walk. The tenth time, he made it three hundred yards. The twentieth time he made it halfway and dropped to his knees, gasping for air.

Instead of turning around, this time Reed stood, caught his breath, and started to run again. When his legs had tightened up so much he couldn't run, he walked. When he was too tired to walk, he moved his legs a step at a time until he could see the boulders. Somehow, he started to run again, beyond the pain, faster and faster, until he reached the road. He was ready to return to civilization.

In mid-August, Reed sent a note to the managing editor of *The Clarion*. The paper gave him a week-long tryout on the copy desk, then offered him a job the day after Labor Day. If the pay was half what he'd made at *The Transcript,* so were the hassles.

He hadn't cared to say why he'd quit his old job, and nobody bothered to ask. There was always room on any paper for a reliable copy editor. One who was willing to work the overnight shift was especially welcome.

Given the circumstances, Reed was fairly happy at *The Clarion*. He was off the bottle, in shape, employed, and virtually invisible. At this point, he couldn't ask for more. . . .

When the bell on the microwave chimed, Reed grabbed the alleged chicken florentine and carried it to an old bleached-pine blanket chest that served as his dining room table. He sat on the burgundy chintz sofa (his ex-wife had gotten custody of the matching loveseat) and ate while Bryant Gumbel and Katie Couric chattered about a new chicken-pox vaccine. He looked at his meal and wondered what the dimples on the chicken were, but dismissed them as harmless.

He sipped slowly from his mug. It still felt strange drinking a beer during *The Today Show,* even though it had been his habit for nearly

two months now. He'd gotten to the point where he could have a
light beer now and again without going off the deep end, and he
considered this a major milestone. He had taken a long time to
realize it, but it seemed that no matter what he did, he hadn't
learned when to stop. It had made him a fast runner and a capable
reporter, but it had also made him a lousy drinker and a lousier
husband.

With the Jenkins story, he had never learned how to stop. He'd
taken his work home, devoted all his energies toward it, to the point
where it was no wonder his wife had moved on. Nature abhorred a
vacuum, and he'd created one in her life. She had merely found a
way to fill it.

Drinking had been the only way to get Jenkins out of his mind,
and now that he'd gotten alcohol out of his mind, he found himself
thinking more and more about Jenkins again. Reed wondered where
Jenkins was at that very moment. What was he up to? What was he
thinking about? Was it time for the killing to start again?

After Reed had finished the chicken, he deposited the plate in the
trash, shut off the TV in the middle of a denture commercial, and lay
down on the sofa. The only sounds were an occasional ranting of a
crow outside, and the constant roil of air bubbles bursting the surface of the ten-gallon fish tank in the corner of the room.

He watched as the four gouramis bobbed to the surface in search
of food, and noticed that the gold one was terrorizing the runt of the
bunch, chasing it from one side of the tank to the other, nipping
ferociously at its tail. Every society, chicken coop or fish tank,
schoolyard or office, had its bully and its weakling. Nothing would
ever change that.

Reed finished his beer, fought the urge to have another, and
turned off the light. A few shafts of light sliced through the gap
between the white vinyl shades and the window moldings, but the
room was dark enough so that Reed couldn't distinguish colors anymore, only shadows and shapes. He threw a lamb's wool comforter
over his head and fell asleep in minutes. He dreamed a new dream.
He dreamed he was in the woods behind his house, stalking Jenkins
as Jenkins stalked a young doe. The dream was in black and white,
flickering like an old silent movie. Jenkins had a rifle.

As Jenkins sighted down the barrel, Reed tried to shout to warn
the deer, but nothing came out of his mouth. Jenkins, unaware that
Reed was behind him, pulled the trigger. In an instant, a chunk of
flesh flew off the deer's left flank and staggered it. The deer regained
its balance and took off toward the stream on wobbly legs. After

forty yards, the doe stumbled, finally collapsing in slow motion beside the still waters. Jenkins turned to Reed and grinned.

The next Reed knew, it was just like the old dream. He was
awake, still screaming, yet unable to utter a sound.

# PART II

# Chapter Three

A year earlier, on a raw October Tuesday, Stuart Reed had discovered the woman who'd changed his life.

The encounter came on his daily late-morning run at *The Riverton Transcript,* where Reed worked as the environmental reporter. The environment was a high-profile beat on a daily newspaper in New Jersey, a state where toxic wastes were the chemical soup du jour and illegal landfills sprouted faster than roadside dandelions. As a result, Reed tried to keep his daily runs as unobtrusive as he could—he'd already taken a raft of grief from the metro desk about his ninety-minute lunch breaks when he had been training for a marathon.

Thus, on mornings when he could spring himself for a run, he'd grab his official blue *Transcript* equipment bag and slip out by way of the rear elevators to the second floor and the pressmen's locker room, where he'd change into his gear. On this day, he recalled the morning chill as he changed into his long-sleeved T-shirt, black Lycra running tights, and red nylon shorts. He grabbed a sweatband and his pair of white painters' gloves from his bag before slamming the thin metal locker door shut.

He looked at his black plastic runner's watch as he left the building: eleven forty-five. If he got a move on, he could reach the track by noon, in plenty of time to run wind sprints with a few of the other regulars. Reed left by a side exit, and decided to avoid running for very long on busy Richards Street. If any editors spotted him there, they'd no doubt assume that he was more interested in running than reporting, and it was futile to try to argue that there was plenty of time for both.

As Reed headed up Richards Street, the cold air presented its usual dose of cotton mouth—car exhausts, factory fumes, the taste of slow death by pollution. The skies were flint gray, and if this were any later in the season, he would have suspected snow was on the way. But this was October, this was north Jersey, and Reed had grown accustomed to worse.

Rain had fallen through the night, a steady downpour, and Reed considered altering his route to the running track at the university.

After long rains, the service road that led past the Department of Parks' shabby gray-green garages and the county police's firing range parking lot was mottled with puddles, and he hated doing his speed work in clammy shoes.

When Reed reached the turnoff for the service road, he looked at his Timex once more. Nearly noon, and that meant risking wet feet or being spotted on Richards Street. He swung right onto the pitted macadam drive, loped easily down the gradual incline past the garages, and hopped over a thick linked chain that blocked the entrance to the one-lane road that led to the pistol range. He darted between the puddles as he went, the star halfback in an imaginary football game that he always won.

No gunfire came from beyond the twenty-foot-high embankment of red clay behind the firing range. Attendance there, like for the sporting events at the university, was totally dependent on the weather.

The tricky stretch of the run was around the corner, just past the range. A three-yard-wide thicket of mud and chest-high weeds separated the range from a complex of low-rise office buildings and classrooms that sat by the river.

Reed was using his forearms to push through a sheaf of brambles when his feet tripped over something and sent him sprawling—through the last of the thorny branches and onto the roadway beyond. He clambered to his feet and inspected the damage. He'd ripped through the Lycra tights on his right knee, and the front of his running shirt was covered with gravel and flecks of dead leaves. The palms of his white cotton gloves, which had absorbed most of the fall, were a soggy gray. And the front of his left Nike, the one that had caused him to stumble, was smeared red. He must have cut his foot during his fall, he decided, but none of his toes hurt.

Then he looked into the weeds from whence he came.

He'd never seen such a scene before—in books, yes, and in a few police photos, but never for real, never up close. He diverted his eyes, clenched his hair, fought back a momentary urge to vomit.

No time for weakness. He had to get help. For an instant, he considered taking off his shirt and draping it over the body before him, but he resisted—he knew that nothing could be touched until the police arrived.

The next thing Reed knew, he was sprinting across the parking lot toward the first office building and nearest telephone. A breeze off the river whipped past his face, making his skin burn. He rubbed his left cheek with the back of his glove, saw blood, and realized he'd nicked himself on the brambles when he'd stumbled over the body. He pushed it from his mind.

Pumping his arms stride for stride, Reed sprinted to the entrance of a smoked glass and brick office building. He took the three front steps in one bound, swung open the glass double doors, and headed toward the reception desk. The woman behind the desk was so startled by Reed's sudden arrival that she sat frozen with her mouth agape and a nail-polish applicator between her fingers.

Reed commandeered the switchboard phone and called *The Transcript*. He reached Claire Green, his assignment editor, and blurted out what he'd found.

As he dialed 911, a hand clamped Reed's right bicep. He swung around to see a thickly built older man in a gray uniform.

"Put down the phone, buddy," the man said evenly, and Reed realized it was a security guard. "Don't start trouble."

"A woman's been killed."

The guard brandished his pistol. "The one who scratched your face?"

Milt Roberts, a *Transcript* photographer and Reed's occasional drinking buddy, was on the scene in five minutes.

"Harry got me on the radio," Roberts explained. "Said you had a cat up a tree for me." *The Transcript* photographers liked to talk in code over the two-way radio, in case another newspaper or a New York TV station was monitoring the conversations.

"Thought you might have trouble finding this place."

"Nah—I shot the mayor at the pistol range the day it opened. So where's our stiff?"

Reed pointed toward the bushes. "I found her in there." Then added sadly: "I hope you haven't eaten in the past couple of hours."

"That bad?"

Reed fought back tears. "See for yourself."

Roberts pushed the clump of weeds aside and inspected the body. He put the Nikon to his face and squeezed off a couple of frames, then stepped back. His face was white. "No point wasting film. I don't think we can print anything from here. Too disgusting for a family newspaper."

Reed was amazed by how calmly Roberts took it.

"Believe me, I seen worse. I used to be assigned to Paterson." Roberts was playing the part of the tough streetwise photographer, but Reed could see from Milt's eyes, and the sweat on Milt's temples, that he was disturbed by what he had seen.

Roberts checked his watch. "Wish the cops would hurry up and get here. I gotta be at my next assignment in fifteen minutes."

"How are the cops going to help you?" Reed asked.

"I can shoot 'em looking into the weeds. Hey, I gotta come back with something."

As Roberts fiddled with a light meter, a Chevy Caprice squad car whipped around the corner of the office building. They parked twenty feet away, and two officers in deep blue uniforms got out. Reed motioned to them and pretended he didn't recognize Kulecz, the taller of the two and a self-important cop who'd written Reed a speeding ticket the week before.

"Officers, I'm Stuart Reed of *The Transcript.* I reported the body. I was on my morning run when I tripped over her." He pointed toward the clump of weeds.

The cops pushed past. Reed called after them: "Look out for the thorns. I cut myself pretty bad on them."

The cops ignored him. Kulecz shouted at Roberts, who was snooping around the weeds, and told the photographer to get the hell out of there. Kulecz stepped past Robert's, looked down, and jerked his head away. The other cop had the sense not to look.

When Kulecz had regained his composure, he was all business. "You with the camera, get out of here. This is a crime scene. And you"—Kulecz pointed at Reed—"you get in the squad car. Now."

"How bad is it, Sam?" The other cop asked.

Waving his arms, Kulecz strode toward the squad car. "We got a butchered body on our hands. I think we'll be handing this one off to the county boys."

"What do you want with me?" Reed stammered.

"I said to get in the squad car. We'll have to take you in for questioning."

"But I have to file a story."

"Better make it good."

# Chapter Four

Stuart Reed spent most of the next two hours waiting at the violent crimes unit's office for somebody to take his statement. He was the only person in the county building annex wearing shiny black running tights and a long-sleeve crimson T-shirt, and more than a few passersby eyed him as though he were some sort of newfangled male prostitute. Whenever he caught them staring, he glared until they looked away.

Reed had hoped to glean some information about the body from the homicide detective who took his statement, but the detective had allowed no room for small talk from the moment he escorted Reed into a small interview room off the reception area and motioned him to sit in a chair with an orange molded-plastic seat. The detective sat across from him at the table.

The detective flipped through a few sheets of white paper in a manila file folder, and when Reed started to ask a question, the detective simply held up a flat palm like a traffic cop.

While Reed waited, he tried to get a measure of the detective. Reed was a firm believer in first impressions. He studied the detective and saw a man about twenty-seven, maybe thirty, six-foot-three, two-hundred twenty pounds. Slightly balding with black hair combed so you weren't supposed to notice. Maybe some Golden Gloves training, judging from the flattened nose that dominated his ruddy face. Neatly pressed white cotton shirt, striped tie, and a slightly shiny brown suit. He wore a rectangular blue plastic nametag that read Aldo Cippriani, Violent Crimes Unit. Reed's first impression was that he was dealing with a prick.

"Young to be a detective, no?" Reed ventured.

Cippriani finally looked up, expressionless. "Yeah, and you're old to be running around in tights. Anybody read you your rights?"

Reed sighed and rubbed his eyes with the thumb and forefinger of his left hand. "Gimme a break, officer. I discovered the girl's body, and I called the police. That's the extent of my involvement. That's all I know."

"Where were you before four and eight A.M. today?"

"Asleep in my apartment in Manhattan."

"Got someone who can corroborate that?"

"My wife."

"Fine. You usually run near the firing range?"

"It's on my way to the track at the university."

"That area's off-limits to civilians."

"I pay my taxes. The public owns it."

Cippriani glared at him and continued. "How often do you run past there?"

"Three times a week."

"Ever see anybody around there that looked suspicious?"

"No, but I move along at a decent clip. I don't usually see much, maybe a cop or two taking target practice if the weather's nice, but it's really out of the way for anybody else."

Cippriani clicked his ballpoint and wrote something in the margin of one of the sheets of paper. "And what do you do for a living?"

"I'm a reporter for *The Transcript.* I was hoping you'd have some information about the girl for me."

Cippriani ignored him. "Ever seen her before?"

"No."

"What do you think happened?"

Reed folded his arms across his chest. "I don't know. Some sicko abducted her maybe. Cut her up. And then dumped her back there."

"What makes you think that?"

"Just guessing. Why, what do you think?"

Cippriani ignored him again. "What kind of gum you chew?"

"I don't chew gum when I run. I don't chew gum, period. Why, did you find any at the scene?"

"You'll have to ask our public information officer."

"Come on, what did the forensics guys find at the scene? Gum wrapper, shoe prints, tire tracks, cigarette butts?"

"You'll have to ask the public information officer."

"And who might that be?"

"You're the reporter. Find out yourself."

"What's the problem, you new here or something?" Reed blurted.

"You're the reporter. Find out yourself."

With that, Cippriani closed the folder, stood, and said: "I'll type up a formal statement and have you sign it later. We'll call you if we need more."

Cold and tired, Reed returned to *The Transcript* at three P.M. and changed into his street clothes, then headed straight for the metro desk to see Claire Green.

"I'm back," he announced with a hint of urgency. "I'm ready to take over the story on the body. Who's been working it for me, and what do they have so far?"

Green turned toward him. The faint smile on the corners of her lips disappeared when she realized Reed wasn't kidding. "Stuart, are in you shock or something?"

Reed furrowed his brows. "How's that?"

"The stiff is not your story. I passed it on to one of the cop reporters, and he'll handle it." She returned to her computer screen.

Reed leaned on the battleship gray filing cabinet next to her computer terminal. "But it's *my* story. Finder's keepers. If I hadn't found the body, we wouldn't have a story."

Green wasn't convinced. "Somebody would have found her sooner or later. You can't write the story because you're part of the story. I don't have to tell you that."

Reed tugged at his tie. "I can't believe this. I do my job day in and day out, writing about waste-transfer stations, illegal ocean sludge dumping, tertiary treatment plants, plus all the garbage I can eat—and I do so without complaint. But when I stumble on a real juicy story, you take it away from me. What kind of message are you sending to your reporters?"

Reed looked to see if anybody else was interested in his plea, but he didn't see any takers. A typical day in the newsroom was like a pro basketball game, picking up intensity as it went along. Three o'clock was akin to the start of the fourth period. Computer terminals that had gone begging an hour earlier were now in high demand, and reporters fresh from the field were jockeying for VDTs so they could input their stories before the first copy deadline at five-thirty.

Reed tried the humble approach. "Please, Claire."

She stood. "Don't be an idiot. It's not on your beat." Then: "I have to go to a meeting."

She walked past him, toward the news conference room. He wheeled and followed her, arguing into her ear. "OK, I know I can't write the story for tomorrow's paper, but what about the follows? Maybe I can help get an ID on this girl if we can't get one tonight."

When Green didn't reply, Reed kept pressing the issue. "I feel obligated here. If you'd been there, if you'd found her, you'd want to find out who she is and who the hell did that to her. It's going to be a great. . . ."

Green walked into the conference room, which was already half filled with editors. Reed stopped at the entrance. Reporters were not allowed in the room. "You'll see," he called.

Reed turned and scanned the newsroom for Dick Black, the assistant editor who supervised the cop reporters. Black stood at the copy machine by the pneumatic tube to the composing room.

"Dick, who you got handling that body that was found by the firing range?"

"Julio Jones."

Reed bit his lower lip. Jones was the last reporter Reed wanted to work with. It was another depressing turn in what had become a thoroughly depressing day.

# Chapter Five

A daily newspaper reflects the personality of its executive editor. If the editor is a former statehouse bureau chief, for instance, you'll probably see plenty of political stories on page one. If the editor has a Harvard MBA, there'll be plenty of financial news. It's never been determined for sure whether this is because the editor asserts his or her own preferences outright, or whether the editors below figure they'll further their own careers by playing up the type of news that should please the boss.

The executive editor of *The Transcript* was Pritchard Majors, a former army man who'd fought the good fight with *Stars and Stripes* in Germany, and who'd had the good sense to marry Constance Quince, daughter of Lawrence Quince, who owned, among other holdings, *The Riverton Transcript*. The other holdings included two magazines and three television stations in the northeast. The glamour that went with them had caught his fancy, and *The Transcript*—which had been in his family for five generations and had once been treated as a sacred trust—had become but one more profit center for a mini-media empire.

Majors had signed on with *The Transcript* five years earlier as assistant managing editor. Ten months into the job, he had taken over the paper in a bloodless coup after the executive editor committed two unpardonable sins. The editorial department went ten percent over budget for the previous fiscal year, and the paper had lost a well-publicized two-million-dollar libel suit to the US representative for the neighboring district.

As a result of a tip, the paper had run a front-page story that the representative had been caught in a nonlegislative caucus with a seventeen-year-old page. The indictment fell through when the page suddenly turned over a new leaf before a grand jury. The congressman claimed that the paper had been gunning for him because his politics were too liberal, and the disclosure had caused him not only great embarrassment but also defeat in the June primary.

With lightning-quick moves, Pritchard Majors mounted an offensive to take command of the paper—he had dinner with his father-in-law and explained how he could save the old man a lot of money if he ran the newsroom. His father-in-law was impressed enough to put Majors in charge.

Majors' first staff meeting set the tenor of his regime. Just hours after his predecessor graciously cleaned out his desk and left to become senior editor of *The Transcript*'s smaller sister to the west, *The Bulletin,* Majors assembled the troops and announced that hence-forth all staffers would follow his orders, foremost of which were to dress correctly, meet all deadlines, and avoid unnecessary expenses.

The result was predictable. A handful of bright young reporters deserted, the rest of the troops grumbled, and the paper went from spunky if erratic to bland and predictable. Deadlines were seldom missed, the operation ran like clockwork, and the editorial floor soon had the feel of a large insurance agency. Most men in the office figured that "dress correctly" meant khaki slacks, button-down shirts, and conservative ties, although a few ambitious souls went so far as to wear shirts with epaulets, in hopes of being promoted to lieutenant. Many of the women in the office followed suit as best they could, favoring attire one step up from flight attendants.

In all, *The Transcript* had become a grim tour of duty. Page one had more international news, particularly items about NATO, and *The Transcript* graphics department soon had seven thousand dollars' worth of official Jane's guides to the world's military arsenals so that when an Iraqi fighter jet strafed a Saudi tanker, the paper could run a front-page graphic that showed the type of plane, the right size tanker, and the exact US naval vessels that were steaming toward the Mediterranean (as the wire services invariably described the maneu-ver).

By attrition, the staff had become homogenized—like a baseball team that was stocked with good-fielding, light-hitting shortstops. Few reporters were encouraged to swing for the fences and hit jour-nalistic home runs anymore, dinking out singles day after day in-stead.

Julio Jones—"the man with the dueling Js," as he was known—was half Cuban, half English, and one of the few remaining rene-gades. Jones, who refused to respond to either "Julio" or "Hulio," was unpopular with management for two reasons. He had that dreadful curse known as the Bad Attitude because he constantly challenged his editors' news judgment and assignments. He'd also taken to snapping to attention and saluting all ranking editors when he passed them in the hall.

Then there was Jones' appearance. Jones weighed about an eighth of a ton and stood six-foot-three, topped by a brambly black beard that he trimmed every *cinquo de Mayo*. His wardrobe consisted of black leather motorcycle boots, faded Wranglers ripped at the knee, a green Sears Roebuck work shirt, and a US army field jacket with a large embroidered patch that read, "Heaven won't take me, and Hell's afraid I'll take over."

Majors no doubt would have fired Jones long ago had it not been for the fact that Jones was a minority reporter on a predominately white-bread staff. It didn't hurt that Jones was an excellent cop reporter. He'd won several awards for stories on a pattern of police brutality against local blacks and Hispanics, and he had earned a reputation for going out and investigating cases himself when the cops were too busy or too uncaring to follow up themselves.

Still, Jones was considered a loner and certainly not the kind of reporter you wanted to team with. Thus, it was with a sense of foreboding that Stuart Reed approached him about the fresh corpse.

"Julio, you doing anything on that dead body I found by the police firing range?"

Jones kept pecking away at his computer keyboard.

Reed tried a different tack. "Jones, you do anything on that dead body?"

"Yeah," Jones grunted. "It's worth a brief at best. Not much to write about."

"Got a name yet?"

"Nope. A Jane Doe."

"Cause of death?"

"Medical examiner's probably checking now."

"Time of death?"

"Get real. Nobody knows that stuff yet, and it's usually a guess at best anyway."

"Mind if I help you on the story?"

"Don't bother. One of the cops was taking bets that it was an Eighth Avenue hooker who'd been free-lancing on her pimp."

"That doesn't add up, Julio."

"Let's get this straight. I go by 'Jones,' and I don't need you to tell me how to cover my beat. And in this case, absolutely nothin' adds up."

"Can I see a copy of what you filed?"

"Why?"

"I talked to Claire, and she said that I could help on any of the follows, seeing as I have a special stake in all this."

Jones sat at his terminal and called up a copy of his story. "If it's OK by her, it's OK by me. I got better axes to grind than this."

Reed read over Jones' left shoulder.

## NEEDS LATE COP CHECK
### By Julio R. Jones
### Transcript Staff

RIVERTON—The battered body of an unidentified young woman was discovered yesterday behind the police department firing range at about 11:30 A.M. yesterday.

Police said the nude body was that of a Hispanic woman, approximately 100 pounds, 5 foot 2, age 18 to 22, with dark brown hair, brown eyes. No distinguishing marks.

According to police, *Transcript* staff writer Stuart Reed discovered the body on his daily jog. County detective Aldo Cippriano said that it appeared that the woman was killed elsewhere a few hours earlier and then dumped at the site. Police have no suspects. They ask that anyone with information on the case to call the County Prosecutor's Office at 555-5899.

"Well?" asked Jones.

Reed scratched his chin. "A few things. One, I'm not really a jogger. I'm a runner. Second, you have two 'yesterdays' in the lead. Third, I think you got the detective's name and title wrong. And finally, I wouldn't describe the body as battered. I think 'mutilated' is the word you're looking for."

"Cippriano said not to use the word 'mutilated.' "

"I think it's 'Cippriani,' with an 'i,' and what are you getting at?"

"They sometimes fudge some of the details in cases like this because of all the cranks. Sometimes it makes it easier to nail the suspect. Besides, one of the other cops I talked with said the body wasn't mutilated."

"Julio, I found the body. Believe me, she was mutilated."

"I didn't say the woman wasn't sliced, *amigo.* I said she wasn't mutilated."

"You lost me."

"Well, to me, mutilation implies some sort of arbitrary slashing job . . ."

"And?"

"The cop said it looked like someone began to dissect her."

"Dissect?"

"You know, like a dead frog in your average high-school biology class. Sliced down the middle, chestbone to navel."

Reed gasped. Earlier, he had been too nauseated to look closely at the body. "Are you serious?"

"Let me put it this way. The cop said this was the first time he'd seen a body in that condition that didn't have webbed feet and smell like formaldehyde."

The image brought Reed back to the moment he first saw the body, and again he fought the overpowering urge to retch. He placed his right hand on his forehead. It felt hot. He started to get dizzy, and leaned on the desk to steady himself. Once Reed had regained control, he asked one more question. "So, Jonesy, what are you saying here?"

"I'd say the cops are hunting a surgeon or a veterinarian maybe, or . . ."

"Or one sick butcher."

# Chapter Six

That night, Stuart Reed arrived home a few minutes after ten-thirty; he'd promised Jeanne he'd be home by nine. Home was a one-bedroom apartment on East Eighteenth between Second and Third. They'd lived there for ten years. The ad in *The Sunday Times* had said it was cozy (tiny was more accurate), convenient (to the methadone clinics south of Fourteenth Street perhaps), and reasonable (if you were independently wealthy). But once they'd settled in, inertia had taken over, and now Reed wondered if they'd ever move. There were far worse places to live in Manhattan, and for far more rent.

Jeanne had talked again last week about starting a family, but Reed had put her off—Manhattan was no place to raise a child, and Reed wasn't ready to move to the suburbs and marry a thirty-year mortgage. He hoped that she would let the subject drop for a few more months, at least until spring, when he'd apply to the *Times*. If he latched on there, moving would be out of the question.

Despite the hour, finding a parking space required three trips around the block, and even then he was forced to settle for a spot by an overflowing dumpster on East Fifteenth. He tried to decide if the spot's proximity to the dumpster made it safer or more dangerous, then realized he was wasting his time. Thieves had ripped the radio out of the Jetta's dashboard months ago. Reed had never bothered to replace it, and the center of the dashboard still sported a gaping hole. At any rate, the Jetta no longer gave crack addicts a reason to break in, and the only thing Reed worried about anymore was bums using the car to sleep or urinate in when temperatures dropped below freezing and the winds picked up.

On his way to the brownstone, Reed stopped by the deli around the corner and bought a single long-stemmed red rose, in the likelihood that Jeanne was sitting home fuming over his late arrival. As he rounded the corner onto their block, he looked to their apartment for any signs of life. Reed detected the glow from a reading light in the living room, and maybe a hall light. Too little to go on.

When he reached the front entrance, Reed checked to see that no one was behind him, then worked his keys in the two locks, eased

the door open, then locked it behind him. He checked the mailbox
—empty—and unlocked the interior door with yet another key, then
climbed the moss green carpeted stairs to the third floor. Although
he wasn't sure why, he walked on tiptoe, as if returning from an
unsuccessful all-night poker game.

Reed unbolted the three locks on the apartment door, leaving the
Medeco for last. The door slid open with a turn of the knob, and he
threw the quarter-inch-thick deadbolt up before turning and calling
the standard "Hi, honey, I'm home" in a voice a few decibels above
a whisper. He walked down the entryway past the darkened kitchen
alcove and into the living room, where Jeanne was curled up on the
sofa. She wore a negligee that Reed hadn't seen before, iridescent
white satin with a lace bodice that barely contained her breasts. She
had tucked her feet under the throw pillows for warmth.

Next to her was the coffee table, a lobster trap they'd bought on
their honeymoon in Maine twelve years before. The thick slab of
glass atop the trap held an open bottle of Spanish champagne, the
pewter ice bucket, and two slender crystal glasses. One glass was
unused. The other was half empty.

Reed bent and kissed Jeanne's shoulder. She didn't respond. He
leaned over to kiss her chest where her fading tan met the soft white
flesh of the tops of her breasts, then got a sudden shiver—the
woman by the firing range had been sprawled in pretty much the
same position. In the dead silence of that room, Reed realized that
the moment he'd found the body would stay with him always. He
knelt by his wife and stroked her long chestnut brown hair, thankful
she was alive and mindful that twenty-odd miles away, lying belly-
up on a slab in the medical examiner's workroom, was a woman
who probably hadn't been all that different from Jeanne or any other
woman, save for the fact that she had picked the wrong bar, worn
the wrong dress, parked in the wrong space, or trusted the wrong
man.

Reed decided that he needed to sit down, and perched himself on
the coffee table. He tried to put the cork back in the champagne
bottle, but like the rest of the day's events, he couldn't manage to
undo what had been done. He tore the thick black lead foil from the
neck of the bottle and molded it over the top. He lifted Jeanne's
glass. The wine tasted flat and watery, not far from day-old beer.
Reed removed the lid of the ice bucket to see a few small lumps of
ice floating in water, and realized that Jeanne must have opened the
bottle much earlier, when he said he would be there. But he'd been
late, and she must have poured herself a glass, then fallen asleep
waiting for the late Mr. Reed.

On the bookcase, the little red light on the front of the stereo glowed. Jeanne must have put on a CD, and he walked over to the stereo to see what she'd selected. "Every Picture Tells a Story," by Rod Stewart. They used to play the album while they made love in Reed's room in college. Reed sighed at what might have been if only he'd gotten home on time. Missed moments. Because of what he'd seen that morning, life now seemed so fragile, so fleeting, so final.

Reed dumped Jeanne's watery champagne into the ice bucket and poured himself a fresh glass. It, too, tasted spit warm, but at least it had bubbles, at least it had life. He shook his head to shake himself of his languor. How long would he let this get to him? Maybe not until they caught the guy who did it, he thought, maybe not ever.

When he finished the glass, he massaged Jeanne's shoulders, then kissed her on the lips and whispered, "Time to go to bed."

She fought to open her eyes. "What time is it?"

"Late," Reed answered.

"I'm sorry. I tried to stay up but . . ."

"Go back to sleep. I'll carry you to bed and tuck you in."

Jeanne rubbed her eyes as Reed slid his arms under her. "Did you say something about a story, or did I dream it?"

Reed whispered that they'd talk about it in the morning, and lifted her against his chest. She wrapped her arms around him, and her bare skin felt inviting. Traces of musky perfume hung in the air as he carried her to the bedroom. He lay her gently on top of the double bed and covered her with the white quilt his grandmother had made as a wedding present for his mother too many years before. The thought occurred to him that the quilt would still be his if he and Jeanne ever separated, and in the stillness of the moment he realized for the first time that the marriage might be over. Tears welled in his eyes.

"Are you coming to bed now?" she asked in a bleary monotone, and fell back to sleep before he answered.

He thought of waking her, of sliding the nightgown's silken straps off her shoulders and nuzzling up against her breasts, as though clinging to her would banish his thoughts, would make things right between them. But he feared it was too late.

Reed undid his tie and draped it over the closet doorknob. He took off his loafers and socks and flipped them under the bed, then walked barefoot toward the living room. He stopped in the kitchen to grab some ice from the freezer, flicked on the CD player again, then sat on the sofa. He hoped the cushion would be warm where his wife had slept, but her body heat had faded. He put the ice in a glass, then poured the champagne gingerly, so it wouldn't fizz over the rim.

He sipped slowly, letting the events of the past twelve hours wash over him. By the third glass, the images of death had begun to recede, gradually becoming blurred black-and-white photographs, then vanishing altogether as he drifted off to sleep. On the stereo, a gravel-voiced Rod Stewart sang a ballad. On the kitchen counter lay the rose, shrouded in tissue paper.

# Chapter Seven

Come morning, Stuart Reed sat down at the breakfast counter to read the *Times* and sip instant coffee. Jeanne had finished her daily grapefruit and tea before Reed had awakened, and she now stood with her back to him, working her way through an assortment of plates and glasses in the sink.

"Leave 'em, Jeanne. I'll get to 'em as soon as I put down the paper."

"It's no bother."

Reed detected a distinct frostiness in her voice. "Look, about last night . . ."

"Skip it. Incidentally, I never got the chance to tell you, but some cop called last night about six."

Reed looked up. "Why didn't you call me at work?"

"He wanted to talk to me. He wanted to know where you were between midnight and eight A.M."

"What did you tell him?"

"I told him the truth." Her voice had a sarcastic edge. "I told him you were here, snoring."

She still faced the sink, and all Reed could see was a pink-and-white quilted bathrobe and her mane of freshly combed hair.

Reed tried to salvage the morning. "Your hair looks nice, long like that."

"It needs to be cut."

"Are you mad at me?"

She rinsed a wineglass, placed it on the drainboard, then turned toward him. "To be honest, last night I felt just like I did that time you stood me up when we first dated."

"Jeez, that's dredging up the past, isn't it?"

"You asked how I felt."

"But it wasn't my fault then, and it's not my fault now."

"Don't get hostile, Stuart. Face it. You screwed up. I was so anxious to see you last night . . ."

"Eager anxious or nervous anxious?"

"Stop with the semantics. Don't lecture me on how words have subtle shades of meaning, or any of that crap, because all you're doing is evading the issue. Do you know how I felt when you stood me up that night, years and years ago? I thought, Would you look at that? We've been dating for three months and he's already taking me for granted. And the reaction is the same this morning. Somewhere along the line we've stopped being husband and wife and become roommates instead."

Reed tossed the newspaper onto floor. "Honey, you're overreacting. You know how much I love you. It goes without saying."

"That's part of the problem. Too much goes without saying anymore. What are we doing together? Where are we headed?"

"I'm sorry. I'll try not to be late again."

"You didn't answer me." She folded her arms and glared at him.

"Honey, it's"—he glanced at his watch—"it's eight-thirty. This is hardly the time—"

"Forget it, Stuart," she interrupted. "We'll talk about it when you're ready. But we've got to do something. We've fallen into a rut."

"I wouldn't mind rutting with you right now." He knew that the comment had clanked before it was out of his mouth.

"Stop it."

Reed tried to think of something to please her, appease her, and suddenly remembered the rose. "You know, I bought you a rose last night, and I can't seem to think where I put it."

"You left it on the counter."

"Then you found it."

"Obviously."

"Then where is it, the bedroom?"

"I put it in the trash."

"You chucked it just because you're mad at me?"

"No, Stuart, not just because of that. You left it out. You didn't cut the stem and put it in water. You don't take care of things, they die."

Her point did not escape him, but by the time he reached the Transcript Building that morning he had more pressing matters on his mind.

# Chapter Eight

Stuart Reed timed his arrival in the newsroom perfectly on Wednesday morning. As he hung his gray herringbone sports jacket on the metal coat rack by the front elevators, he spied Claire Green entering the city editor's office for the ten-thirty news meeting. At *The Transcript,* the only thing done with true efficiency was meetings—the ten-thirty meeting was an unofficial meeting of assignment editors, designed to make sure that everyone was on the same page for the eleven-thirty news meeting. There, from what Reed had heard, the next day's paper would begin to take shape and the executive editor would hold court, asking his usual raft of questions and generally making his underlings' lives miserable.

Buoyed by the thought that Green might be out of his hair for at least a few minutes, Reed went straight to his desk. He logged on to his computer and read his electronic mail. The first note was a universal message—one that went to everybody on the system— about new stylebook additions. The second note was from Claire Green, reminding him to update his list of nondeadline stories by five P.M. that day. He skipped over the next message, even though it was from Pritchard Majors, because it looked like the twice-monthly everybody-clean-up-your-desk note. Instead, Reed's eyes jumped down to a note from his buddy Clancy Collins, who'd been working night rewrite of late.

> Yo, bro.
> FYI. Production boys were less than thrilled with the story you filed last night. Said the story didn't support your lead, etc., etc. But you already knew that. At any rate, they fobbed it off on me to fix up, which I did. They were still pretty pissed about it and wanted to fire off a note to Claire Green, but I talked 'em out of it. I say all this for two reasons:
> 1. Better get on the stick, because you're getting a reputation with the night crew as being a sloppy writer.
> 2. Better bring your wallet next time we go out beer drinking, because you owe me, buddy. You owe me quite a few.
> Cheers,
> Clancy

Reed scanned the rest of the messages, then stored them as a new file. He opened his red leatherette appointment book to see what he had going for October 28. On the appropriate page was scribbled some information about a conference, two P.M. at the Expressway Hilton. He turned to the computer again and called up the budget for the next day's paper. Sure enough, Claire Green had already entered a budget line for him, entered for page three:

CLEANAIRSR (Reed)—Coverage of the Friends of the Earth conference, "Clearing the Air about Pollutants"; looking for local angle. Developing. 50 lines.

It would be a nothing story, about a nothing conference, a story no worse than countless others that filled newspapers across the country every day. But it would shield him from last-minute grenades—general assignments like a story on what the best-selling Halloween costumes were so far this year, or the arrival of the latest *Farmer's Almanac,* or the city fire commissioner announcing the winners of the grade-school poster contest for fire prevention week.

What's more, the environmental conference would free up his morning to work on follows to the mystery body story. Reed turned to the latest edition of *The Transcript* and flipped through the news section in search of Jones' story. No luck. He leafed through the regional pages. Zip. He skipped the living section and sports in favor of the last section, a pot-luck serving of financial news, editorials, obituaries, classifieds, and stories that didn't find a home elsewhere. Jones' story was at the bottom of the page that faced the obits.

DEAD WOMAN FOUND NEAR FIRING RANGE, the headline announced in eighteen-point type, the smallest permitted by the stylebook. The story itself didn't appear to run more than three inches. Reed didn't read farther, for fear of getting more exasperated.

He inhaled deeply, until air seemed to fill his stomach, then he slowly exhaled. He'd learned to breathe that way to calm himself before a major race, to keep himself from hyperventilating while the official issued final instructions to the runners. He found that the deep breathing helped calm him when he was under any sort of pressure, and he also found himself using it more and more—at work, during his commute, at home. Relax, his mind whispered, but his emotions wouldn't listen.

The moment he saw Claire Green leave the news meeting, he sprang to his feet. "Claire!" he shouted across the newsroom, and headed toward her clutching a copy of the paper. "Claire, did you see where they played the dead body story?" For emphasis, he slapped the newsprint with the back of his hand.

"Yes, I saw it. What did you expect? You get a dead body story, you bury it."

"That's a big story—a woman found murdered."

Claire Green's reply sounded half wistful, half impatient. "I wish that it were big news when a body's found, but it's not. Not even when a star reporter like yourself trips over it."

Her sarcasm wasn't lost on Reed, and he was glad when she changed the subject. "More important than dead bodies are live stories. What you got working today?"

Reed clumped the newspaper into a big ball. "Why bother asking? You already put it in the budget—that ecology conference at the Hilton."

"That's this afternoon. What you got working this morning?"

Reed had expected the question, since she asked almost every day, and he responded with a list of Mickey Mouse stuff—expense reports, time cards, a letter to the state DEP to request documents. Reed stood, tried to gauge the heft of the wad of paper in his hand, and took a mini-jumper at a metal wastepaper basket ten feet away. It caromed off the rim and landed two feet away.

Green smirked. "And your enterprise budget. I mean it."

"Yeah, yeah. And I'll be upfront with you. I'd like to make a few quick calls about the dead girl."

When Claire Green started to go into her official lecture about sticking to one's own beat, Reed deflected her with a promise to keep the calls short.

"Look, what's your exposure here?" he argued. "If nothing turns up, then we've only wasted a few minutes of my time. But if it turns into something big, then we'll sell a lot of papers."

Claire Green responded that naked corpses may sell copies of papers like *The New York Post,* but not *The Transcript,* where words the likes of "naked" and "battered" rarely found their way past the copy desk, let alone onto page one.

Reed realized he was getting nowhere, so he simply said thanks, as if she'd agreed to let him make the calls, then walked away before she said no. Back at his terminal, he shot off an electronic message to Julio Jones via the computer: "Any more on the dead girl?"

Jones's reply appeared on Reed's CRT screen moments later. "Nope. Still naked. Still dead. Buzz off."

Reed started to take deep breaths again. Had to keep cool, had to stay on Jones' good side, had to cultivate him if Reed wanted to keep the story alive.

He walked to Jones, who was sitting at his terminal, his feet propped up on his desk. Reed managed to catch Jones' eye and forced a smile. "Jones, don't get me wrong. The reason I asked about the girl is I want to help. I'll call the cops for you and let you know if I hear anything, OK?"

"Yeah," Jones grunted. "You want to waste your time, be my guest. Just don't get the cops any more pissed at me than they already are. But let me give you a word to the wise. Don't be so damned lazy. You want something from the cops, pay 'em a visit. They hate giving out stuff over the phone."

"Good idea. Know anything about Cippriani that might be of help when I talk to him?"

Jones stared out the window for a few moments, and Reed couldn't decide whether Jones was thinking of a reply or daydreaming about something else altogether.

"Jones?"

"Yeah, I'm here. Just trying to describe him for you, so you know what you're in for. He's new, so he's probably not crooked yet. He does things by the book. Got an advanced degree in criminology or something and let's people know it, so he's not exactly Joe Popular at the cop shops. You don't shit him, though, and he don't shit you."

"I already met him. Anything else?"

"Don't get too psyched up about this case. A Sherlock Holmes he ain't."

# Chapter Nine

The city of Riverton (population 70,000) was an anomaly, a sprawling urban area with ghettos and low-income housing projects plunked down in the middle of one of New Jersey's wealthiest counties.

Since its beginnings as a trading settlement on the banks of the Oritani River in the early seventeen hundreds, Riverton had always been an immigrant town. Over the years, its complexion changed with each new wave of arrivals. Dutch, then English, then central European, then black, and now mostly Hispanic.

To each group of first- and second-generation Americans who had landed in New York City and saved enough money to seek a better life, Riverton represented the first stepping-stone toward the middle-class American dream—to escape the tenements for a place of their own, even if it meant a mortgage larger than the patch of yard in front of their semidetached homes. They worked hard, saved their money, and then made the jump to the suburbs beyond—selling their houses to the next group of newcomers.

For nearly two centuries, Riverton had meant jobs in the factories and mills along the Oritani. In the fifties, the factories began to close, unable to compete with cheap imports and the cheaper labor available elsewhere, and the stepping-stone turned into an urban island cut off from the suburban mainland that surrounded it.

Aside from the brick town houses within walking distance of the university and the legal hub at the north end of town, most of the housing stock in the area reinforced the notion that you lived in Riverton only when you couldn't afford to live anywhere else.

The only business that continued to grow was the business of county government, and the workers who profited from it lived elsewhere. In recent years, Riverton's main drag bustled only during the day, and then only on weekdays. Most of the storefront businesses—luncheonettes, video rental stores, shoe repair shops, hair cutters, newsstands, office supply stores—catered to commuters who worked in the county buildings and offices during the day and beat a swift retreat to the safety of the nearby suburbs come dusk.

The shopping district lined Main Avenue for nearly a mile, with the county courthouse, the county administration building and annex, and more than a dozen attorneys' offices clustered at the north end of town, by the commuter college and the interstate.

The farther you progressed south on Main Avenue—it was a one-way, two-lane street that led out of town—the more blighted the buildings became. The other end of the avenue was known simply as the district, the bad part of town, filled with auto repair and body shops, taverns with boarded-up windows, pawnshops, and bodegas.

Main Avenue after sunset might as well have been midnight. The sidewalks were deserted. The stores were padlocked shut. The only signs of life were the reflections of passing headlights on the shop windows or an occasional hooker who wandered out of the south-side taprooms when business was particularly slow.

As Reed walked up Main Avenue toward the county building annex, he thought of the district and wondered if the dead woman had been a hooker who climbed in the wrong man's car, but something inside told him no—even in death, she didn't look hardened enough to work Riverton's meaner streets.

Reed's progress along the narrow boulevard was slowed by cars and pedestrians. The digital clock on a pole outside the bank read 10:37, 50 degrees, and Reed figured that he must have hit the avenue at coffee-break time. To his left, a magazine shop was packed with customers. In one long line were people queued up to buy state lottery tickets. In front of the next cash register, a string of people stood with newspapers, candy bars, and takeout coffee. Across the avenue, two window dressers were putting up Christmas decorations next to the Halloween display in the five-and-ten, and Reed shuddered. Autumn, barely arrived, suddenly seemed all but over.

To avoid the sidewalk congestion, Reed walked a block west, off the main drag. A few minutes later he arrived at the county building annex, a square three-story building with a fake stone face and glazed yellow brick sides. Until two years before, it had served as the administration building, but the politicians had finally gotten themselves a shiny new glass and steel headquarters in the new county court complex, and the prosecutor's homicide detectives quickly claimed the old place.

The first thing they did was stake out all the parking spaces in a two-block radius as their own. Next they converted the old county courtroom into a rec room, replete with two Ping-Pong tables and a pool table they'd confiscated in a raid. Newsroom cynics joked that turning a court into a rec room was symbolic of the way justice had deteriorated in these parts, and Reed suspected that they weren't too wide of the mark.

Reed reached the annex at ten-forty-five, and a secretary directed him to a set of stairs that led to the second floor, where the detective bureau took up two-thirds of the space. Reed was told that Cippriani's office was just inside the violent crimes section, and Reed relaxed a little when he saw that Cippriani's door was open. Reed rapped on the doorjamb and leaned into the doorway. The room smelled of stale cigarette smoke. Cippriani sat facing him, behind a gun metal gray desk piled with paperwork in sloppy foot-high stacks.

"Got a minute?" Reed said with a reporter's best smile.

Cippriani stared blankly at Reed for a moment, then waved his index finger at him. "I got it. You're the guy who found that girl's body—Reed, wasn't it?"

"That's right. Mind if we chat for a few minutes?"

Cippriani looked at his watch theatrically. "You're a reporter, right? You here on your own or on business?"

"Does it matter?"

"I'm tight on time. If this is business, then I can spare a few minutes."

"It's business then."

"You don't sound so sure."

"Just cut me a little slack. A few minutes is all I ask."

"OK, but it'll still have to be brief. I'm up to my elbows in forms and reports, and they have to be done by noon."

Reed took a seat before answering, to let the detective know he wouldn't be rushed. "To be completely up front with you, I'm here unofficially, but what I learn from you may well find its way into a story. I'm interested in who the dead girl was, how she died, who killed her. Anything you want kept off the record, you got it. And whatever I can do to help you . . ." Reed flipped open his notepad, to let the detective know that this was on the record unless he was told otherwise.

Cippriani grew restive and replied that he didn't need help from the press, nor did he need to spend his time talking to a reporter. "We're still trying find out who the young woman was. She doesn't match up with any missing persons reports, either local, state, or New York metropolitan area. We got no clothes or wallet or jewelry or anything to trace her with. Hell, the ME's office said she didn't even have any cavities, which makes trying to match dental records a huge pain in the ass."

Reed scribbled frantically on the notepad. "Cause of death?"

"At this point, we go off the record. Suffocation, apparently."

Reed closed his writing pad. "Suffocation? Looked to me that she was filleted with a Ginzu knife."

"She was, later, but don't take my word for it. You can come back at five or so, when the ME's office drops off the autopsy. I'll give you a peek—off the record—but at least you'll have the official word, and you won't be wasting your time on second-hand information."

"Search of the crime scene turn up anything?"

Cippriani began rooting through the papers on his desk, finally finding what he was looking for in the In basket. "Look, tell you what. I'll give you all the stuff I have on this thing—not for publication, of course—and you can sit at the table over there and sift through it to your heart's content."

Reed's eyes brightened. "Fine. Can I ask you some questions when I'm through?"

Cippriani handed the folder to Reed. "Like I said, you're better coming back at five when I can tell you all the good stuff—time of death, what she had for dinner, any evidence of sexual assault, needle marks. . . ."

The report weighed more than Reed had expected, and he felt his heart race as he sat on a folding chair and lay the report open on a beat-up oak table that had the look of a hand-me-down from the city library.

Page one was the uniform crime report, which resembled a loan application. Reed opened his reporter's notepad again, then went over the report line by line. It contained little he didn't already know, since most of the form was blank—nameless victim, one not too enlightening witness (himself), no suspects, no vehicles, no clothing.

The second page was a preliminary report from the evidence technicians at the scene, and it, too, was on the scant side. They'd found no fingerprints, tire tracks, or any sign of a struggle. They'd made plaster casts of four partial footprints, three of which belonged to Reed's pair of size eleven Nike Wind Runners. The other was from some sort of rubber boot (a note said that a photograph of the print was attached).

Also found: one old candy wrapper, a small wad of pink chewing gum, and three soggy cigarette butts, all Marlboros. The report said that none of it was likely linked to the woman or her killer.

The next page was the statement Reed had signed the day before.

After that came the reason the file was so thick—eight-inch by ten-inch glossy photographs of the victim and the crime scene. The photos were in color, grainy and overdeveloped, with a purplish hue that made them seem even more macabre. Reed saw photos of similar quality at *The Transcript* all the time—the film and prints had been run through automatic processors. The up side was that you got the photos quickly. The down side was they looked as though they'd been stored in a hot attic for two decades.

In the photos, the woman's flesh had the appearance of polished marble—cold, motionless, milky white. Sweat formed on Reed's temples. He flipped through the pictures until he got to the print of the rubber boot tread. The tread looked familiar. Reed thought he had boots with a similar tread. He mentally ran through the shoes on the floor of his closet. Yes, his L. L. Bean duck shoes, which he kept in his car to dodge the puddles in the parking lot at the Transcript Building. They had that same row upon row of parallel chainlike treads. He jotted it in his notepad. He leafed through the papers once more, then stood and tapped on Cippriani's doorway again.

Cippriani looked up from his paperwork: "So, Mr. Reed, what do you think?"

"What I think isn't important. What do you think?"

Cippriani looked at his watch again. "What I think we have here is a hooker who was probably picked up in New York City, probably by some sicko in a van, who suffocated her, carved up her stomach to get his jollies, and dumped her on this side of the Hudson, just off the interstate.

"Further, strictly between you and me, I think we're probably drilling a dry well here. In solving almost any crime, there are two key elements. First and foremost is the information provided by the victim or witnesses to the crime. What we have is a dead victim and —no offense—no witnesses worth squat. The second element, usually linked to the first, is the speed of the investigation. The first few hours are crucial. The longer it takes to develop leads, the worse our chances are. It's geometric. It's been over twenty-four hours already . . ."

"Where do you go from here?"

"The next step is to get the autopsy and toxicology reports, add them to the folder, and give it to the chief, who will determine how high a priority we put on it."

"Meaning what?"

"Well, it is a murder investigation, like I said. That means that officially it will remain active until it's solved, but don't hold your breath. It all depends who the corpse belonged to. Since it's a homicide, it'll be top priority for a little while, no matter what. If the corpse turns out to be some suburban kid, it'll stay on the front burner a lot longer. I know that sounds callous, but that's the way it is. The squeaky wheel gets the oil, and the richer you are, the louder the squeak."

"Any predictions?"

"Maybe we'll get lucky. Maybe someone will come forward with information. We have two investigators showing a photo of the dead woman's face to people in the area—the university, the office buildings, bars. Maybe someone will recognize her.

"If we don't get lucky, my guess is this gets quietly plunked in what I call the SUC bin. Short for "suspended unsolved cases." We've had a hiring freeze for a year now, and we just don't have the manpower to spend on marginal cases."

Reed interrupted. "But—"

Cippriani talked over him. "I know, we have a murder here. We'll keep looking into it, following up every lead. But the bottom line is we have jack shit here, and when we eventually ID this woman, we'll still probably have jack shit. So unless we come up with a similar MO in other murders . . ."

"What about the boot print?"

"Got any idea how many boots have soles like that? What do you suggest, a door-to-door search from Paterson to Poughkeepsie?"

Reed suddenly felt heavy, like a deflated basketball, and he trudged out of Cippriani's office a disconsolate man. He sensed his story, his primo shot at the big time, was about to be buried in a stack of files in a storage room somewhere.

Instead of running during his lunch hour, Reed went to the Pasta Depot, a small bistro near work, and had a burger and a mug of beer. He thought of the afternoon ahead, and ordered another brew.

# Chapter Ten

In the warehouse district on the western outskirts of Riverton sat a drab one-story stucco building the cops called the body shop. Most locals knew it as the morgue, but the name in foot-high burnished aluminum letters by the glass double doors out front was its official title: County Medical Examiner's Office.

It was the place where the county's recently expired were taken in an effort to determine what had made them permanently horizontal. When any death occurred without an attending physician, state law required an autopsy be performed within twenty-four hours of death or the discovery of the body.

The mustard colored building sat at the front of a square lot, with a row of diagonal parking spaces on both sides. In the back, the ground had been carved out to allow a macadam driveway to curl its way down one flight to a windowless garage door.

The first floor housed an antiseptic reception area, a viewing area, four offices, and a huge records room. On the lower level were a refrigerated body storage room, three autopsy rooms, and a supply room. Connecting the two floors were stairwells front and back. A freight elevator ran between the body storage room and the viewing area, where the bodies were identified by next of kin.

Bodies entered through the delivery entrance in the back. Upon their arrival, the bodies were stripped, placed on large stainless steel carts, shrouded in pale blue disposable sheets, and wheeled to the storage room to await dissection.

Aldo Cippriani arrived at the ME's office at three that afternoon in hopes of learning about the life and sudden death of a young woman found dead in a clump of goldenrod and briar by the Oritani River.

Ordinarily he would have stayed at headquarters and waited for the afternoon courier from the ME's office, who usually dropped off autopsies and other paperwork at half past four, but one of the lessons Cippriani had learned at detective school was that cases that attracted media attention needed special handling.

The appearance of a well-run investigation was nearly as impor-tant as the investigation itself, and if a detective sounded stupid or lackadaisical or uninformed in the local press, the prosecutor would raise hell, and the department would spend more time dodging flak than getting its job done.

Ordinarily, reporters made cop checks over the phone twice a day. When a reporter appeared in person, the rule was to get on the stick. Cippriani also learned from his classes on media relations that a reporter with a fresh story was like a four year old with a new toy. Once the novelty wore off, it was forgotten.

Cippriani reckoned that this was how it would go with the reporter from *The Transcript.* The guy was interested only because he'd found the body, and he'd move on to other stories if the case seemed to be moving along—or going nowhere—by the book.

Thus, if and when this jerk Stuart Reed called later this afternoon, Cippriani would be able to say that he'd been to the morgue, talked to the assistant ME who did the autopsy, and gone over the findings top to bottom. Reed would grin to himself at the "top to bottom" line, write down the information he needed, and be gone.

After Cippriani showed his ID, a secretary buzzed him through the interior glass door that separated the reception area from the offices. The security measure was there not to stop body snatchers but to prevent youths from sneaking in and stealing pocketbooks, which had become fairly common in the area now that crack had become the intoxicant of choice among the local youth.

The secretary was a bleached blonde, slender, about thirty, with Mediterranean features, and Cippriani flashed a smile as he walked past her desk. He glanced at her left hand. On her ring finger was a small gold band set with three red stones. That could mean anything from a friendship ring to an engagement ring from a cheap suitor, but as Cippriani ambled down the hall he decided it was open season and made a mental note to stop and chat with her on the way out. Even if he didn't score, at least he'd have another name to call when he needed a favor.

Halfway along the carpeted corridor, Cippriani was greeted by a fairly stout Hispanic woman in a knee-length white lab coat. Her gray black hair was tucked in a bun off to the side, and her face was barren of makeup. Cippriani figured that when you worked with stiffs all day, there was no reason to get dolled up.

The woman introduced herself as Dr. Silvera and ushered him into her office, which wasn't much bigger than his own. "Take a seat and look these over for a minute, then ask all the questions you want," she said. "Can I get you some coffee?"

The thought of warmed-over morgue coffee made his stomach heave, and he quickly declined. He perused the autopsy report, which had been filled out in neat blue ink block letters. The gist of it was that the unknown woman was in her late teens, that she died of asphyxiation, that the lacerations on her chest and stomach were post-mortem—all of which he'd heard over the phone.

"Feel free to ask questions," she reminded him.

"OK. I'm confused by the description of the incisions."

"You're clear on the point that the incisions were made after death? The victim's heart had already stopped when the cuts were made, or she would have lost a lot more blood. The tissue samples we took confirmed this. What I found when I examined the cuts, though, was that they were done with two instruments."

Cippriani stiffened in his chair. "Run that by me again."

"From the nature of the incisions, I've concluded that two instruments were used. The skin was cut smoothly, by a scalpel or a razor blade. The deeper lacerations, through the muscle and tissue, were made with a thicker edge. I'd suspect a knife was used, most likely a hunting knife."

"Have you seen any corpses with similar cuts?"

"No. I haven't really had a chance to ask the other two assistant MEs, though. I wish I could tell you more, but to be honest, yesterday was not a good day," Silvera continued. "I don't know if you heard, but the mayor's brother-in-law died of a heart attack in a compromising position at a local motel yesterday morning, and, well, you get the picture. I was pulled off this autopsy to get the mayor's in-law processed and shipped to the funeral parlor."

Cippriani asked to borrow a sheet of paper and a pen, then began writing down Silvera's comments on the two blades. He spoke as he wrote. "The report says she died of asphyxiation. What's that mean —strangulation, suffocation?"

"The latter. We found petechial hemorrhages—tiny flecks of blood in the eyelids—which suggests acute asphyxia. We found no ligatures, no bruises about the neck. We're not talking carbon monoxide, by the way. We're looking at something as simple as a pillow over the nose and mouth, or something like a rag shoved down her throat."

"But there was no sign of a struggle, right?"

Silvera looked at her report. "We found several small contusions on her neck, but nothing to indicate she was strangled. Plus there was no foreign blood or skin under her fingernails, and no sign of sexual assault, no semen anywhere."

"Any sign of a condom?"

"No traces of any lubricant, so I doubt it."

"Time of death?"

Silvera let out a long breath. "As you know, that's always a crap shoot. At least when you know who the victim is, and when they had their last meal, you can make an educated guess. But her stomach had been cut open and cleaned out. We did find some food in the intestines, fairly well along in the digestive process, but that's meaningless. Based on the degree of rigor mortis and the temperatures two nights ago, I could take a guess, but I'd be lying if I gave you anything more precise than, say, between midnight and six A.M.— and like I said, that's a guess. But the body was remarkably intact. If she'd been out there very long, the muskrats and river rats would have gotten to her."

"We figure she was killed somewhere else and dumped there."

"That would make sense."

"And since we doubt anybody dumped her off in broad daylight, we'd have to figure it was before six-thirty A.M. Your comment about the condition of the body means she wasn't out there long. So she was probably dumped just before dawn."

"It was raining, though, wasn't it?" She thought out loud. "I'll see when it stopped."

Cippriani ran his fingers through his hair as he tried to think of what to ask next, and how to ask it. "Too many question marks here, to my way of thinking. I don't like the cuts or the fact that the stomach had been cleaned out. I can't get a bead on any of it. Did she eat some weird dinner that we could use to connect her with the killer or something?"

"I just process 'em and leave the detective work to you. But I don't know of any murder being solved by what the victim had for dinner."

"How about this: she wrote the name of the killer on a piece of paper and swallowed it."

"Like I said, I leave the speculation to you." Silvera closed the report and put it aside. "It's a one-way street. If you catch the guy, maybe he can explain it. But I doubt if you can come up with an explanation and then use it to lead you to the killer."

Cippriani started to ask another question, but Silvera interrupted. "Not to be rude, but it's almost quitting time and I still have a lot to do."

"OK. One last thing. I didn't see any record of needle marks."

"Right."

"What about the blood tests? Alcohol, drugs?"

"Negative. The breakouts on the blood are on the last page."

"Can I take that with me, along with a copy of the autopsy? And I can call you with any more questions, right?"

She nodded, and he stood to leave.

In the parking lot, Cippriani sat at the wheel of his white Ford Escort and wrote the following on his yellow legal pad:

- See if anyone in area of offices, campus, firing range noticed any vans between 5:30 and 6:30 A.M. Tuesday, October 27.
- Do a computer search for similar MOs.
- Follow up on footprint.
- File what you've got into one report first thing tomorrow and fax it to the FBI in Quantico.
- Call Sally D'Ambrosio for a date.

Cippriani placed the notepad on the seat next to him and turned the ignition key. As he drove to headquarters, he visualized the pictures of the dead woman and decided to have a vegetarian dinner.

At five-ten P.M., Cippriani got the call from Stuart Reed. He told Reed that the investigation was moving along as fast as possible, but that it was hindered by the lack of a positive ID. When the subject turned to the autopsy, Cippriani took command, going over detail after detail. Cippriani mentioned that the woman had no dental cavities again, figuring that was the kind of detail that would appeal to a reporter. He didn't tell Reed about the double incision—that might get him pumped up. He tried the joke about going over the body with the assistant ME "from top to bottom," but Reed didn't respond.

Still, Cippriani felt the call went well. He'd answered all the reporter's questions and sounded self-assured. When Reed asked for the autopsy off the record, however, Cippriani faltered for a moment, then mumbled something about making him a photocopy. It was a no-win situation. If he refused, he'd pique the reporter's interest. If he gave Reed the autopsy, he risked the reporter finding out about the cuts, which would pique the reporter's interest even more.

Before hanging up, Cippriani threw Reed a little mind zapper. "By the way, you really ought to take a few days off. When you see a body as badly cut up as that, the way you did, it affects you without your even knowing it. I'll leave the autopsy at the front desk. It's pretty standard stuff—nothing you haven't heard already—but you're more than welcome to it. If you're really certain your stomach can handle it."

# Chapter Eleven

Stuart Reed never liked dining at the Chinese restaurant next door to the pet shop, but the evening was cold, the place was only two blocks from the apartment, and he couldn't beat the price. Jeanne had offered to treat.

She seemed to be over her morning snit, and Reed had decided against rehashing the night before. After they ordered, he took her hand in his and gently massaged her palm with his thumb. Sitting in rush-hour traffic earlier that evening, he had vowed to be conciliatory and attentive, but already his thoughts were drifting back to the police detective and the dead girl.

Jeanne was recounting her day at school. "Inez came in with her baby," Jeanne said, and he nodded as though he were listening.

"You remember me telling you about Inez," she explained, then paused while the waiter placed a pot of tea and ceramic handleless cups on the white tablecloth. "I had her in my fourth-grade reading class two years ago. Bright kid. She came in today with her month-old baby, and all the other teachers were gushing about how beautiful the baby was—right there in front of the other kids. I guess I must be a bitch, but I refused to make a fuss. Then, later in the lounge, Trudy and Yolanda said they thought it would be nice if all of us pitched in and got the baby a gift, and I just blew my stack."

A strand of hair slipped down across her forehead, as was its wont, and she brushed it back unconsciously. She looked in Reed's eyes to see if he were still paying attention, then continued. "Was I wrong? I don't have anything against Inez or her baby, but what happened is terrible. Inez is twelve. She's too young to raise a baby. She's too young to quit school. Twelve years old, and her life is wrecked.

"The other teachers—even Lois—couldn't stop talking about the baby, and why didn't I want to see it. I let 'em have it. I said, yeah, real cute baby. A baby who will be attending PS Sixty-four before her mother finishes high school. Maybe, I added, mother and daughter could walk to class together.

"The teachers said I was just jealous because I don't have my own child, but I don't believe that. You don't think so, do you?"

Reed seemed distracted by something, then started to get up.
"Crap, I'm sorry, honey, but I have to call the office. I forgot to give
Julio Jones the information I got from the cops today. I hope he's
still there. It won't take more than a minute."

He slid out of the red vinyl upholstered banquette and walked to
the pay phone toward the back of the narrow dining room. When he
returned to the table, she was on her second helping of lo mein.
Reed joked about being able to look into the kitchen from the pay
phone, and seeing the cook prepare poodle gai pan.

Jeanne Reed was unamused. "What was that all about?"

"The dead girl. I got some more info about the body today, and
I'd forgotten to pass it along to the other reporter. Then the metro
desk corraled me to answer some questions on the story I filed this
afternoon."

She wondered why it couldn't wait till they got home.

He sensed her irritation and apologized, adding, "Did I tell you I
got a copy of the autopsy?"

"Yes, Stuart. You told me once when you got home, and once on
the way over here."

"You ever see an autopsy?"

Jeanne shook her head no.

"I can show you when we get home."

"Stuart, I'm trying to eat my dinner. And I might as well eat as
talk, because I've been wasting my breath talking to you."

"No you weren't."

"Then what was I talking about?"

"School."

She began to tap her fork on the dinner plate. "Go on."

To buy some time, Reed poured some tea into the two cups and
took a sip. "Tea's getting cold."

"You haven't answered my question. What did I say?"

"You said Inez brought in her baby, and you were pissed."

"And what do you think?"

"About what?"

"About a twelve-year-old girl bringing a baby into this world.
What kind of life is that baby going to have?"

Reed tried to calm her. "You shouldn't take your work so seriously."

She glared at him, the kind of glare that would de-ice a twenty-
pound roast. "I guess you mean that teaching isn't important, is that
it? At least not serious like working for a daily newspaper. I mean,
it's OK that you let dinner get cold while you talk to another reporter, but my job—"

"Forget that I mentioned it." As he spoke, he sensed that no matter what he said, he'd only make her angrier. He had to shut up and let the storm blow itself out.

Sure enough, she jumped on the latest comment. "What do you mean, forget it? Why? What you do is more important? Do you know how far apart we are this moment? Do you have any idea? You're upset because a life has been taken, and I'm upset because a life has been created. Well, I don't give a flying fig about your dead body, because it's dead and done with, and from what you say, the killer will never be caught. Let's worry about the living."

Against his better judgment, Reed went into a sermonette about the need to investigate the murder, lest the killer go unpunished.

She responded that Reed was supposed to be an environmental reporter, not a cop. Cops got paid to find killers, and he would be wise to let them do their job without butting in.

"I guess I'm not explaining myself right." He took a sip of cold tea. "I have to confess that there's a selfish motive involved here. Once, maybe twice in a reporter's career, a story comes along that can win awards, make you a star—change your whole career.

"I want to work for the *Times.* I'm not a woman or a minority hire, and there are a thousand other good white male reporters who want to work for the *Times,* too. So I can cover toxic spills and sludge and illegal landfills well into the twenty-first century and I'll still never get a job at the *Times.*

"But yesterday might change all that. When I stumbled over that girl's body, I stumbled onto a story, *the* story. A story so big that it might put me in the big time. On the way home tonight, I realized that the guy who dumped that cadaver never expected it to be found so soon. I mean, it was dumped in the bushes behind a firing range that probably won't be used again till spring. How many other bodies have been carved up and dumped in out-of-the-way places, and chewed up by animals, and nobody ever found out about the cuts? I think those cuts were the killer's signature, as sure as he'd signed his name. He never thought anybody'd ever get to see them."

Jeanne started to say something, but Reed was getting worked up. "Just hear me out now. I have this feeling that if I handle this story right—ask the right questions, interview the right people, think real hard—I will take a nothing story, an insignificant three-paragraph police brief, and turn it into a page one story that will win awards and vault me straight to the *Times.*"

Jeanne Reed took her red linen napkin from her lap and placed it by her dinner plate. "And on the third day, Stuart, you will ascend into newspaper heaven and sitteth on the right hand of Punch the publisher almighty, where ye shall judge . . ." She broke into a grin.

"Enough."

"Or maybe the skies will part and you'll be beamed straight up to the promised land. I can see it now—the assumption of Stuart Reed, patron saint of ace reporters."

She slid out of the booth and stood. As she put on her overcoat, she turned serious. "I think, as you'd put it, that you're pissing into the wind."

Jeanne Reed turned in early that night, having made it clear on the way home that she didn't wish for her husband to join her in the bedroom. That suited him just fine. He still had the autopsy to go over, and he didn't feel very attracted to her at that point anyway. So after she retired to the bedroom, he got a cold Miller from the refrigerator and sat at the kitchen counter. Before him lay the autopsy, a latter-day Rosetta stone for him to decipher.

After a while, he took out a notepad and jotted down a few questions. Some of the medical jargon on the photocopied report baffled him, and he made notes to himself to ask for clarifications on several points. He was confused by the term "petechial hemorrhages," and the description of the cuts. The autopsy implied that maybe two blades were used. What were they?

As he read through the autopsy, he developed a sense of urgency. The story was going cold. In a day or two, it'd be forgotten by the cops, the newspaper. He also sensed that something in the autopsy wasn't right.

He got another beer, then went through the form again, line by line, until a one-syllable word jumped off the page.

In the box marked "eye color," the medical examiner had printed "brown." Julio Jones' story had said the same thing, but Reed hadn't really thought about it. Now, though, Reed remembered the frozen expression on the girl's face—those vacant blue eyes—and he knew somebody was dead wrong.

# Chapter Twelve

In Pritchard Majors' three-year reign as executive editor, *The Riverton Transcript* may not have become a better newspaper, but Majors' subordinates all agreed that Majors had made a significant impact in the three areas that he had targeted.

The editorial department was consistently under budget, the staff dressed better, and meetings—like Mussolini's trains—ran right on schedule.

Thus, at three P.M. sharp on Thursday, October 29, down to the very tick of the second hand on Majors' gold Rolex, the afternoon news meeting commenced. Although Majors sat at the head of the oval conference table and began the proceedings, he usually passed the leadership role to Claire Green, who had kept tabs on the wire services and the stories the metro reporters were working for the next morning's paper, and therefore could best brief the production editors and graphics department on where various stories should run in the paper, what kind of photos and graphics were needed for each, and when the various elements had to arrive if all deadlines were to be met.

Majors usually limited his participation to an occasional question, usually along the lines of "Anything libelous here?" "Have you run this by the lawyers?" and "Do we really want to go with this story?" The last question invariably arose when a story might be perceived as casting an advertiser in an unkind light.

Majors had learned his lesson the hard way only two months into his tenure as executive editor. *The Transcript* had broken the story that Crazy Bob, the area's largest car dealer, was setting back the mileage on his demo fleet and selling the cars as new. The story's results were immediate. The paper won three investigative-reporting awards, the advertiser canceled its million-dollar ad campaign in *The Transcript,* and the reporter got reassigned temporarily to the copy desk to "give him more seasoning."

Coupled with the libel suit that had brought down Pritchard Majors' predecessor, the "Crazy Bob mess" compelled Majors to second-guess half the stories that went into the paper. And after a few irate Catholics threatened to cancel their subscriptions over an editorial cartoon that portrayed the pope as less than infallible, Majors took to reviewing all the cartoons in the paper, from Pat Oliphant to Charles Schultz.

Although Majors disliked news meetings—he always sat slightly sideways, toward the door—Claire Green had grown to enjoy them. When she was on her game, she wielded tremendous power, shaping popular opinion around the conference table as to which stories should be played on page one and which stories should go in the low-rent district near the classifieds.

Along the way, she'd found another major benefit of the news meetings. When she would ask Majors a key staffing question in private, he invariably waffled, postponed his answer, changed the subject. But in a meeting, Claire found, Majors was loathe to evade questions lest he create the impression that he wasn't in complete command.

Thus, when the latest follow on the mystery-corpse story came up, Claire made her pitch: "While we're on the subject, Pritchard, I've got an idea that I really need your guidance on. Stuart Reed's been doing a lot of reporting on the dead girl—lots of behind-the-scenes stuff. Don't you think it would be a grand idea to turn the story over to Stuart completely?"

Majors straightened his navy blue rep tie, stalling for time as he tried to remember who Stuart Reed was. "Why can't the cop reporters handle this?"

"Because Stuart found the body, and he's all fired up to see the story through."

"Isn't that a conflict of interest?" asked Mike Tyburski, an assistant editor from the regional staff and Majors' main toady.

Claire scowled. "Who's going to accuse us?" She glanced around the table to see if anybody supported her idea and realized that none of her colleagues had a whit of interest in the discussion. The business editor was busy doodling dollar signs on a yellow legal pad, the wire editor was looking at her watch, and the living section editor was stealing glimpses at the home section of *The New York Times.* Only Majors and Tyburski seemed to care.

"What's the point, Claire?" Tyburski asked. "We can't reassign reporters willy-nilly."

Majors followed up. "That's right, Claire. I don't want us going into the daily newspaper wars with a medic doing an infantryman's job."

Claire was undaunted. From experience, she knew she could win if she kept pressing the issue. "Pritchard, I couldn't agree more, but I was thinking about that great remark you once made—I'm trying to remember if it was from your army career or your stewardship of *The Transcript*. How did you put it? The fiercest warriors are the ones with the most at stake."

She knew that Majors had never said any such thing, but she knew that Pritchard would be happy to accept authorship of it. He started to demur—"In all modesty"—but Claire kept talking.

"And in this instance, Pritchard, I believe your theory has already paid off. I think Stuart may have broken open the case today."

"Pray tell," said Tyburski the toady.

"Stuart saw something in the autopsy that didn't jibe with what he saw when he found the body. The girl's eyes were a different color. He questioned the cops on it, the cops questioned the assistant coroner and—voila!—the assistant coroner suddenly remembered that she'd forgotten to write in her report that the corpse had been wearing blue-tinted contact lenses."

Pritchard tapped his pencil on the table. "So?"

"So the cops ran the contacts through some tests at an eye lab, and found out that the manufacturer was a small supplier who custom makes them on order for opticians. We have the manufacturer going through their files to see how many pairs of contact lenses matching that tint and prescription were made and for whom. The bottom line is our mystery corpse should soon have a name."

The business editor looked up from his legal pad long enough to ask, "Will that put the cops any closer to finding the killer?"

"That'll be part of Stuart's story tomorrow, the Lord and Pritchard willing . . ." She looked over at Majors, who was flicking his fingers impatiently.

"Yes, yes. Let him get on with it. Just make sure we can't be sued for anything."

Claire delivered the good news directly after the meeting. To her great annoyance, Stuart Reed not only took the news for granted but wanted to pull a clerk off the news desk to do some legwork for him. "Give reporters an inch," Claire mused aloud, "and they write another foot of copy. What do you have at this point, Stuart?"

"For tomorrow?"

"Yes, for tomorrow. Don't go assuming anything here, Stuart. I didn't say we were turning you loose on this story. I only said you could do the follows on the mystery woman until you play out the string."

Reed played dumb. "Meaning what?"

"We'll play it one day at a time. Write up the contact-lens information for tomorrow's paper, and we'll see if it leads to a positive

ID. I see an opportunity to do a real writing job on this down the road. I mean, at some point the next of kin will be notified, and they'll have to go to the ME's office to make an ID and claim the body. Should make the perfect epiphany to the story."

Reed scrunched his lips like a catfish, an unfortunate habit he displayed whenever he was confused or deep in thought. The thought in current question was what "epiphany" meant. He'd always thought it was a book in the Old Testament, somewhere between Elastics and Episiotomy, but it didn't make sense. Finally, he gave in and asked Claire what she meant.

She said that the story of the parents claiming the body might provide a moment of revelation, when the clouds part and a shaft of sunlight shines upon who the girl was, how she lived, and maybe how she died. "Through the parents' anguish, Stuart, perhaps you might give readers some insights into what it's like to lose a daughter, or you may even make them contemplate their own fleeting mortality—"

"On this spinning giant orb we call earth," Reed added with a smirk. "That's OK by me, Claire de lune. I can write you up a storm on that one—jerk some real tears for you. But I'm more interested in who killed the girl than who claims her. Unless, of course, they're one and the same."

Claire reminded him that he and she had had this conversation before, and that he should do his job and let the cops do theirs. "And don't ever call me Claire de lune again," she said, and walked away.

# Chapter Thirteen

"When you hear hoofbeats, think horses not zebras."

On his commute to *The Transcript* Friday morning, somewhere in bumper-to-bumper traffic, Stuart Reed had recalled that ancient bit of wisdom from the editor of the first newspaper he worked for.

Every time he tried to come up with a theory on how the girl had been murdered, Reed kept returning to that advice—don't think of some elaborate plot, consider the obvious. In that light, Cippriani's contention that the girl probably had been murdered in New York City and dumped in Riverton just didn't wash. The pistol range was too isolated, too off the beaten path for a zebra—for someone from Manhattan to stumble upon. Hell, even Riverton residents weren't aware that the pistol range existed; how could a stranger with a body in the back of his van happen upon the area?

No, some connection had to exist between the firing range and the dead girl. Who but somebody who had used the firing range would have known that it would make a handy-dandy spot to dump a corpse?

That theory led to a corollary: if the killer had used the firing range, chances were good that he or she had signed some sort of guest book or attendance sheet. As Reed recollected, the local and county cops liked to take target practice a couple of hours a month, since they had to requalify with their weapons at least twice a year by law. And the police department, bureaucracy that it was, no doubt kept records of who took practice and when.

As soon as Reed arrived at work, he logged onto *The Transcript*'s electronic library to get more information on the firing range and on any other discarded corpses.

First, he did an electronic search for stories that contained the words "body" and "found" and "examiner." The computer went blank for thirty seconds, then said that 17,621 stories contained the word "body." Another 6,783 contained the word "found." Another 938 contained the word "examiner." Only seventy-eight contained all three words. He pecked out the word "display" with his right forefinger and hit Execute. In fifteen minutes' time he had scrolled through the seventy-eight stories. Three of them dealt with murdered women whose bodies had been discarded in the county in the past three years.

A fourth story he had written himself—about a corpse that'd been found by a bulldozer operator at the Fresh Kills landfill on Staten Island. Julio Jones had called in sick that day, and out of convenience Claire Green made Reed handle the story on the grounds that the landfill made it an environmental story. He made printouts of all four stories, and in the margin of his yellow legal pad he made a note to himself to check with the cops on the status of each case and to check with the reporters who handled the stories.

Reed recalled the story he'd written—about a not-yet-cold corpse dumped by the entrance of the landfill. He'd handled it by phone and had never done a follow, and now he regretted his lack of discipline. Maybe there was a clue to the new killing, a similarity, a pattern.

The Fresh Kills case had involved a slain and discarded young woman as well, and getting a positive ID had been difficult because the gulls and Norway rats had nibbled for several hours before a trash hauler found her. It had made a big splash at first, and, as Reed seemed to recall, *The New York Post* ran a banner headline that read "Fresh Kill at Fresh Kills" with a subhead that proclaimed, "Mystery Blonde Devoured by Rats."

Reed decided he'd need to make some calls on Monday and see if the woman had ever been identified (the rodents had chewed her fingers to the point where fingerprinting wasn't in the realm of possibility). The case had probably never been resolved, but he knew he couldn't assume anything at this point. He made a note to himself in the margin of the legal pad again, then drew a big star in blue ink next to it as a reminder.

He placed the pad and felt-tip pen beside the computer keyboard and returned to the electronic library. He did a search on "Riverton" and "firing range." The screen went blank again for half a minute, then spewed its findings. Some 14,432 stories had references to Riverton. Another forty-one had at least one reference to a firing range. Only two had references to firing ranges and Riverton.

As fast as he could, he tapped out "display" on the keyboard, then punched the Execute button. Reed slumped in his chair. The story that appeared was the story he'd written the day he'd found the body. One more chance. He typed "N," for "next story" and hit Execute again.

The screen went blank, then—bingo—there appeared a police brief from April 13 of that year, detailing the ribbon cutting of a new county police firing range on DPW property. The electronic file said that the story had run on page B-12 all editions.

Reed ordered a printout of that story as well, then exited from the library system. Next he logged off the computer and headed to the library, where a laser printer would be spewing out copies of the stories he'd requested. En route, he stopped by the bank of electric LekTriever files containing staff black-and-white photos, stored in manila envelopes and arranged alphabetically by subject.

The envelope marked "Police—Riverton" contained twenty-five glossy eight-inch by ten-inch photos dating as far back as 1969. The one Reed wanted was fourth from the top—a basic ribbon-cutting shot of four middle-aged white men sporting say-cheese smiles. Three of the men he recognized, county cop honcho Glenn Brenner and Mayor Leon Kadowski, and none other than *The Transcript*'s own Pritchard Majors. The fourth face, slightly gaunt and patrician with its upturned nose and high cheekbones, looked vaguely familiar.

Reed turned the photo facedown so he could read the cutline affixed with rubber cement to the back. The mystery man's name, Culp Jenkins, didn't jog Reed's memory, but he could always check the electronic library later. Reed walked to the printer, picked up the printouts he had ordered, then threw the photo into the "TO BE FILED" bin on his way out.

As Reed strode out of the library, he broke into a grin: he had his first four suspects, and at least two of the four were potential front-page news. He gave Majors the benefit of the doubt.

# Chapter Fourteen

Detective Aldo Cippriani grabbed his hat and car keys and took three steps out his office door, only to hear the phone ring on his desk. He plunked the gray flannel hat atop his head and leaned against the doorjamb. He had no intention of answering, but he wanted to see how many times the caller would let the phone ring before giving up. He'd found that five rings usually meant his mother, eight his ex-wife. After the tenth ring, he picked up the receiver. He knew he should have invested in an answering machine the instant he recognized Stuart Reed's voice. Only a pain-in-the-ass reporter would let the phone ring for a minute.

"Can't it wait, Mr. Reed? I was literally out the door when you called. . . . No, Mr. Reed, there's nothing yet, but it's only a matter of time. . . . No, I can't give you any theories on the cuts on the victim's stomach. Like I told you, I'll call you as soon as I hear anything."

When Reed asked another question, Cippriani took off his hat and cleared a spot on his desk where he could sit. "Like I told you yesterday, contact lenses of that specific type are few and far between. Soft, blue-tinted lenses with that exact prescription just aren't that common. . . . We haven't heard anything yet, but I should have some word for you on Monday. I hate to cut you short, but it is Friday, I've had a long week, and I have a very important appointment across town in a few minutes."

He waited while Reed made one more request. "I'll have to get back to you on that," Cippriani replied, wondering to himself why callers always waited until four-thirty on a Friday afternoon to bug him. "What do you need the logs for?"

Reed's explanation didn't go over well. "Mr. Reed, that's preposterous. Look, I don't know for a fact that the logs exist, and even if they do, I doubt they're part of the public record. I'm sorry. I have to go."

Cippriani reached for his hat, only to be interrupted again. "What did that reporter want, Al?" The voice belonged to Cippriani's boss, Glenn Brenner, who now stood between Cippriani and the weekend.

"Oh, hi, boss. Nothing much."

"What's nothing much?"

"He asked about the cuts on the stomach of that dead girl we found the other day."

Brenner was a career cop who'd gotten ahead in the department more through his political connections than through any sterling performances in the line of duty. Five-foot-six, with broad shoulders and thick forearms, Brenner must have been one tough cop in his day, Cippriani figured. But Brenner's reddened, pitted nose and generous waistline said that those days were long gone.

Brenner had started in Riverton by walking the beat at age twenty-one, jumped to the county department a few years later, and progressed slowly through the ranks to the point where he pulled strings and got to head the prosecutor's Violent Crimes Unit. Now, at age fifty, he was one year from a nice fat pension, and he had his antennae up for any problems that might botch his plans. And from the way Brenner was snooping around at the moment, Cippriani figured that Brenner saw the dead girl as a potential mine field.

Thus, Brenner just stood in the doorway, waiting for Cippriani to tell him everything the reporter had said.

But it was too close to quitting time for Cippriani to play his boss's game. He shrugged. "That's all. Look, it's getting late . . ."

Brenner reminded Cippriani who signed whose time card, and that he'd ask all the questions he wanted—like why was the reporter interested in the cuts on the girl's stomach.

Cippriani told him that the reporter—Reed was the guy's name—must have gotten tipped to something by the ME's office.

Brenner turned to close the door. A bad sign, thought Cippriani.

"I think we'd better sit and talk about this, Aldo—see if we can't do a little damage control."

Cippriani scratched his ear out of annoyance, then walked around his desk and sat down. Brenner sat across from him.

"Aldo, is your desk always this sloppy?"

"No, boss." He knew that Brenner liked to be called "boss." "I've been getting buried in paperwork the past week or so. I let it go on account of more pressing matters—like covering the mayor's ass on his brother-in-law's riding accident."

"I thought the jerk died in a motel."

"Yeah, but he was in the saddle." Cippriani laughed. Brenner did not.

"Well, a sloppy desk doesn't send a very good message to the public. Makes you look disorganized. The reporter come by and see the desk like this?"

"I get your point. I'll clean it first thing Monday."

"Fine, just see that you do. Now bring me up to speed on the dead girl."

Which Cippriani did. He explained how the assistant ME had talked of the double incisions on the girl's belly, how the contact lens situation would probably lead to a positive ID, and how the case might die down or get solved once this happened.

"The reporter's turning up more than you are. Not good, Aldo. Not good at all. Don't let it happen again—I don't want this guy sinking his teeth into anything or we'll never be rid of him, you understand?"

Cippriani nodded. He hoped that Brenner wouldn't bring up the attendance logs at the firing range, but they were the next question out of Brenner's mouth.

Cippriani stole a glance at his watch. "Yeah, I figured that you'd overheard that. Reed wants to see the logs. No big deal."

Brenner clenched his right fist and pounded Cippriani's desk so hard he rattled the spoon in an empty ceramic coffee mug that proclaimed, "Cops Do It with Authority."

"He what? What the hell is he driving at—that a cop is involved? He can go—"

"I cut him short, boss, as you no doubt heard. I haven't had a chance to figure out what he's after, but if you stop to think about it, it does add up. I mean, the firing range is in a fairly remote spot. It would make sense that the person who dumped the body might have been there before. It's not unreasonable, although he's forgetting all the workmen who built the range last year, the guys who leveled the ground and poured the gravel on the driveway, all the DPW employees who clean up the place. At any rate, I'm certainly not going to give him any logs. In fact, I'll drive over there first thing Monday morning and pick 'em up."

"Why don't you get them now?"

"You want to pay me overtime? Look, I don't want to cause any trouble on this, but the firing range is locked up for the season. It's got a master lock on the front gate, and a Medeco on the door to the little office. You think the reporter's going to try to break in? No way. He'll wait till Monday, raise a stink, then go sniffing in other directions once we get an ID on the body."

Brenner pounded the desk again and started firing more questions —who was this reporter anyway, wasn't the reporter a suspect himself at one point, what was in the logs that might be damaging, what progress was being made toward solving the girl's death, and so forth.

Cippriani felt like a kid in a batting cage, facing a mechanical pitching machine for the first time. He tried to swing at every pitch, make contact, but knew he was overmatched.

"Boss, look, I understand your concern. I'll get on all of this first thing Monday, I promise. But at five P.M. on a Friday? Let's be realistic. To be honest, the importance of all this escapes me at the moment."

"In two words, Cippriani: bad press. I can sense we're going to catch hell on this stupid case, and I want answers in case the prosecutor starts reaming me out."

"I don't want to talk out of turn, boss, but I say to hell with the prosecutor. He knows we're doing our best on a nickel-dime budget. The only damned person who cares is the reporter, and his boss isn't going to let him waste too much time on this penny-ante story. Besides, when it comes to blame, we didn't screw up. It was that assistant ME who botched the contact lenses."

"Maybe so, but the reporter found the mistake, not us. It just doesn't look good. And get that logbook tonight, would you? I'll feel a whole lot better."

Cippriani said he'd give it a shot.

After Brenner left, Cippriani called the ME's office. "Hi, Sally. It's Al Cippriani. I'm running late. How about I pick you up at your place, and we'll grab some dinner from there."

She said if he hurried, she'd give him a special appetizer, and giggled.

Cippriani dialed the desk sergeant and asked who had the keys to the firing range. The desk sergeant said that the range was locked up tight for the winter and the only readily available keys were at the Riverton Department of Public Works. A county cop who had the other set wouldn't return from vacation until Monday.

Cippriani looked at his watch again: Ten-to-five. There was no way anybody'd be around at the DPW building on a Friday at that hour, but he dialed anyway. He thought about Sally while the phone rang and rang, imagined her getting undressed. He let it ring ten times, as the reporter had done to him, but the technique didn't work. He hung up and went to tell Brenner that the logbook would have to wait till Monday, but Brenner had already bolted for the weekend as well.

On his way to Sally's apartment, Cippriani reached into the glove compartment and retrieved a bottle of musk-scented cologne. At a red light, he unbuttoned his shirt and sprayed his chest, then returned the amber bottle to its usual resting place. For a moment, he thought about driving past the firing range just to make certain that all was quiet. Then he looked at the directions Sally had given him, and decided that if he went to straight to Sally's, there was always an outside chance she'd be just getting out of the shower when he knocked on her door.

Six blocks northeast, by the county police department firing range, Stuart Reed was jumping from the roof of a Portosan onto the top of a ten-foot-high cinder block wall. He swung his body up to where he could get a foothold on the thin ledge, then pulled the rest of himself up until he was lying on his stomach. He took a breath, grabbed the top of the wall with his hands, then dropped to the ground as gently as possible. From there he moved quickly. He wanted to be on his way before darkness fell.

Three miles south of the firing range, Sally D'Ambrosio was in the bathroom of her apartment. Clad only in a bright pink bath towel, she leaned against the sink and studied her reflection in the mirror as she applied the last daubs of mascara to her eyelashes.

She had been delighted that the county detective had called, what with the week she'd had—to have a lover die right in the middle of making love, and the mayor's brother-in-law no less. She figured she'd be better off with a younger guy like this county detective, and she figured that having a guy die in the sack with you was like falling off a bicycle—the best thing you could do was get back in action as soon as you could. All she had to do now was make it appear as though she were getting out of the shower when the cop knocked on her door.

# Chapter Fifteen

Stuart Reed found the phone conversation annoyingly brief. At 8 P.M. Friday night, Jeanne Reed called from a pay phone in the West Village to say that she was going out to dinner with a few teacher friends, and that Stuart should go ahead and nuke himself a frozen dinner in the microwave.

Reed placed the receiver in its cradle on the kitchen wall, then placed the ends of his just-drained beer can between his palms and crushed it flat. It didn't take a genius to figure out what the call was really about. Going out with her pals on a Friday evening was a female ploy, a means of getting his attention.

He fetched another beer from the refrigerator and slumped against the kitchen wall. He'd been so eager to get home so he could tell her about his exploits—how he'd sneaked into the firing range, how he was going to solve the crime of the century—and she wasn't there for him.

Once he turned his attention to the photocopies he'd made of the firing range logbook again, he felt the adrenaline pumping. He finished the beer in three swift gulps, swung to his left, and put up a jump shot with the empty, which caromed off the far kitchen wall and the front of the dishwasher before landing in the tall yellow plastic wastebasket. Reed clenched his fists, flexed his biceps, and let out a war whoop. Jeanne wanted to play her mind games, to hell with her. Reed sensed he was about to embark on something major, something that would make him famous, and if she didn't want to stay on board, it would be her loss.

He opened a third beer, returned to the photocopies of the logbook, and grinned a smug grin—Jeanne wouldn't ruin this moment with her absence. But if she only knew what he'd accomplished, Reed decided, then she'd have been there to bask in his reflected glory. Imagine: he'd had his hand in the cops' candy jar and gotten away with it.

Surprisingly, the caper had gone according to plan. Once that lieutenant had waffled about the attendance logs when Reed phoned that afternoon, Reed was sure he was halfway home. The cop's hesitation not only verified that the records existed, but it seemed to indicate they were still at the firing range under lock and key.

From there, it had been as easy as getting into a locked playground after school when he was a kid. After buying a small flashlight on Main Avenue, Reed had changed into his sweats, put on his painters' gloves, and jogged to the firing range just before dusk. He had run past the range often enough to know that one glimpse at the parking lot and through the chain link fence would tell him if anybody was there.

The eight-foot-high fence had strands of barbed wire looped across the top, but the two cinder block walls on either side had no such deterrent, and it seemed like only seconds for Reed to climb atop a Portosan and scale the wall.

Over the summer, when he jogged past, Reed had noticed that cops arriving at the steel door to building would stop to tie their shoes before unlocking the door. About the third time he saw it, Reed concluded that a spare key had to be somewhere by the door— too many cops from too many departments throughout the county took firing practice to supply each one with a key, and common sense dictated that an extra key lurked nearby.

Sure enough, Reed found the key immediately, in the midst of an assortment of dead bugs, under the thick bristle doormat. Nobody had ever accused cops of cornering the market on ingenuity, but then who would have thought anybody would want to break into an office at a pistol range?

The smell of flat beer and dead cigarettes struck Reed when he entered the dark room. The stench reminded him of his old fraternity, of hangovers and lost weekends, of one snowy Saturday night in particular. Three buddies had been drinking sixteen-ounce cans of malt liquor—tall boys, they called them—and in their stupor had decided to go trolling for a hooker on Oswego Street. They returned twenty minutes later, and Reed had grabbed a glimpse of her from the card room as the three boys hustled her toward the back stairs.

From her throaty laugh, which erupted when one of the boys grabbed her as she wiped the snow from her shiny black galoshes, Reed decided she was probably as drunk as they were and aiming to earn some money for her next quart. From the looks of her, the price would be right. An apple red scarf covered her hair, and a long brown cloth coat covered most of the rest of her. In profile, she looked to be in her mid-thirties, with a hook nose, raw cheeks, and only lipstick for makeup.

The boys brought her to a room directly above the card room, and every so often over the next hour Reed heard muffled shouts and cheers, then the woman's voice, hoarse, gravelly, desperate, pleading with them to stop. She groaned, and the room above fell silent. Moments later, one of the boys ushered her down the stairs to the door. He wore jeans, but his feet and chest were bare. She was bundled up in her coat. When she stopped short, to ask for more money, Reed detected a drop of blood under her nose. The boy opened the door and pushed her away. After he slammed the door, he saw Reed and gave a thumbs-up sign. "Cheap slut," he said by way of explanation.

As the boy headed upstairs, Reed went to the window and watched in silence as the woman trudged into the snowy darkness.

Reed moved out at the end of that semester and rented a small apartment off campus. Later, he heard how the three boys had tape-recorded the events of that night, and every so often they'd buy a case of tall boys and play the tape. Fifteen years later, as Reed stood in the darkness of the firing range office, he felt the same nausea coming over him. Something was not right;he wanted to be any place else.

Reed turned on his flashlight so he could see the room better. Clearly, the place was more clubhouse than office. Dead beer bottles sat next to an empty pizza carton on a picnic table. Above the table hung a life-sized nude poster, pasted to the traditional black silhouette target. Reed looked closer. Several bullets had ripped through each breast, and a few more had just missed.

He walked to the far wall. Next to the venetian blinds on the mullioned window that faced the range, stood a soda machine. A white cardboard sign above the coin slot said MILLER 75 CENTS in thick black marker. Reed made a mental note to check the soda machine in the rec room at the prosecutor's offices as well.

Reed knew he had entered reporter heaven. A bullet-pocked poster of a naked woman, an illegal beer machine—taxpayers would have a fit when they read about this next week in *The Transcript.*

He continued to survey the room by flashlight. Not much beside the picnic table and accompanying benches was in the room. An aluminum trash can that contained the remains of a case of Miller. Reed held up a clear glass bottle to the light from his flashlight; the beer on the bottom had long since dried. He rooted through the can until he saw several used condoms. Jackpot.

As he turned to face the door, Reed saw the four-drawer metal file. Atop it, a big round glass ashtray brimmed with cigarettes. He looked for brand names on the butts, but they were too hard to see in the thin light. Next, he tried the top drawer of the file cabinet, and it slid open. It was empty, save for a black leatherette three-ring binder. He read it by the slender beam of the flashlight barely discerning what appeared to be dates and names and a few comments.

The second drawer had some rolled-up targets. The third drawer contained an empty Winston carton and two dozen red and yellow matchbooks that offered stamps from around the world. The bottom drawer held a well-drained fifth of Jack Daniel's, a stack of plastic cups, and a half-open box of condoms.

On his way out, Reed made a mental note of the pizza shop on the empty cardboard box. After locking the door, he returned the key to where he'd found it, jogged to the wall, and jumped high enough to grasp the top. From there, he hoisted himself up and over. In a half hour's time, he had jogged to *The Transcript* and photocopied every page of the log. He jogged back to the range and returned the log to the top drawer of the filing cabinet. A textbook caper.

That same night, while Reed finished his third beer in his apartment, he began to daydream about Monday, when he would drop by the county annex with a photographer and ask Cippriani to go get the log. Reed figured the resultant story would be decked across the top of the front page Tuesday, with a headline the likes of: "Cops' Pistol Range Orgies," except the chief copy editor would probably tone it down to "parties."

Reed could feel the beer starting to cloud his brain, and he knew he was at the crucial point: if he didn't stop now, he'd lose his self-control and go through another six or seven before passing out. Instead, he went to the sink and splashed some cold water on his face, then returned to his required reading.

He started to approach the logbook as a guest list of who hung out at the range. He got out the notepad where he'd begun to write his short list of suspects, then went over the logs line by line. He had thirty pages to go over, and most of the names had initials in the Comments column. Reed figured these were from actual target practice, and didn't bother to write down the names involved in those instances. He could always go back to the copies if his theory didn't pan out.

Reed finished the list and opened a fourth beer. The list had yielded two leads. The man in the photo of the ribbon cutting, Culp Jenkins, had returned once more. And in the last entry, dated two weeks earlier, someone named Dotty Bannister had signed in. Under Comments, someone had scrawled "The Force was with her." Four names were underneath, and Reed remembered from earlier entries that they were cops. And dumb ones at that.

Reed wondered what Dotty Bannister looked like, whether she

had brown eyes and blue contact lenses, and decided she didn't. No one would be dumb enough to leave a body so close to home. But Dotty had the potential to provide another great story, and Reed smiled at the thought. In fact, Reed would have been downright ecstatic over his afternoon's work were it not for one more name he'd come across on the logs.

It belonged to Pritchard Majors.

# Chapter Sixteen

Saturday was Halloween, and one of those rare days when Manhattan seemed just short of paradise. A storm front had pushed through overnight, cleansing the streets and sidewalks, and leaving the sky so clear and blue that New Yorkers actually took notice of the clouds—billowing high and cotton white above the midtown office towers.

The air tasted crisp. Vermont weather, Jeanne Reed called it as she and her husband walked toward the West Village in the late morning. They were holding hands for the first time that either could remember, and it felt right. The walk had been Stuart's idea, to head for the Village and visit their favorite haunts, a way to recapture their old magic, a way to soothe the bruised feelings of the past week.

Stuart had passed out on the sofa by the time Jeanne had gotten home Friday night, and he hadn't bothered to ask what time that had been. He had awakened the next morning before she did, still in a bit of a huff—Jeanne hadn't called him to bed—but his weekly Saturday long run and the new weather lifted his spirits. And when he passed the Strand Bookstore on Broadway and a book he had been looking for caught his eye in the front window, everything clicked: he'd take Jeanne on a flashback tour to all the places they used to call their own the summer that they'd met. On a quick guess, he'd figured it had been a decade earlier. When he did the arithmetic, it turned out to be fourteen years, and he felt a pang. They were growing older, and further apart.

But the thought of going to the Strand, the old record shops on West Fourth, the antiques shops on Bleecker, revitalized him, and he breezed back to the brownstone without breaking into a sweat. While Jeanne rearranged the utensil drawer in the kitchen, Reed took a quick shower and changed into his favorite denims—the Levi's with the torn pocket. He opened the bathroom door and called to Jeanne to see what she thought of his plans for the afternoon ahead. Today Jeanne would get his undivided attention; he vowed that he would not think of the dead girl or the pistol range or Aldo Cippriani. Jeanne said that the idea sounded great.

First stop was the Strand, jammed with the usual Saturday throng of browsers and bargain seekers. Near the cash registers, on a table piled high with half-price review copies, Stuart found a copy of an old novel he'd seen in the window, *The Fast Men,* by Tom McNab. He read the dust jacket and slid the book under his arm. While Jeanne scanned the art book shelves, he wandered from stack to stack until he came to the Crime section.

Ten minutes later, Jeanne found him.

"All set?" She said, and gave him a tug on the torn pocket of his Levi's.

She caught him by surprise. "Oh, hi. Yeah. Just three more shelves to go through, and I promise we're out of here. This is unbelievable. I found two books on forensics, and another on how to conduct a murder investigation."

Jeanne asked how much the books cost, and Stuart replied not much. She thought of suggesting he take the books out of the library and save some money, but decided not to press the matter. Instead, in her sweetest voice, she said: "C'mon, honey. It's too nice a day to be in here. This is a gloomy rainy-day place. Besides, do you really want to carry an armful of books all over the Village?"

Reed couldn't argue. "OK, but maybe we can stop on the way back." She humored him, and they left.

Perhaps it was the sunshine, or the motley assortment of early Halloween revelers, or the mug of Bass ale he'd had at the old tavern on University Place, but Stuart Reed passed the next few hours in a mild state of euphoria. At one record shop, he found an old Eric Clapton album that he and Jeanne used to play so much that they'd worn it out. At a print shop on Sixth Avenue, Jeanne bought an Ansel Adams poster. At a candy shop, Stuart bought red shoestring licorice, and they ate one strand from opposite ends until their lips met—when a bum who was scavenging through a nearby trash can for returnable cans told them they were making him sick.

They laughed, and Jeanne skipped a few steps ahead and whirled, her skirt lifting enticingly in the breeze. "I have an idea."

"Don't tell me. Let's go home and fool around—is that your idea?"

"Well, that's not bad, but I was thinking tomorrow morning we could have coffee and bagels and do The *Times* crossword in bed, then go to the Museum of Modern Art. Isn't that a perfect idea?"

He scrunched up his face. "Can't."

She stopped swaying and folded her arms, and the city seemed to grow silent around them. "Because . . . ?"

"Because I thought I might run a five miler in Riverton tomorrow morning, then use the paper's library to do some research on my mystery corpse."

"Thanks for letting me know so soon."

"Well, it's a helluva lot earlier than you told me about your soiree with your girlfriends last night—if it indeed was your girlfriends."

"What's that supposed to mean?" She turned and started to stride up Sixth Avenue before he could respond.

Reed caught up after a few steps and clutched her arm. "I'm sorry. Forget I said anything. Let's not spoil the rest of the day."

She said it was already too late for that, but when he offered to buy her an early dinner at their favorite Greek restaurant, she softened a bit. "But let me choose the wine, OK?" she said, and held his hand again. If she felt the grasp had changed, she didn't mention it, but Stuart knew that the tenderness between them had evaporated. After a few blocks, Stuart took his hand away to rub an itch on his nose, and the hand-holding had run its course. She waited outside the Strand while he paid for his books.

At the restaurant, the waiter uncorked the bottle of red table wine they'd bought at the corner liquor store. Stuart lifted his glass to Jeanne. "To a nice day," he offered.

She clinked her glass against his. "That toast was real clever."

"What did you want me to say—'Here's to a good race tomorrow'? Let's give it a rest, OK?"

She gave him an unconvincing nod, and reached for her menu. He looked at his, announced "I know what I'm going to order," then opened his bag from the Strand and started to scan the table of contents of the book on fingerprinting. "I'll only take a peek," he said by way of explanation. "It'll take a second."

Jeanne excused herself to go to the bathroom, and Stuart leafed through the first few chapters.

He was on chapter four when the waiter asked if he was ready to order. Stuart looked around, but Jeanne wasn't in sight. "Have you seen my wife?" Stuart asked the waiter. "She went to the lady's room maybe five minutes ago."

The waiter put his pencil behind his ear. "I may be wrong, but I believe your lady left about fifteen minutes ago."

Stuart Reed stayed and killed the bottle by himself, to wash down a Greek salad. He staggered home around ten, after a three-tavern detour. He lay down on the sofa without announcing his arrival, and fell asleep soon after.

Sunday morning, Stuart Reed awoke at nine A.M. When he realized what day it was and what time it was, he went back to sleep. He had missed the race in Riverton—not that he was in any condition to run it—and he decided he might as well sleep off his hangover.

When he woke again, three hours later, Jeanne had gone. The note taped to the front door reminded him to move his watch back an hour and informed him that she had headed for the Museum of Modern Art. She wrote that he could meet her there at noon if he liked, by *Hide and Seek*—his favorite painting—or he could spend the afternoon in the library at *The Transcript.*

Reed smiled to himself—Jeanne still knew which buttons to push to get to him. *Hide and Seek* had been painted during World War II in England by a Russian emigré, Pavel Tchelitchew, and Reed loved to stand in front of it for so long that his legs would cry out for a rest. The massive oil painting—it filled an entire interior wall of the museum—took on added meaning each time Reed studied it.

At first glance, the painting was of a gnarled oak. Upon second look, the branches became a monstrous hand. Then the tortured faces of young children emerged from the outlines of the branches, and the images became three dimensional. Flaming yellows and reds, lush greens and sinister browns. The first time he had studied it, several years earlier, Reed had assumed it must be a Holocaust painting but later on he'd read up on the painting and learned that it was meant to represent the mystery of life.

A book about MOMA's greatest paintings described *Hide and Seek* as an artwork about metamorphosis—seeing one object in another—which was the key to perceiving an image in its totality. "The tree becomes the clock of the seasons," the art critic had written. "Its greens and fiery reds and wintry blues celebrate the annual cycle of death and rebirth."

Reed felt that the painting's meaning went deeper—the naked children on the canvas looked tortured or dead. The painting was not a celebration of anything. It represented the darkest side of nature, which preyed on the young and the weak. . . .

While Reed threw on his Levi's and an old denim work shirt, he thought about the painting's meaning and realized that the same notions of seeing one object in another held true for the image that had haunted him for the past few days—an image that could have easily fit in Tchelitchew's masterwork.

For the county detectives, the motionless girl in the brambles was one more job in an overwhelming caseload. In Reed's mind, the image of the girl's anguished face superimposed itself on the painting, representing a mystery that plumbed the depths of depravity—and society's indifference to it. To bring the killer to justice meant more than a scoop and the accolades that surely would follow. Solving the mystery of this unlamented death, he felt certain, was a first step toward comprehending that depravity.

Jeanne Reed was surprised when her husband met her at the Museum of Modern Art at noon sharp. She was more surprised when he presented her with a red rose (he was nothing if not persistent, she decided) and, after he'd studied the painting for ten minutes, insisted on treating her to a Lowenbrau in the cafeteria that looked out on the sculpture garden.

"This rose doesn't let you off the hook, you know," she said as they sat down. "It's a nice gesture, granted, but you're doing it purely to get back into my good graces, and you're not going to get off that cheap."

Reed apologized for the incident at the restaurant. He conceded that it had been rude of him to look at the book, and he said that he was sorry. "But," he added, "you could have told me to stop any number of ways—rubbed your leg against mine under the table, asked to hold my hand. It takes two to quarrel, and it takes two to mend fences. You didn't have to up and leave the restaurant."

Jeanne poured her beer, watching the foam inch toward the rim of the cup rather than look at her husband. "You're just not there for me anymore, Stuart. That's got to change."

"You're not listening. I am there for you, if you'd only make an effort to meet me part of the way. I do the slightest thing to annoy you—like glance at that stupid book at dinner—and you flip out. This is a tough story I'm dealing with, and I'm under a lot of pressure to see it through."

Jeanne took a long sip of the Lowenbrau. It tasted bitter. When she placed the cup back on the table, it was half empty. She'd had only a bagel for breakfast, and the beer was beginning to make her feel light-headed. "I thought nobody at work cared about the damned story. The only pressure is in your head."

Reed drummed his fingers on the table. He realized it was pointless to explain that for the top reporters, the pressure to excel came from within. They forced themselves to do more than what was needed just to get by, and it paid off in the long haul. He was stunned that Jeanne would think otherwise.

He gulped his beer, then excused himself to go to the bathroom. He didn't say that the bathroom he had in mind was at *The Transcript* in Riverton.

# Chapter Seventeen

On the drive to *The Transcript,* Stuart Reed fretted over his little pay-back gesture at the art museum. Jeanne would no doubt consider the way he skipped out without telling her to be bush league, if not unforgivable, but hadn't she done the very same thing the night before? He had merely returned the favor. Tit for tat.

Jeanne wouldn't see it that way, of course. And coming on the heels of yesterday's futile attempts to mend fences, his latest stunt would accomplish nothing less than destroy those fences completely. Reed slammed the steering wheel with his palm. The last thing he needed was to play kiss and make up with her. He needed to give his undivided attention to all the follow-up stories about the dead girl. What he needed was breathing room, and Jeanne was suffocating him.

Clancy Collins, his pal at *The Transcript,* had always said that the key to a successful relationship was "keeping your stock up." Collins had explained that if you wanted to keep a woman happy, you had to do things that made her think that you valued her—perfume, earrings, flowers, a new record album that she wanted. What you did didn't matter so much as the appearance of it.

Collins had used a TV set as an example. He and his wife had owned the same thirteen-inch portable for the five years of their marriage, and Collins decided that he needed a bigger set to watch pro football. One night, as they were watching *The Cosby Show,* he announced that she didn't deserve to watch her favorite programs on such a cruddy TV. Tomorrow, he would buy her a new one—just in time for the weekend games, naturally. Thus, as Collins later explained to Reed, he got the new TV he wanted, and raised the value of his stock in her eyes in the process—"just like eating your cake and having it, too."

Reed didn't disagree with Collins' philosophy, but he thought that the other half of the equation was that the woman had to try to keep her stock up as well—otherwise you were only spoiling her. Flowers for Jeanne were a fine idea, but how come he seldom got a little

surprise in return? In any event, the Stuart Reed stock index was at
an all-time low, and he sensed a major depression in the offing.

He got his mind off Jeanne by mapping out his workload for the
afternoon, all the leads that needed to be followed up. He divided
them into four areas: other murders, the dead girl, the firing range
improprieties (including Dotty Bannister), and Culp Jenkins.

Reporters at *The Transcript* called Sunday duty "the baloney shift."
The usual generators of news—government agencies, the courts, and
PR firms—were closed on Sundays, and the newspaper had on a
skeleton crew of two assistant editors, four reporters, and two rewrite
people to handle the trickle of news. Fatal fires and other natural
disasters were few and far between, and reporters typically had to
cover such events as ethnic fairs, home and garden shows, and four-
generation family reunions—hence "the baloney shift."

What it meant for Reed was a perfect afternoon to go rummaging
in the newspaper's library without distractions, and to find a free
terminal to work at. With a bit of luck, maybe a cop reporter who
had covered one of the earlier unsolved murders would be working,
and Reed could get some details that hadn't found their way into any
stories.

Reed stopped at the diner next to the paper and bought four cups
of coffee, two for himself and two for the pair of assignment editors.
If his stock had fallen in Jeanne's eyes, he might as well earn a few
brownie points with the bosses. He'd be working the Sunday shift
next month, and the editors decided who would get the choice assignments and who would get saddled with the Ukrainian Festival in
the Vet Stadium parking lot. Getting a story that made page one often
meant cultivating your editor as much as cultivating your sources.

After dropping off the coffee and schmoozing with the editors for
a few minutes—how's that baby daughter of yours? see that Notre
Dame game yesterday?—Reed found a terminal on the far side of the
newsroom, out of the editors' sight. If disaster did happen to strike,
he wanted to be out of the line of fire.

First on tap were the laser printouts of the stories on the earlier
unsolved slayings. He pored over each story, underlining the information that struck a resonant chord. The four deaths had come over
the past two years, approximately six months apart. In each case, the
body of a teenage girl had been found in an isolated spot—in a
picnic grove in a county park in December, by a dumpster in a
shopping mall parking lot over a three-day holiday, in an industrial
park on a Monday morning, and, of course, in the Fresh Kills landfill. There was no telling how the girl had ended up there.

In each case, the killer's trail had dried up by the time the police had gotten positive IDs, and the follow-up stories were obligatory at best. The victims were all in their mid to late teens; most had come from poor families. Two had had a history of prostitution arrests. Because the turnover rate among cop reporters was so high, no one at *The Transcript* had thought to connect the killings, and if someone in Violent Crimes over at the county building annex had done any work along those lines, they certainly weren't saying so. Homicide dicks never had anything to say unless they had solved a case, and then you couldn't shut them up.

The news budget for the Monday paper listed the Sunday reporters, and Reed tried to match the bylines from the murder stories to anyone who might be in the newsroom today. Alas, two of the stories were too short to merit bylines, and the reporter who had covered the third murder had since left the paper for greener paychecks. As for Fresh Kills, that would have to wait till Monday. He'd need to call the NYPD, and nobody would be around on a Sunday to give him any information.

He was in a similar situation with the county detectives and the dead girl; nobody would be able to give him squat on a Sunday. But if this were the work of a serial killer, maybe the electronic library could help. He logged onto the library system, then did searches on "serial" and "murder." The system went back several years. He found wire stories on the Green River slayings out west, some murders in Connecticut (an arrest had been made), and several others in Great Britain.

Next, Reed did a search for the words "culp" and "jenkins." He found five stories, one by the hunting columnist, three in the television section, and one on events at the local malls. He got printouts of the stories, ten in all, then underlined items of interest. Maybe he'd call Jenkins on Monday, once he fleshed out the guy a little more. The stories said that Jenkins was a hunter and conservationist, and perhaps Reed could call and say he was working on an environmental story—a new green acres proposal or something.

Halfway through his second cup of diner coffee, he had a brainstorm. He got the Riverton phone book and looked up Dotty Bannister, the woman whose name had surfaced in the pistol range logbook. To his mild surprise, she was listed. The address was in the southern part of town, a block from the projects. He started to dial the number, then thought of Julio Jones' advice about interviewing people in person. He hung up and dialed Jeanne. It was five P.M. She'd be back from the museum, if she wasn't off to a girlfriend's, still fuming over his stunt. The phone rang eight times before he gave up.

On his way home, Reed drove past Dotty Bannister's place, a two-story semidetached home with two boarded-up windows and asbestos siding the color of cigarette ash. A light was on in the front room, but the shades were drawn. In the narrow drive was a rusted-out Plymouth station wagon on cinder blocks. It had no wheels, the perfect transportation for a part of town that was going nowhere.

Reed circled the block twice. He tried to think how to approach her, what questions to ask, whether to identify himself as a reporter. Play it by the book, he decided, and hope for the best.

He parked two doors down from the address in the phone book, made sure he had locked both car doors, then walked slowly to the front entrance of the Bannister household. The door was plywood that had begun to delaminate, and a hollow thunk sounded when he knocked on it. He heard a TV set, the sounds of a football game. The hall light flicked on, and the door opened two inches, the length of the chain. Reed could barely make out a woman in her mid forties. She wore a floral housedress. Reading glasses teetered on the tip of her nose.

"What you want?"

"Hi. My name's Stuart Reed, and I'm looking for Dotty Bannister. She home?"

Reed heard an infant crying in the background, and the woman turned to tell the child to shut up. She turned back to Reed. "She ain't hookin' no more, so get lost." The door slammed shut.

Reed knocked again. "I'm a reporter," he called through the closed door. "I need to talk to Dotty Bannister about a story. It's important, or I wouldn't be coming by to see her."

The door opened a crack. "No good never came to nobody by talking to a reporter. She ain't talkin' about it. She weren't hurt that bad, and she wants to forget about it. Now get lost."

# Chapter Eighteen

The moment Stuart Reed and Milt Roberts, the *Transcript* photographer, set foot in the pistol-range office on Monday morning, Reed smelled something wrong: the unmistakable scent of Pine Sol had replaced the stale aroma of spent tobacco.

The moment that Aldo Cippriani opened a venetian blind and daylight poured into the room, Reed's fears were confirmed. Someone had been hard at work. The trash can had been emptied. The nudie poster was nowhere in sight. And, most irritating of all, the ashtray on the filing cabinet had been replaced by a Bible.

When Cippriani turned his back and headed for the filing cabinet, Reed bit his lower lip, tilted his head ten degrees, and shrugged apologetically at Milt Roberts. The photographer replied by tapping his watch and motioning toward the door.

"I think they keep the log in this cabinet over here," Cippriani said. "Yes, here it is."

Cippriani reached into the top drawer, retrieved the black notebook, and cheerfully gave it to Reed. "I'll need it back this afternoon."

Reed ignored the cop's bonhomie. "This place sure is immaculate for a pistol range, isn't it?"

"You should have been here two hours ago, before I cleaned up. It was a sty."

"What do you mean?"

Cippriani explained that two weeks earlier, some of the city cops apparently had thrown a bachelor party for a patrolman, and had never come back to clean up. He said he had been pissed to find the room in such disarray, but added, "It could have been worse. I could have discovered the mess now instead of at eight A.M., and then where would we all be?"

"You tell me."

"Well, off the record, I found a case of empty beer bottles. That's not exactly according to regulations, you know?" Cippriani paused. "Is something wrong there, Mr. Reed?"

"Not at all. I think I'll find just what I need in here," Reed replied, holding up the looseleaf notebook.

"And what might that be?"

"Just a hunch. I figure that whoever dumped the girl might have been at the pistol range at one time or another. Stands to reason: this place is pretty out of the way for anybody else to even know about."

Cippriani leaned on the picnic table. "I guess I should be offended by your theory, because what you're implying is that a cop killed that girl."

"I'm not implying anything. You're inferring it."

Cippriani waved a forefinger in Reed's face. "You want to play word games, go play Scrabble with your mother. All I'm saying is that nobody—even people who are supposed to be as stupid as us cops—nobody shits where they eat. A cop ain't that stupid that he'd bring a dead body to a place he hangs out. And what's more, I don't like you bringing a photographer along today. You didn't say anything about him when you called. I don't like surprises."

Reed stepped back and pushed Cippriani's finger aside. "Jeez, if I'd known you'd be upset, I'd have had Milt here stay in the car. It just so happened that we're on our way to another assignment."

"What'd you think you'd find in here, that you insisted on coming along when I got you the logs—the murder weapon or something?"

"No, but you never know until you check. In fact, would you mind if I look through the file drawers? If the killer was here, maybe he left a clue."

Cippriani took a deep breath, then exhaled slowly through his nostrils. "Okay, pal, have your look, then get out. You're getting me extremely pissed."

Reed opened the second drawer from the top. It contained several rolled-up targets. The next two drawers contained a first aid kit, a jar of instant coffee, a stack of plastic eight-ounce cups, a few packets of evaporated milk, and a big yellow Smile button.

Reed decided not to press his luck, and skipped checking the soda machine for cans of beer. He'd been had.

On the way to the staff-photographer car, a white Nova, Milt Roberts asked Reed to explain what had gone down moments earlier in the pistol range office.

"What do you think happened? Cippriani cleaned up the place so we wouldn't find anything, then rubbed my nose in it. But it doesn't matter. We're in fine shape."

As he swung the Nova out of the parking lot and down the pitted roadway to Richards Street, the photographer asked Reed again to explain what was going on.

"All our answers are right here," Reed said, holding up the log-book.

"But if that guy cleaned the office, he must have gone through the log and removed anything incriminating."

"You got it. All I do is compare this to the copy I made on Friday. If it's different, then I make a list of the names that conveniently happened to disappear over the weekend, and I have myself a list of suspects."

At four P.M., after copying the logbook and comparing it to the earlier list, Reed drove to the county building annex and returned the book to Cippriani.

The homicide detective seemed in excellent spirits. He gently tossed the book on top of the paperwork piled on his desk and then announced: "We got an ID on your mystery bitch. Contact lenses did the trick, just like you said. We confirmed it through her dental x-rays and from fingerprints we lifted from a bracelet we got from her bedroom in her parents' home in Brooklyn. It turns out her parents reported her missing last Monday, and the NYPD never inputted the information until today."

Reed got his notepad out and asked for details.

"What do you need to know?" Cippriani inquired.

"Everything."

"OK, first things first. Her name was Diana Diaz." Cippriani spelled it for him. "Eighteen years old. Freshman at Columbia. That's right, Columbia, not Barnard," Cippriani added, before Reed could interrupt. "She modeled in her spare time, which wasn't much. All-American kid, especially for a Puerto Rican."

Reed glowered, which caused Cippriani to grin. "C'mon. Lighten up. I meant that in the best sense of the word. She was a real goody two-shoes. Sang in the church choir, tutored poor kids. Her parents were fairly well-off. Father owns a chain of laundromats, or so he says.

"The girl was last seen late Monday afternoon, leaving her freshman English class. We'll send somebody there tomorrow to see if her classmates saw anybody suspicious. Apparently headed toward the subway station near the campus and was never seen again. Until you found her, I mean."

"She commuted?"

"Her parents weren't that rich for her to live in a dorm, I guess. Besides, her father said he didn't think it was safe for her to live in that area. I mean, everybody at Columbia calls it Morningside

Heights, but you're still basically talking Harlem. At any rate, he was obviously right."

"When did you talk to her father, when you got the bracelet to check for fingerprints?"

"No, when he came and identified her. A half hour ago."

"What? The guy was at the ME's office to identify his daughter, and you didn't call me?" Reed stopped, trying to comprehend what it all meant. Then he glared. "You knew all that this morning, when we met at the pistol range. Why didn't you say something then?"

Cippriani shrugged theatrically. "You were so fired up about the logbook here, so fired up with all your implying and inferring. I thought you that's all you cared about."

"You shafted me."

"Not true. All you had to do was ask. That's what you're supposed to do for a living, is it not?"

"You got it. And I have one more question before I go."

"What might that be?"

"Just exactly whose ass you trying to cover?"

# Chapter Nineteen

Claire Green called Stuart Reed into a debriefing session as soon as he returned to his desk at *The Transcript*. He'd been logged on to his terminal for less than a minute when "message pending" began to blink in the upper right-hand corner of the green computer screen. He knew what the message would say before he called it up: "See me first chance. CG."

Reed hated such encounters with Green. They invariably took place in a tiny conference room just off the newsroom, and colleagues always assumed that whoever Claire had invited there was about to be chewed out. A few of Reed's colleagues had taken to calling the room the woodshed. Reed had seldom found it that severe, but he had taken note of Claire Green's knack for asking questions that he couldn't answer about a story, and he understood why other reporters cringed when Claire called them in. Not this time, Reed thought. This time he knew he held the aces.

"What have you got for tomorrow?" Claire asked, probably for the ten-thousandth time in her editing career. She shut the door behind them, not a good sign.

But Reed saw no reason to worry. "We have a positive ID on the murdered girl, thanks to my scoop on the contact lenses. Her name is Diana Diaz. From Brooklyn. Eighteen. Nice girl. Columbia freshman. Lived with her parents. Never came home Monday night."

"What does the Violent Crimes Unit have at this point?"

"Do you mean, what does the prosecutor's office have at this point, or what do I think they're holding?"

"Both."

"They say they're tapping an empty keg, and officially they don't much seem to care—another instance of New York City dumping their trash in our backyard. Our boys say they want to push the case off on the NYPD, who had a missing persons report last week and never put it in the computer."

"And what do you think our county detectives actually have?"

"I think they have plenty to hide. On Friday I happened upon the logbook for the pistol range—which is twenty yards away from where I found the girl. At any rate, I copied the whole thing, and guess what I came across?"

"Enlighten me."

"First of all, the range is supposed to be off-limits to everybody but cops, but the log had the names of three civilians. Including our own Pritchard Majors, if you can believe it. A guy named Culp Jenkins, who turns up on our electronic data base a half dozen times. Hosts a weekly outdoors show syndicated on independent TV stations across the country. Need I remind you that the ME's office said the girl might have been cut up with a hunting knife? Interesting, no?"

Claire shrugged and motioned Reed to continue.

"And then there's an entry marked Dotty Bannister, with some sly comments by four of Riverton's finest registered underneath. On a Saturday, when the range is supposed to be closed. I did a search on her in the data base and—surprise, surprise—she's been in a few police briefs for prostitution collars. I stopped by her place yesterday —on my own time, I might add—and talked with her mother or aunt or somebody. I got the impression the cops must have played rough with her."

Claire Green stifled a smile. "So you're saying she was in a few more police briefs at the pistol range?"

"You got it. But here's the grabber. I asked for the logbook again today, on an official basis, and somebody had removed the pages that contained all three civilian names. The pages were loose leaf, and somebody just yanked out the entire pages."

"That's not surprising, under the circumstances. No big deal. We can always use the copies you made on Friday. But I think the only story worth going after at this point is Dotty Bannister."

Reed blanched. "One problem. Promise not to kill me?" Green agreed with a nod. "I stole the log from the range on Friday, brought it here, and made myself a copy, then sneaked it back before anybody knew it was gone."

Green inspected the polish on her fingernails and spoke without looking up. "That'll be all. You're off the story."

"What?"

Green looked him in the eye. "You broke the law. I really ought to fire you on the spot. If you'd been caught, the paper's credibility would have been down the drain. For now, all I'm going to do is pull you off the story, but let it be known you're on my shit list. Anything else happens, you're gonzo. Got that?"

Reed stood in silence.

"I asked you if you understood."

Reed nodded a halfhearted yes. As Claire Green stood to leave, Reed asked if this meant that the paper wasn't interested in any more stories about the murdered girl.

Claire Green thought for a moment and corrected herself. "I want a police brief for tomorrow's paper, saying that the girl has been identified. See if Jones will write it up. Beyond that, even if you hadn't compromised the paper, I agree with the cops. This is a New York City problem and not worth filling our news hole with. I don't want to see any other stories from you on this."

Reed couldn't resist firing one last salvo. "You know, Claire, all I want to do is find out who killed that girl—before he slaughters somebody else. The trouble is that you're so caught up in procedure and circulation areas that you've lost sight of what we're here for—the truth."

Claire Green glared at him and asked, "How much can the truth be worth if you have to break the law to get at it?" She didn't wait for a response.

As soon as she had left the room, Reed broke into a grin. Bad luck had turned good once more. According to *Transcript* policy, if an editor didn't want a story, a writer was free to sell it elsewhere. And once Stuart had gathered the goods on Culp Jenkins, he'd sell the story to *New York* or *Esquire* or even *People.* Then he'd work on the book and screenplay.

Stuart Reed was in too upbeat a mood to allow the marital discord of the past week to spoil his evening. He arrived home at seven, on time, cradling a bag with one arm, carrying a bouquet of pink carnations with his free hand.

He craned his head past the front door. When he heard Jeanne in the kitchen, he ventured: "Are you speaking to me yet?" In fact, neither had said one word to the other since Reed's disappearing act at the museum. She had been in the bedroom when Reed returned home the night before, and refused to answer when he had called to her.

Tonight was an improvement. "Depends," Jeanne replied from the kitchen. "Are you willing to apologize and listen to what I have to say to you?"

Reed took off his sports coat and hung it on a hook by the door, then stood next to Jeanne. "You got it. I'm sorry for the stunt I pulled at the museum, but at the time I thought I owed you one—turnabout is fair play, and all that. Now tell me what you have to say. Can I get you a beer for our talk?"

"No, Stuart, that's part of what I have to say to you." She led him to the sofa, and over the next ten minutes proceeded to tell him that:

A. He'd been taking her granted, and worse.
B. He'd been drinking too much lately, and it upset her.
C. He'd been taking his work home too much.
D. He had two weeks to shape up or move out.

He said fine, then got up and poured himself a beer.

Under the circumstances, the evening went better than Stuart Reed could have expected. Although Jeanne frowned upon the beer, she didn't make an issue of it. She let Stuart cook the spaghetti, begrudgingly conceding that he could still cook better than she. She made the salad at his side, and the kitchen seemed cozier than it had in months.

After dinner, they went for a walk. The weather had grown brisker, and Jeanne said, as she usually did this time of year, that if it weren't early November, she'd be predicting snow. Stuart said he guessed that this meant he didn't have to treat her to an ice cream cone tonight. He placed his arm around her (he said it was to keep them warm) and they walked around the entire block arm in arm. They watched TV until eleven, and then Stuart sprung the big question: was he allowed back in bed yet?

She said yes, but not to get any ideas. Later, after she'd fallen asleep, he lay beside her, thinking about how to go about catching Diana Diaz's killer. He had a hunch he should concentrate on the hunter, Culp Jenkins, until proven otherwise.

Finally, Reed curled up next to his wife, reached over her shoulder, and cupped her breast through her flannel nightgown.

She rolled over, away from his grasp, and said wearily, "Forget it."

He replied, "Your loss," and meant it.

# Chapter Twenty

Detente arrived mid-morning on Election Day, wearing Gucci loafers.

Reed was at his computer terminal, writing a budget line about a state Department of Environmental Protection announcement scheduled for one P.M. the next day. Reed had just confirmed through a second not-for-attribution source that the number 2 man at the agency was jumping ship to become a vice president of a toxic-waste disposal company. That was the rule—if you couldn't get someone to speak for the record, then you had to find a second source who'd confirm the story. Thus, Reed would have a nice scoop for the Wednesday paper, especially if he could imply that some conflict of interest might be involved.

After Reed's disastrous Monday, when almost everybody he knew had given him some sort of ultimatum, he knew he had to rebuild bridges. Any kind of "beat," or exclusive story, would help with the damage control. It didn't matter that his exclusive would be public knowledge anyway a few hours after the papers hit the newsstands —or that no one would give a damn about the story a week from now. The goal was merely to beat the competition, the ultimate trivial pursuit.

Then Aldo Cippriani called from the receptionist's desk in the lobby, and Reed forgot all about toxic waste, the DEP, and conflicts of interest. Cippriani said he wanted to talk. In person, outside, and off the record. Reed logged off his computer, grabbed his tweed sports jacket, and raced down the four flights to the front lobby.

Instead of his usual House of Polyester wardrobe, Cippriani was decked out in big-ticket threads. Camel-hair topcoat with the collar upturned to display the Burberry plaid. Dark blue pin-striped suit, white shirt, red rep tie, and glove-leather loafers. Reed thought Cippriani looked like he was straight out of *Gentleman's Quarterly,* save for the toothpick that dangled from his lips.

Reed decided to gloss over the bad blood between them, offering his hand and kidding the cop about his wardrobe. "Detective, it's nice to see you, but your clothes are above and beyond the call of duty. You got a lunch date with a freeholder's wife or what?"

Cippriani forced a smile and asked whether they could talk outside. Reed said sure, and inquired whether this was off or on the record.

Cippriani looked puzzled.

"Today's Election Day. Don't you have the day off?"

Cippriani looked at Reed as though the reporter were nuts. "Those days in this county are long gone."

Once they'd seen their way through the revolving door, Cippriani explained: "Just had a meeting with the prosecutor. Or, should I say, had a reaming from the prosecutor. I go to the trouble to dress for success for the joker, and I might as well have dressed like one of the slobs in the county-cop squad room. Prosecutor was furious, said I hadn't accomplished squat on the Diaz investigation, and now that we found out she's not from our jurisdiction, we should cut our losses and quietly table the case."

When the two men reached the corner of the Transcript Building and turned onto Richards Street, they were buffeted by a raw north wind, and Reed wished he'd worn a heavier jacket. He tucked his arms inside his jacket and walked slightly crouched to fight the wind. "Detective, I know where you're coming from," Reed said, raising his voice against the stiff breeze. "I've been pulled off the story myself. So why don't you just tell me what you're driving at, and I can go someplace warm?"

They crossed the street at the traffic light and headed toward Main. "Yesterday," Cippriani said, "remember when I said you forgot to ask whether we'd gotten an ID yet for the girl? You forgot to ask the other big question—whether we'd heard back from the FBI on whether any pattern was involved."

Reed suddenly warmed up. "What's that again?"

Cippriani explained that the FBI had a research facility in Quantico, Virginia, called the National Center for the Analysis of Violent Crime. Police departments sent them the particulars on murders and sex crimes, and the agency would run the data through their mainframes to see if it rang any bells. Reed had read about the center in a story he'd fetched out of the electronic library on Sunday, but chose not to say so. He'd learned long ago that when a source wants to talk, you keep your mouth shut.

Just as Cippriani was about to go into details on the Diaz case, he stopped mid sidewalk and turned toward Reed. "Here's where you and me reach an understanding or we go our separate ways. The way I see it, I need you, and you need me."

Reed gave him a puzzled look and suggested they talk inside a luncheonette a block away. Cippriani's feet were freezing, and he agreed. They walked to the luncheonette and took the booth farthest from the door.

Over coffee and cinnamon doughnuts, they cut a deal. Cippriani would feed Reed exclusive information in exchange for glowing coverage of Cippriani's investigation. And when the case was solved, the two of them would come out holding nothing but aces.

"What exactly do I have to do?" Reed asked.

"Two things. I may ask you from time to time to check out some leads from your end. Do your usual reporter number. And when I crack this case, my boss and the prosecutor are going to try to hog the limelight like they always do. You have to promise to give me all the credit, all the glory. That's it."

Reed wanted to know why Cippriani picked him. "Three reasons," Cippriani replied. "You work for the biggest local paper, you seem to care about the case, and you strike me as a sneaky son of a bitch."

Reed was indignant. "What are you talking about?"

"You tried to screw me and the police department yesterday morning. At the pistol range with your photographer pal. You must have broken into the office over the weekend and found all the crap —the beer and whiskey bottles, the defaced nudie poster, the condoms, the Dotty Bannister entry in the log. And you thought we'd walk in there together yesterday morning, you'd take pictures of all that crap, and I'd look like a clown. Am I right?"

Reed finished his coffee and looked for the waitress, a wide-bodied woman in her fifties who was flirting with a postman two booths over.

Cippriani tugged Reed's sleeve to get his attention back. "You don't have to answer the question. I know the answer already. I'm not stupid, and I'm not going to arrest you for breaking and entering. I'm just saying you're a closet sleazeball. I like that in a reporter."

Reed smirked. "Thanks."

"The only point I'm trying to make is that if we're going to be partners on this, we gotta be straight with each other from now on, and I gotta say something's on the record before you go ahead and write it, agreed? Are we partners?" Cippriani extended his right hand.

Reed shook Cippriani's hand, then confessed to the pistol range heist. He finished by asking: "And now I'll give you the same question I threw at you yesterday. Off the record, partner, whose butt you protecting?"

Cippriani stood and took his coat from the hanger. "Get something straight here. You want to help me catch the murderer, great.

But don't go throwing cops' asses in a sling because they had an after-hours party at the pistol range with some slut. In the grand turd pile of corruption, it doesn't amount to a fart.

"What I was about to say before is that I got the word back from the FBI on the Diaz murder, and they figure there's an outside chance—and I emphasize the word 'outside'—that it matches up with at least two rape murders in the metropolitan area—one where a body was dumped north of here, the other on Staten Island."

"At Fresh Kills?"

"The dump over there? Yeah, that's it. How'd you know?"

"I had to do a story on it. Never followed up on it, though. Out of *The Transcript*'s readership area. What are the similarities—the knife wounds?"

"Couldn't tell on the other two bodies. They were out in the elements too long. I know there was no sign of rape with the Diaz girl, but other than that . . . All three were teenage girls, suffocated and dumped. Their stomachs had been cut open, although in the other two cases it took a bit of conjecture—the stomach cavities were wide open when they were found, and how else would have they gotten that way?"

Reed crushed his paper napkin into a ball. "Crap. Sounds like a bit of a stretch to me. But should be enough to get me back on the story. Claire's going to flip."

"Who's Claire?"

"My boss. She's the one who told me that I was off the story, and that if I didn't watch my ass, she'd fire me. I guess she'll hum a different tune when I tell her this. Sex crimes. Serial murders. Front page, all the way, even with the off-year elections. Where do we go from here?"

"You write a story for tomorrow that my investigation has uncovered similarities between the Diaz murder and two other dumped corpses in the area, and that the FBI has confirmed that possibility. Then say I'm pursuing several strong leads."

"Are you?"

"Not really, but I'll cast a bunch of lines in the water and see if I get any nibbles. I'll check with the usual informants and see if they've heard anything about a sex killer. I'll go through the files and see what we got in terms of sex offenders who like to play with knives. And I'll check my connections with the NYPD and see what they turn up. FBI's running some data through their computers as well."

Cippriani's mind was racing now. "And we got those cuts on the girl's stomach to work with. I doubt that the killer knows that the wounds were intact when you found the girl. That gives us an edge. Figure out why he used two blades, and we're halfway home."

Reed was pumped up. "And we'll follow this wherever it leads, right?" Reed mentioned the photo at the pistol range—with such local celebrities as Mayor Kadowski, Glenn Brenner, and Pritchard Majors.

Cippriani chuckled. "Yeah, sure. The mayor, my boss, and your boss. A fine list of suspects. And, if you want my opinion, a fine waste of time."

Reed shrugged. "Maybe. You never assume, because you never know. And if you don't mind, let's look into a guy named Culp Jenkins. He was in that photo, and he's been to the pistol range on at least two other occasions—probably enough to know that it was secluded and closed for the season after September."

Cippriani told Reed to get the firing range off his brain.

Reed ignored the comment. "According to *The Transcript*'s data base, the guy's a host of a TV outdoors show. A hunter. I'd say he's a prime suspect. Can you check and see if he's got a rap sheet? I'll check with my sources at the Department of Wildlife, see if he's had any hunting or fishing infractions that might set off a few alarms."

Reed and Cippriani parted with another handshake, and Reed didn't notice the blustering north wind as he hurried back to the newspaper. One thought stuck in his mind: the crow he was about to make Claire Green have for lunch.

# Chapter Twenty-one

She stood at Stuart Reed's desk, arms folded and foot tapping impatiently, while he hung his sports jacket on the coatrack just inside the newsroom. Reed had spotted her as he walked in, and now he was dawdling, irritating her, savoring the moment.

He sauntered over, pausing to joke with a fellow reporter along the way. "Hi, Claire. What's shaking?" he asked with a half-concealed grin.

"Where were you? You're aware, of course, you're not to leave the newsroom without telling an editor where you'll be. The news meeting starts in five minutes, and you were supposed to get me that budget line an hour ago." In typical Claire fashion, she hadn't yet given him an opportunity to respond to any of her accusations. "Have you forgotten the little discussion we had yesterday?"

"Sorry, Claire. I'll do it now." He was all smiles and sunshine.

Reed sat at his desk and logged onto the computer system. He ignored the "message pending" that blinked on his screen and created a new file:

MURDERS (Reed) Riverton homicide detective links Diaz slaying to at least two others in the area, including one three months ago in North Ridge. Exclusive. A-1. Developing. Eighty lines. Due: 5 P.M.

He sent the file as an electronic message to Claire. It took ten seconds for her to read it and return to his desk. "I'm sorry I was harsh. The story sounds great. Do we have any arrests yet?"

"Pull up a seat, boss. We need to discuss a few things before we go further."

"The news meeting's about to start. You know how Pritchard is about beginning on time. I have to print out your budget line and get in there. We'll talk as soon as the meeting's over."

Reed put his feet up on the desk. "We'll talk now. Unless you want to go in there and make a fool of yourself."

"You lost me, Stuart. What are you talking about?"

"I think it's high time we threw out some old rules and made ourselves some new ones. First of all, yesterday you told me that I was off the story permanently. You haven't told me otherwise."

She hesitated. "Well . . . OK. You're back on the story. What else?"

"I want to make a deal. Strictly between you and me. What Pritchard doesn't know can't cause him *agita*. Before I go any further, you should be aware of the fact that I'm the only reporter with the connections to get the story for you, and I want guarantees from you that you'll keep me on the story until it plays itself out."

Claire assented, with a frown.

"Furthermore, I want temporary leave from the environmental beat so I can work on this full-time. I'll file that DEP resignation story for you, and then that's it. And when I break this story open, I want permission to write it up for a national magazine as well—on *Transcript* time. Finally, I want you to back off for a while. From now on, I come and go as I please. I'll do my job, I'll give you your blessed budget lines, and I'll make every deadline. In return, you'll save your raft of crap for somebody else. Agreed?"

Green folded her arms. "I hardly believe that I give anybody a raft of crap, as you put it." With each parry, her voice grew louder.

"Look around metro," Reed countered. "All I see is a bunch of sailors, trying to stay afloat."

At this point, a few reporters had stopped what they were doing to listen. Claire's face reddened. "Stuart, this is insubordination."

"You want the story, or you want me to write it for another publication?"

"I'll fire you."

"Try it. We'll see who gets canned. If you get over your snit fit here and look at the situation objectively, you'll see that even a wimp like Pritchard would want me to go after the story. You have a reporter with great inside sources in the Violent Crimes Unit—sources that won't speak to anyone else. Believe it. And what they have to talk about is the possibility of a serial killer on the loose right here in our dear, safe environs. Son of Sam does the suburbs. It's probably the most important story you'll ever have the chance to handle. So be a sport. Take a chance. Live a little. Say yes."

"You have one week free and clear, and that's it."

"Thanks, Claire. You're a sweetheart. And I mean that sincerely."

She stormed off to the news meeting. When she disappeared from sight, several reporters broke into applause.

Reed filed the story by three P.M. He led with Cippriani's information, mixing in a few quotes from an FBI spokesman in Quantico who said he couldn't comment on current investigations but did explain what the National Center for the Analysis of Violent Crime did. Reed recapped the Diaz case, mentioning she was to be buried that very day, and threw in a few paragraphs on the other cases that Cippriani thought might be connected to the Diaz slaying.

Near the end of the story, he invented a quote from an anonymous law-enforcement official, saying that this could turn out to be the biggest one-man killing wave in the metropolitan area since Son of Sam roamed the outer boroughs in the seventies. Claire cut that quote, lest the paper create a panic, but she left in the statements from the prosecutor and Brenner that the Violent Crimes Unit was the best around, and Detective Cippriani's current investigation was just another example of that. She also left Reed's lead paragraphs and the copyright untouched:

By Stuart Reed
Staff Writer
© The Riverton Transcript

RIVERTON—A county homicide detective yesterday linked the Diana Diaz slaying with two other brutal murders in the region in the past year.

According to Detective Aldo Cippriani, the FBI has confirmed the lethal connection: all three cases involved teenage girls who were assaulted, slain, and dumped in remote locations.

Once Claire Green OK'd the Diaz story, Reed banged out the DEP resignation story in forty-five minutes, then went full tilt on learning all he could about Culp Jenkins.

His first call was to the state Department of Wildlife. "Hi, Helen. Stuart Reed calling from *The Transcript*. Got a favor to ask of you. I've been assigned to do a profile of the TV sportsman, Culp Jenkins. It's going to be a pretty favorable piece, and I want to make sure he doesn't have any skeletons in his closet that might make me or the paper appear foolish when the story comes out. . . .

"You might start by checking the records to see if he had his hunting or fishing license revoked for any reason—raping rabbits, catching too many trout. Tell you what. Why not just dig out whatever files you got on him and fax it up to me tomorrow morning? Great. I owe you lunch. . . ."

Reed headed over to the features department to talk to the clerk who handled the daily TV listings. He wondered if there was a press kit on Culp Jenkins' wildlife show. There was. He copied it.

Next stop was the sports department, to see if the hunting and fishing columnist was around. He wasn't. Never came into the office; always filed by phone. Did anyone know of any other hunting fanatics on staff? Yes, the sports editor said, Dick Yerkes, a nightside copy editor, used to hunt small game, and Milt Roberts the photographer still hunted deer with bow and arrow.

Reed picked up a phone and dialed the photo department's extension. Milt was out shooting enterprise weather shots. Wouldn't be back until tomorrow morning. Would he stop by Stuart Reed's desk? Certainly. They'd radio Milt the message now.

Back at his desk, Reed reviewed the bio of Culp Jenkins included in the press kit.

Culp Jenkins, the writer, producer, and host of *The Wild Life,* has been an international sportsman and celebrity since 1980, when he made the acclaimed documentary, *The Deer Stalkers,* about a hunting trip that turned into a tale of survival in the wilds of northern Maine.

The fifty-one-year-old Kentucky-bred Jenkins has been an avid hunter and outdoorsman since the tender age of five, when his father took Culp along on hunting trips. During his teen years, he worked as a hunting guide's apprentice in Montana. In the Vietnam era, he served three years in the armed forces. He is the author of three books on hunting, as well as the new, acclaimed video encyclopedia of deer hunting, *The Sportsman's Primer.*

In 1982, the independently wealthy Jenkins founded the National Wildlife Conservancy, a nonprofit group dedicated to protecting the environment and endangered species. He has won the National Police League Citizenship Award for his campaign against the legalization of Teflon-coated bullets. He has been a guest at the White House on numerous occasions. He currently lives in a suburb of New York with his two Labrador retrievers, Winchester and Colt.

Reed underlined a few areas worth following up on, then dialed the New York City syndication company that handled *The Wild Life* show and asked for the publicity department.

"Hi. This is Stuart Reed calling from *The Riverton Transcript,* over in Jersey. I'm the paper's environmental reporter, and I'm told that

Culp Jenkins would make a great interview for our features section. Is Mr. Jenkins available for interviews?"

The PR woman said she'd have to check with Mr. Jenkins. But, she added, as luck would have it, Mr. Jenkins lived in *The Transcript*'s circulation area and had wanted a story in the TV section for more than a year. She said she'd see what she could do.

Reed wanted to know if there were any videotapes of the show or *The Sportsman's Primer* that she could Federal Express to him, or— better yet—leave for him to pick up.

Would the eight-volume *Sportsman's Primer* be too much? she asked. No, Reed replied, that would be perfect. He arranged for her to leave it at the night desk. The office building stayed opened to nine, she said.

He arrived at eight-forty-five and double-parked long enough to retrieve the carton of tapes. At the first red light, he looked through the titles of the ten tapes. Volume six caught his eye: *After the Kill: How to Field Dress and Skin Your Deer.*

# Chapter Twenty-two

Tuesday night, after his wife had gone to bed, Stuart Reed slid the forty-minute tape into the VCR. He had expected to see a redneck in camouflage talking awkwardly into a hand-held mike. What Reed got was a smashing performance by a man who was one-part bank executive, one-part helpful neighbor, and two-parts Billy Graham.

The credits rolled with some classical music and a shot of Culp Jenkins in the background—Reed recognized Jenkins from the photograph taken opening day at the pistol range. The silver-haired sportsman sat in a cordovan wing chair in a library and turned the pages of a leather-bound volume. Jenkins wore a blue blazer, gray flannel slacks, a white button-down dress shirt, and a necktie the shade of red favored by TV newscasters.

Reed leaned forward on the sofa and laughed—what was this show supposed to be, *Masterpiece Hunting*? When the credits ended, the music faded, Jenkins looked up from his book and smiled easily, as if an old hunting companion had just joined him. He casually held the book so viewers could see the title, *The Call of the Wild,* by Jack London.

"Hi, I'm Culp Jenkins, and this is part six of *The Sportsman's Primer.* He spoke in a deep baritone as smooth as good Kentucky sour mash, and every bit as Southern. Although he had no doubt gone to a voice coach—an amateur couldn't possibly come across that polished—"Jenkins" sounded like "Jinkins," and he drawled a final consonant here and there.

"I'd like to offer a brief welcome to any new folks out there that haven't seen any of the other videos, and I'd like to ask my old friends to bear with me for a moment to talk to you about the concept behind *The Sportsman's Primer.* But if you're in a hurry to get to the good stuff, then please feel free to hit the fast forward button. You won't hurt my feelings."

Jenkins proceeded to go through the predictable blah-blah-blah about how the series of videos were designed to give hunters who care about their sport not only some good field-proven advice on various subjects of interest but also "a set of values to hunt and to live by." Jenkins talked grandly of conserving the natural resources that America had been blessed with, and developing "a sense of appreciation for all of God's creatures." He talked of the National Wildlife Conservancy, a nonprofit organization that donated thousands of dollars every year to help protect the environment. As he prattled on, the video cut to scenes of waterfalls, amber waves of grain, deer frolicking in a verdant forest.

"Before we discuss the subject of this video, field dressing and skinning your buck, I'd like to say a few words about the importance of hunting. I realize I may be accused of preaching to the already converted," he said with a self-deprecating grin, "but some things need to be repeated. I share them with you in the event that you someday find yourself at a social function and some pantywaist antihunting, antigun zealot starts to condemn us hunters for slaughtering defenseless animals."

Reed opened a beer and watched a while longer while Jenkins stood, walked to the bookshelves, and invoked the names of Hemingway and London as he described how hunting was not only part of man's innate nature but part of the great American tradition as well. When Reed found himself about to gag, he fast forwarded through the rest of the library sequence.

In the next scene, Jenkins was in a forest, his back to the camera. He wore bark-colored camouflage overalls, a navy blue baseball cap, and a fluorescent orange hunter's vest with a hunting permit displayed in a clear plastic pouch.

Jenkins was standing behind a thick tree. As he looked through the scope of a hunting rifle, the camera zoomed down the barrel and across a stream to reveal a large buck loping through a harvested cornfield. The video cut to a close-up of Jenkins' right index finger squeezing the trigger, and—*blam*—as the rifle fire reverberated in the stillness, the video cut to the buck, which stumbled for an instant then broke into a run.

The camera followed the deer's progress as it lurched toward a ridge. Two other deer joined him in his flight but soon scampered past him on the rocky ground. The buck began to move in slow motion, then stumbled and slumped on its haunches.

The video cut to Jenkins, looking into the camera lens now. "I think we nailed him," he said excitedly, giving the thumbs-up sign. "We'll soon find out."

A hand-held shot followed Jenkins as he walked cautiously up the slope. In the crackling leaves underfoot, Jenkins' chatter was barely audible. "He should be right up here, a big gorgeous buck."

The next shot was of a deer lying motionless on its stomach, with its chin buried in leaves. Jenkins approached his quarry gingerly and used a long stick to prod the deer several times. It didn't so much as twitch. Jenkins turned to face the camera. "This is great. I was shooting slightly downhill, which is preferable from a safety standpoint. And I shot him clean, as you saw. He didn't suffer long. See, he's not bleeding much."

Jenkins kicked the deer in the side, then raised the deer by its antlers. "Let's see. One, two, three, four—an eight-point buck. Gorgeous."

He tied a tag around the antlers.

The video cut to a wide sloping lawn. Jenkins stood in front of his trophy buck and discussed his hunting techniques. "You'll note that I didn't shoot as soon as I got this big guy in my sights. I checked the terrain to make sure there weren't any other hunters about, and I waited until the buck slowed to inspect the cornstalks so I'd have an excellent chance of hitting the mark and killing him clean. If I hadn't, the deer might have fled for a half a mile or more, and we'd have had to track his trail of blood. This way's so much better, so much easier, so much better for the buck, don't you think?"

Jenkins bent over the dead buck, narrated a brief deer anatomy lesson, then went into field dressing—"a fifteen or twenty minute job if you know what you're doing." He rolled the deer on its side, its legs pointing down the slight grade, then talked about what knives were best for the upcoming procedure. Reed reached for his pen and notepad.

"Before I use my knife, I use a razor blade that I always keep wrapped in my pocket. This way I can shave away the thick hair on the deer's underbelly and cut the first layer of skin smoothly."

Jenkins then straddled the deer and used his hunting knife to make a slit from the bottom of the deer's belly clear to the rib cage. He peeled back the skin on the stomach, cut through a milky white membrane, and tugged gently on the deer's innards. Intestines, stomach, liver, heart—all slid out in one bloody mass.

Reed stopped the tape and took a slug of his beer. Jeez, Reed thought, this guy really gets into it, or gets off on it. Reed had seen enough of the tape but wanted to review one section again—the part where Jenkins used a razor blade, then a hunting knife, to cut open the deer's belly. It was almost too good to be true.

# Chapter Twenty-three

The funeral of Diana Diaz began at eleven A.M. Wednesday in an evangelical church, a dozen blocks from Prospect Park in Brooklyn. Stuart Reed arrived ten minutes late—he'd taken the wrong turn off the BQE—and spent most of the hour-long memorial service scanning the mourners for he didn't know what.

Reed had held out little hope that he'd come across any new leads for his investigation here, but he tried to make a mental note of the various faces in case it came in handy later. You never knew, Reed mused, you just never knew. The mourners were mostly Hispanics, dressed somberly for the occasion and coping poorly with their grief. Three women in the row across from him dabbed their eyes with white tissues throughout the service, and someone down front— Reed couldn't see who—had become hysterical during the sermon when the preacher made reference to the murderer.

The minister was a small-framed man, but his rich baritone filled the room as he swung into his windup, his arms out-stretched. "May the Lord bring this fiend to justice," the minister solemnly intoned, and the congregation erupted into a chorus of "amens" and "Good Gods" but, as Reed noted, nary a "Lord have mercy."

When the chanting stopped, a young man jumped up and pulled violently on his hair. "It's not fair," he shouted, then sobbed uncontrollably. The preacher paused for two ushers to lead the distraught man to the doors of the church, where he seemed to regain control of his emotions.

The all-news radio stations had been reporting Reed's story about the murder ever since the first edition of *The Transcript* hit the news kiosks in the Port Authority at sunrise, and no doubt the thought that the girl had died at the hands of a methodical madman had heightened the highly charged atmosphere in the room. Reed fumbled with his shirt collar nervously, unbuttoning the top button and loosening his tie. He figured that this was no place for a stranger.

Reed breathed easier when the congregation sang the recessional, and he slipped out the back doors during the final verse of "Amazing Grace" so he could position himself on the stoop to study the mourners as they filed out.

They did so in rapt silence, puffy eyed and disconsolate. As he watched them, his head slightly bowed, Reed's heart raced and he reflexively balled his hands into fists. Although a cold blustery wind snapped at the mourners' topcoats and had them holding onto their hats and black veils, Reed's cheeks burned hot. In his brain flashed the image of Culp Jenkins, straddling the dead deer and slicing open its stomach. Reed would ease these people's grief, he vowed to himself. He would bring that son of a bitch to justice. Then, and only then, could anyone be able to rest in peace.

As the dead girl's father trudged solemnly past, his elbows locked with the minister's, Reed considered talking to him outside, but thought better of it. For once he would take Claire Green's advice and leave the police work to the police.

A good thing, too, for near the end of the procession Reed spotted a familiar face, that of Aldo Cippriani. Reed fell in beside him.

"You going to the cemetery?" Reed whispered.

Cippriani said no.

"Can we talk for a second?"

"Only a second. I've got to get back to work before I get buried in paperwork. Don't you have a story to file or something?"

"Not till four. I've got something extremely important to tell you."

The two men walked alongside a line of cars in the funeral cortege, and nodded grimly to mourners who happened to glance at the two men as they went by.

Reed pointed to a bakery sign on the corner, and he and Cippriani headed inside. The place smelled of fresh doughnuts, reminding Reed that he hadn't had breakfast yet. He ordered a cinnamon doughnut and a large container of coffee. Cippriani stood by the window, watching the mourners.

Reed tore a hole in the container's plastic lid, took a sip, and joined Cippriani by the window.

"I think I tied Culp Jenkins to the killing last night, Aldo. In fact, I'm sure of it."

Cippriani grunted, waiting to be convinced. His eyes still looked out at the sidewalk.

"I borrowed a hunting video, a Culp Jenkins deer-hunting video called—get this—*After the Kill.* A forty-minute program about how to gut a deer. In the video, Jenkins demonstrated the best way to slit open a chest cavity."

Cippriani turned toward Reed, eyes opening wider.

"Jenkins says the way you do it is to use a razor to cut through the first layer of skin, then your hunting knife. Sound familiar?"

Cippriani grunted again and turned toward the window. "Doesn't mean dick."

"What do you mean? We know Jenkins was familiar with the pistol range, and now we finally know why two different blades were used to cut the girl open. I'd say we're on the right track, wouldn't you?" Reed bit a large chunk out of the doughnut, then used his coat sleeve to wipe away the crumbs on his lips.

Reed saw from Cippriani's flat expression that he was unimpressed by Reed's information. "I'd already figured out the knife bit," Cippriani said. "It's fairly common among hunters. Besides, if you saw the video, so have hundreds of others. That's not enough to link Jenkins to the murder—it's not even close. I checked his background. He's clean."

"But—"

"Look, you don't solve a case like this by singling out a possible suspect and trying to make a positive match. You follow time-proven procedures, working from the body of solid evidence and going where it leads you."

"And where's that?"

Cippriani's nose had started to run, and he rubbed it with a Kleenex. "Right now? Nowhere. But we're going to keep on following through, playing it by the book."

"And wait until another Diana Diaz gets sliced? Hopefully in another police department's jurisdiction."

Cippriani grasped the door handle. "I don't need your garbage, you know. You want to play ball with me on this, you play by my rules or you don't play at all."

As Cippriani opened the door, Reed grabbed the detective's sleeve. "What the hell's bugging you today?"

"You are. I got a call from Quantico right before I came over here. Their field office up here faxed them a copy of your effing story in today's *Transcript.* Let's just say they're extremely pissed, and leave it at that."

"What?" Reed demanded.

"You overwrote that story in today's paper. You overplayed the FBI and serial killer crap. You shouldn't have attributed it to me. The FBI has now completely ruled out any links between Diaz and the other killings. You're fishing up the wrong creek. I gotta go."

"But I have more to tell you."

"Not now. I'm swamped. We'll talk later, when I find the time. If you want to get me up to speed in the meantime, write me a memo on what you got. That way when we talk, we don't spend half the time going over your stupid theories."

Reed grabbed Cippriani's sleeve again. "You didn't think they were so stupid the other day when I pointed out that discrepancy in the autopsy—the contact lenses."

"You got lucky, pal. Don't press that luck too hard." Cippriani pushed Reed's hand away, and there was a split second when Reed thought the detective might take a swing at him.

Instead, Cippriani poked his index finger into Reed's chest and raised his voice a notch. "I'm looking out for you on this as much as I am for myself. Believe it or don't. I saw the body, too. You think I enjoy the fact the creep is still out there somewhere? I want to catch whoever did it as bad as you do, maybe more. You already got a story out of it, and you made the Violent Crimes Unit look like a bunch of deadheads in the process. Now sit back and let me do my job. If I do catch the guy, I don't want my case shot to hell because you screwed things up."

Reed stood inside the doorway and watched the detective walk down the sidewalk until he disappeared around the next corner. Reed saw a red neon Budweiser sign in the window of a taproom across the street, and told himself it was too early in the day.

# Chapter Twenty-four

Claire Green was in one of her uglier moods, which could mean anything from getting scooped by another paper to discovering that a reporter had gone to lunch without checking with her highness first.

She had little to say to Reed, only that she had decided to go with a photo and cutlines on the funeral unless Reed could come up with something more substantial that afternoon. The editors at the news meeting were getting tired of the story.

Reed replied that the editors didn't know what they were talking about, and that he hadn't seen any photographers at the church.

"Maybe you would have if you'd been there on time. Photographer had another job in the city, at noon, so she took a few frames of the girl's father entering the church, then split. You got anything working that I should know about?"

"Nothing for tomorrow, but I may be onto something big."

"Care to clue me in for once? Before you say anything, just tell me it doesn't involve the FBI. Because someone from D.C. called Pritchard just before lunch and read him the riot act—or at least tried to. Pritchard played hard ass and told the guy to piss on somebody else's leg."

Reed's eyes widened, but Claire Green squelched his hopes. "But that doesn't mean that you're not on Pritchard's shit list. Pritchard *hates* that kind of call. He said that from here on in, he's going to read every inch of your copy with a magnifying glass to make sure you get it right."

Reed gave her a phony smile. "That's great. I'd like Pritchard to read my copy. Then maybe he'd realize what a star he has on his hands."

Claire glared at him. "You're on *my* shit list, too," she said, and returned to her VDT. Discussion over.

Reed sat at his work station and inputted the caption information for the funeral photo. Moments later, "msg pending" blinked in the command field on his VDT. He called it up. It was from Claire. "Don't forget to mention the status of the investigation. FBI told Pritchard that the serial killer theory was the biggest pile of horse crap this side of the Central Park riding stables, and you sure as hell didn't get confirmation from them. So you might say that the Violent Crimes Unit is pursuing several leads, and leave it at that."

Reed spiked the message and gave the VDT a healthy whack with his open palm, which was more mature than his initial reaction—to send her a message that she was on his shit list as well. If Claire had gone to the trouble to send him an elaborate electronic message instead of just talking to him, it meant that either she was:

a. pissed off at him
b. trying to distance herself from him and the story
c. saving a copy of the message and keeping a file on Reed's coverage of the ongoing story, just to cover her own ass if he screwed things up. Under Pritchard Majors' regime, getting good stories into the paper took a backseat to damage control.

But he hadn't screwed up yet, damnit, he thought. He may have embellished the FBI stuff, but that didn't mean his assessment had missed the mark. He got the feeling that too many people were more concerned about covering their butts than finding Diana Diaz's killer —and he would prove them wrong.

If it wasn't a serial killer, it wasn't any skin off anybody's back. At the very least, Reed's story had kept the murder in the public eye a week after it had happened, and it forced the police to keep up their investigations.

And if a maniac really was on the loose, his stories might make more people double-bolt their doors, stay on their toes around strangers, and stay away from strange bars and isolated parking lots.

Reed finished the story on the funeral and shipped it to the news desk for processing, then called his contact at the state Department of Wildlife.

"Helen, it's Stuart Reed. Got anything for me?"

He heard a shuffling of papers on the other end. "Yes, I do in fact —off the record. Culp Jenkins was apparently stopped a few years ago for bagging an underage deer."

"What?" Reed pressed the phone hard against his ear to make sure he didn't miss a word.

"A couple of forest rangers stopped Jenkins' truck during deer-hunting season a few years back. Four years ago, according to the report. He had a young doe strapped to his roof, and he hadn't tagged it or taken it to a check station as the rules require."

"And?"

She said that she had followed up with the ranger who had filed the report, and that he had told her that Jenkins was rattled when they'd stopped his truck, that he had explained that he hadn't realized that the deer was too young until after he'd killed it, and that rather than report it, he had panicked. He pleaded with the ranger not to write up the incident.

Reed scribbled frantically on a yellow legal pad. When he asked Helen to continue, she balked, and Reed had to prod it out of her. She said that strictly off the record, the ranger had struck a deal with Jenkins, taking into account that it hadn't been intentional and that Jenkins was a hunter of some renown. The ranger would write up the incident and put the report in the pending file. If Jenkins stopped hunting in New Jersey for five years and kept his nose clean, the report would be shredded.

"That stinks," Reed said, making no effort to mask his disgust.

"It's not uncommon. Hunters accidentally kill underage deer from time to time, just as fishermen get caught with undersize trout. There are bigger sins in this world. Rangers are often hunters themselves. They're not out to pillory some fellow hunter for messing up once, especially someone like Jenkins. The punishment fits the crime."

Reed swallowed hard. "I bet he paid 'em off. Can you fax me that report? Off the record. Just for background," he lied. "Please, Helen, ol' pal, ol' buddy?"

She refused. It was against department policy, she said.

Could he drive to Trenton and look at it? he asked, thinking that he might be able to sneak a photocopy of it or photograph it.

No.

"Could you tell me if the deer had been gut—"

She hung up before he finished the sentence.

Reed went to the cafeteria and got a large container of coffee. He knew that he was on to something, but he couldn't decide how to proceed. What he knew and what he could write for publication were two different stories, and what he could write for publication was a big fat zero.

He dialed Jenkins' TV production company and tried to do a little fishing. He had called earlier about an interview, he explained, and wondered if next Monday would be OK. The assistant said that Mondays were no good.

Why?

Because Jenkins taught a class at Columbia every Monday.

How about tomorrow then?

The assistant said she'd have to get back to him.

Reed gulped his coffee, opened a computer file, and pecked out a memo to Cippriani that listed all the items that linked Jenkins to the murder: his familiarity with the pistol range, the technique used to slice up the body, the incident with the underage doe, the fact that Jenkins taught at Columbia on Mondays, which would have put him on campus the day Diana Diaz disappeared.

In conclusion, Reed wrote, while none of this would convict Culp Jenkins of anything, it meant that Jenkins was a suspect worth pursuing. He printed out the memo on the laser printer, and sent it to Cippriani by fax machine.

# Chapter Twenty-five

Stuart Reed spent the rest of the afternoon going over a week's worth of notes, computer printouts, and newspaper clippings. As he sifted through the material, he kept a list of loose ends to be nailed down by Friday afternoon. He compiled a list of questions for Cippriani. Had the detective received faxes of the other two autopsies in question yet, and if so, what did they say? He also needed Cippriani to call the dead girl's father and get a list of courses that Diana Diaz had been taking at Columbia—you never knew when you might get lucky.

He was picking up the phone to call Cippriani when Ray Michel tapped him on the shoulder. "Got a minute?"

Reed said OK. Michel was the paper's investigative editor. He handled the mob stuff and consumer rip-offs, including the local auto dealer who had canceled his million-dollar ad campaign in *The Transcript* after Michel had done a series on how the dealer had rolled back the mileage on demo cars and sold them as new. Michel was presently an outcast, as the current regime frowned on stories that hurt ad revenues, but Michel still mined his beat and quietly produced stories that exposed crooked TV repairmen, fly-by-night travel agencies, and the like. For Reed, the bottom line was that Michel knew the ropes and might be of help.

Michel's office was an oversized closet behind the photocopying room. It had no sign on the door, save for a Vote Libertarian bumper sticker. The office itself had no windows, no bookcases; just two desks, three chairs, and a metal table piled high with folders, documents, and microcassettes. Scotch-taped to the wall was a sign that announced, DEADLINE FOR COMPLAINTS WAS YESTERDAY. Michel pointed to the chair, then sat on the edge of his desk. "So you're working a murder story. Pritchard took me aside and asked if I'd help you out. I said no, that I hate sticking my nose in other reporters' stories, but that I would offer any assistance when asked."

"And so you're asking me to ask, right?" Reed forced a smile and tried to guess what Michel was up to—trying to horn in on a good story? Pumping him for information to relay back to Majors?

Michel scratched his beard, a Brillolike Vandyke that, like his hair, was in bad need of a trim. He said that Reed shouldn't get defensive —that any investigative editor would be curious how Reed was doing.

"I'm doing fine, thanks," Reed replied.

"Can I ask what you got so far?"

"You can, but I'm not going to tell you."

"Oh?" Michel folded his arms, then crossed his legs. One leg began to swing rapidly.

"Nothing against you, Ray, but I don't want too many chefs stirring my pot."

"Or jerking your chain, right?" The leg swung faster. "Well, I'll give you some general advice, and don't be put off or offended. Mind if I smoke?"

Reed said it was OK, even though smoking was prohibited everywhere on the floor except for a very small lounge unofficially known as the cancer ward. Michel lit up and inhaled. The leg stopped swinging.

"A few things, Stuart. First, with this kind of story the tendency is to publish every scrap of information as you get it. That's a bad idea, and I'll tell you why. Nickel-dime stories get lousy play, and editors begin to think of the whole thing as a lousy story. They figure that you're hanging on to it so you don't have to go back to your beat. What's more, every time you print some bit of information, you're tipping your hand to the other papers, who may be working on the story themselves."

Michel inhaled on the cigarette, and told Reed that murder investigations were mine fields. That if Reed wrote the wrong thing, or wrote the right thing in the wrong words, he could open up the paper to libel charges.

Reed nodded. This was why he'd been called in. He noticed a microphone suction-cupped to the phone receiver, and wondered if this lecture was being recorded as well.

Michel continued: "Don't write anything that could be considered libelous, not in your notes, not even in the name of the electronic file you're writing the story in. One reporter was doing a story on a sleazoid councilman, and he slugged the story 'slimeball.' Majors saw the slug 'slimeball' on the news budget, hit the roof, and spiked the story. Know why?"

"It showed intent to smear the guy, right? Those are the guidelines these days, right?"

"And so is anything—anything at all—that could be similarly misconstrued in your notes. If you got sued for libel on a story, little things make great ammunition for the plaintiff's lawyers. And given the gun-shy atmosphere around here, you just might have to hand those notes over. I mean, can you see Majors paying lawyers two hundred bucks an hour to defend you in some shield law case? You'll be left to hang out to dry by yourself."

"Good advice, Ray," Reed said, standing up. "I mean it. I'll keep it in mind."

"Indulge me one more minute, Stuart. Two more things. One is if you've been fabricating any quotes—and I'm not saying that you have been—stop it before you get burned."

Reed looked down, focusing on a coffee stain on the carpet, and said nothing.

Michel waited for eye contact before continuing. "As for my last bit of advice, I've done investigations for a dozen years and helped on countless others, and I need to warn you of a trap you can easily fall into if you're not careful. In ninety-nine successful investigations out of a hundred, either we got the meat of the story on the initial sniff or we had an insider supplying us with the goods.

"My advice is to take a good sniff, but if nothing turns up right away, don't go looking under every rock in the county. Reporters mess up when they spend weeks trying to come up with something. Because at that point, then they're out to prove that they weren't wasting their time, and they reach conclusions that mean either the spike or disaster."

"I hear you."

"How long you been looking into this murder, a week?"

Reed nodded yes.

"If you don't find the smoking gun in another day or two, well, take my word for it—the gun won't be smoking anymore."

# Chapter Twenty-six

As soon as Stuart Reed returned to his desk, he spiked the electronic copy of the memo he'd written to Cippriani. Then he called the detective.

"You get my fax?"

"Yeah. Read it ten minutes ago."

"Great. Read it again, then rip it up and burn the pieces."

Cippriani grunted. "Sure. You want to be paranoid, I guess it's your privilege. Anything else?"

Reed asked him to check with Diana Diaz's father on what courses she was taking at Columbia, then inquired about the autopsies.

Cippriani said he'd received them, and that they were inconclusive. The bodies had been out in the elements too long. Cippriani agreed to meet with Reed around five P.M. to compare notes, and hung up.

Reed called Culp Jenkins' office again. An interview had been arranged for eleven the next morning at Jenkins' house in River View, a fifteen-minute drive from the Transcript Building—and the murder scene.

Later that afternoon, Reed's chat with Cippriani took less time than he had expected. Cippriani had gotten the list of the Diaz girl's courses—none would have put her on the same part of the campus as Jenkins, let alone in his classroom. Cippriani said that he found Reed's information interesting but unsubstantial, and cringed when Reed told him that he'd arranged an interview with Jenkins for the following day.

"Crap. Don't go playing Nancy Drew on me, Reed. I warned you already. You'll only screw things up."

"I'm not an idiot. I'm not going to mention the murder. I just want to meet the guy close up, see what makes him tick. I could be dead wrong about him, and if I am, I'll be the first to admit it."

At the apartment Reed found a note on the fridge from Jeanne. Tonight was another parents' night, and to expect her around nine. Reed went to the D'Agostino's on Third Avenue and bought some salad fixings, a couple of baking potatoes, and the best sirloin he could find. He bought a bottle of French Bordeaux at the liquor store, and had dinner waiting when Jeanne arrived a few minutes past nine.

She noticed the table settings but said nothing. She hung up her coat, walked past her husband, and poured herself a glass of wine. "I wish you hadn't gone to the trouble," she said. "I grabbed a bite at six, and I'm just not hungry."

Reed sensed that they had acted out this scene before, and experience told him that it never had a happy ending.

"Parents night always depresses me," Jeanne said, swirling the wine in the glass. "It's the same every time. The parents of the kids who are doing fairly well always show up, and the parents of the hotel kids are nowhere to be found. So why bother? I'm beating my head against the wall."

Reed sat next to her. "But where would those kids be without you? You're making your mark. You just don't realize it."

Jeanne told him to stop patronizing her.

"If I don't patronize you, who will I patronize?"

"If that's supposed to be a joke, I'm not in the mood." She gulped the wine. "And I thought I told you to stop drinking."

"Only a glass of wine with dinner. No harm in that."

"But I know you. You'll knock off the whole bottle tonight."

"You're wrong. I've got too much work to do."

"When has that stopped you?" She put the glass on the coffee table and curled sideways on the couch, her back to her husband.

# Chapter Twenty-seven

Culp Jenkins' home was off Oritani Road, a narrow oak-lined lane that ran parallel to the river and dated from the early days of the colonies, as evidenced by the exquisitely restored stone colonial residences that sat by the road every quarter mile or so. The area was home to the county's old money and—to judge from the glass and cedar contemporaries sprouting up on the hillsides—new money as well. The town was close enough to New York to draw some of Wall Street's heavy hitters, plus a smattering of pro athletes, entertainers, and mobsters.

Stuart Reed never would have found the Jenkins place without directions. Even with explicit instructions from Jenkins' assistant, Reed had twice driven past the driveway, which was obscured by two massive oaks that must have been around ever since the Dutch had settled the area in the sixteen hundreds.

The drive sloped gently down toward the river and a modest one-story center-chimney colonial on its banks. The house was white-painted cedar shakes, with slate blue shutters and a glossy varnished wooden door.

Off to the side were parking spaces for five cars. A British racing-green Jag with a PBA sticker in the rear window occupied one space. A gray panel truck sat in another. Reed pulled his Jetta alongside the van, and wondered what a forensics expert might find inside it.

Reed got out of his car, decided he didn't need to lock it, and took a deep breath. Ten miles away from Riverton, and already the air began to taste like New England. He reached for his briefcase and the set of hunting videos.

At the front door, Reed read a brass plaque engraved THE MILL HOUSE. BUILT 1747 TO LODGE WORKERS FOR THE VAN STRANDER MILL. He looked for a door bell, then rapped on a heavy wrought iron knocker. Culp Jenkins opened the door moments later, full of pleasantries about the great autumn weather and the white crane he'd seen down by the water earlier that morning.

Jenkins was taller than Reed had figured him, six-foot-four, with a farmer's handshake strong enough to crack walnuts. Reed squeezed back in self-defense and felt relieved when Jenkins released his grip.

"So you want to do a story on me, huh? I dare say the timing couldn't be better. I see you have my new series of hunting videos, my syndicated cable show is in its fourth season now, and I'm clean up to my eyeballs in some important environmental projects."

Jenkins took Reed's coat and the videocassettes, and ushered him down a flight of narrow stairs. The room below was right out of *Colonial Homes* magazine—a huge bay window looked out on the river, wide-plank pumpkin pine floor, exposed-beam ceiling, a fireplace that occupied an entire wall.

"This place is beautiful," Reed said, genuinely taken aback. "From the road, it looks so small, a cottage, but . . ."

"Yes, isn't it something? It's called a bank house. It's built into the hill, so you really don't see much house from the front, but believe me, it's big. Three thousand square feet.

"Come outside and you'll get a better idea of what I mean." Jenkins opened a Dutch door and led Reed onto a brick patio as long as Reed's entire apartment. Reed turned to see three stories of glass—sweeping picture windows, dormers with skylights, a two-story greenhouse.

"Must be a pain to heat," Reed blurted.

Jenkins laughed. "I suppose it is, but the early settlers were pretty dang smart. This side of the house faces south and catches the sunlight. And since it's built into an embankment, it's cool in the summer and sheltered from those harsh north winds in the winter."

"Belongs in a magazine." Reed placed his hands under his armpits to warm them from the chilly autumn breeze.

"I've been approached but . . . I'd rather keep it a secret. Afraid some burglar might read about it and get ideas. Can't be too careful, as my pappy used to say. . . . You look cold. I shouldn't have been so hasty to take your jacket. We can go inside."

Back in the room, Jenkins lit some kindling in the enormous stone fireplace, then disappeared into the next room. Reed had been so taken by Jenkins and his house that he'd momentarily forgotten why he was there. He remembered, and quickly looked around the room for anything that might connect Jenkins to Diana Diaz. Nothing in particular, but no harm in checking. All he saw was money well spent. A wall filled by leather-bound books and Steuben crystal, what looked like a genuine Andrew Wyeth watercolor over the mantel.

Jenkins returned with a sterling silver tray laden with matching creamer, sugar bowl, and coffee pot, red linen napkins, and two spatterware mugs. "Hope you like coffee. Brewed it just before you got here."

"I didn't expect the royal treatment."

Jenkins set the tray on a butler's table. "I'm an old buddy of your boss, Pritch Majors. Can't have word getting back to him that I treated one of his men shabbily."

Reed feigned a smile and changed the subject. "How'd your parents ever come to name you Culp?"

"Have a seat, make yourself at home." Jenkins ushered Reed over to two cordovan wing chairs that faced the bay window, then poured the coffee. "My pappy's name was William, and he said he didn't want any son of his to go through life with the same name as a thousand other Jenkins. Culp was my mother's maiden name. He used to call her that when they were courting. So Culp I was."

When Jenkins got up to tend to the fire, Reed reached into his briefcase and fetched a tiny tape recorder. Reed decided that Jenkins' little Southernisms, like calling his father "his pappy" and tossing in an occasional "dang" had seemed forced. In fact, Reed thought, Jenkins good ol' boy routine was a tad too calculated. Still, it was a pretty good act.

"Mind if I tape our conversation?" Reed enquired. "It's a lot easier than writing frantically the whole time."

Jenkins said that it would be fine, and asked what Reed wanted to talk about.

Reed began with the hunting videos, how they were selling, then touched on Jenkins' outdoors show and the celebrities that Jenkins had hunted with. Jenkins answered expansively, and Reed decided that Jenkins talked for a living because he was so good at it—lacing his comments with anecdotes that were brief enough to make great quotes for the profile yet got across the point that the self-effacing Mr. Jenkins was a well-connected chap, and a philanthropic one at that. There was the fund-raiser where he had managed to spill champagne on Nancy Reagan's borrowed gown, and the time he went duck hunting with Jimmy Carter and fell out of the rowboat.

After thirty minutes of yarns and sermonettes on the environment, Reed turned the cassette over and pushed the conversation onto trickier ground. "Deer season's almost here—you hunt much in Jersey?"

"Used to, some years back. Herd in the north of the state has thinned out to the point it's not worth my while."

"I didn't know that. Ever had an embarrassing moment deer hunting—along the lines of falling out of Jimmy Carter's boat?"

Jenkins flicked a piece of lint from his corduroy trousers. "I don't get what you mean. Why do you ask?"

Touchy bastard, Reed thought. Then he looked into Jenkins' eyes and saw cold steel. "No reason, Mr. Jenkins. You've been telling me some great tales—thought you might have some more."

"No. I take my deer hunting very seriously." Jenkins shifted his weight and sat rigidly in his chair.

Reed noticed that the interview had turned frosty. Jenkins was weighing his words now.

"So where do you go deer hunting these days?"

"New York State. I own a hunting lodge in the heart of deer country. I've got a favorite spot, a stand of trees overlooking a corn-field just half a mile from my place. Usually manage to bag a big buck first day of the season every year."

"I'd love to go with you sometime—see the master in action."

"I'm not sure you'd be suited for it, Mr. Reed. Hunting is a waiting game. You do weeks of homework, studying your quarry's habits, then you just wait at the right place for the perfect moment. The real work is the preparation. Pulling the trigger is easy."

"How about after the kill? You like to field dress them yourself?"

Another glare. "I can take it or leave it. Again, seems like a bizarre question for you to be asking for a story."

"I was watching your video, and it struck me—"

The phone rang in the next room, and Jenkins rose to answer it. "You're out of time, my friend. Have I answered enough questions?"

"Yes. Thanks so much. Get the phone. I'll see myself out."

"When will your article appear?"

Reed's face turned red. "Not sure. I'll let you know. I'll probably have to call you to fill in a few things anyway."

"Good enough. Good-bye."

Reed hurried up the stairs, thankful that he had been spared a farewell handshake but worried that he had overplayed his cards. Doubtful. Just being paranoid, he decided.

At the top of the staircase, he located the coat closet. As he reached for his jacket, he noticed a pair of L. L. Bean duck-hunting shoes on the floor. He picked one up to see what size it was.

"Can I help you?" Reed froze, then turned to see Jenkins holding a portable phone at the base of the steps.

"No. Just dropped my briefcase, and a pen rolled out. Thanks again." Did that sound like a bullshit reply? Reed asked himself. No, just more paranoia. And a size eleven shoe. How long before Jenkins would notice that it was gone?

# Chapter Twenty-eight

Stuart Reed walked quietly into Aldo Cippriani's office and tossed the neoprene-soled shoe on the detective's desk.

A coffee mug went flying, and Cippriani stood bolt upright. "Crap. What the hell you think you're doing?" Then he looked closer at the shoe. "Where'd you get this?"

"Culp Jenkins' house. Must've accidentally put it in my briefcase as I was leaving my interview with him this morning."

Cippriani grabbed the leather-topped shoe and flung it into the hall, narrowly missing Reed's head and a clerk who happened to be walking by. "You're nuts. Absolutely certifiable. What good's this damned shoe going to do?"

"Use it to match the partial, damn it. I risk my neck and this is how you thank me?"

Cippriani clenched a fist. "It's worthless. Even if it matches, it's worthless. Inadmissible. You stole it. It'll never see its way into a courtroom, and neither will your cockamamie suspicions. Man, you're torture. You got a hearing problem? I tell you not to screw things up, and you go into a klepto act."

Reed stormed from Cippriani's office. His heart pounded. His face was beet red. He needed a beer.

He ended up drinking four. From a barroom down the block, he called Claire Green from a pay phone, said he was sick. She asked where the hell he'd been all morning. He lied and slammed the phone onto its cradle. He ordered a coffee, and when he felt sober enough, he drove home.

On the way, he kept replaying the conversation with Jenkins. Kept returning to that one snippet of conversation, one thing that Jenkins had said. "Hunting is a waiting game. You do your homework and get to know your quarry, then you wait for the perfect moment."

Reed would play the waiting game now, back off, wait for Jenkins to screw up. It was only a matter of time.

When Reed neared Fourteenth Street, he had an idea. He'd stop by Jeanne's school and surprise her. Perhaps they could call a truce, spend the rest of the afternoon in the sack. He double-parked in front of a candy store to buy some mints. Didn't want her to smell beer on his breath. He turned on to Twelfth Street and parked down the block from the school. Jeanne would walk by on her way home.

He took out his notepad and jotted down a few ideas. Around three-thirty, he saw Jeanne leave the school with another teacher, a male teacher that Reed had met at a Christmas party once. Reed tried to remember the jerk's name but came up empty. The pair stood on the concrete steps for a minute, chatting amiably. Then the man put his arm around her and gave her a kiss on the lips. They departed in opposite directions. Jeanne was smiling like a schoolgirl.

Reed waited a few moments, then hit the horn. Jeanne saw him, looked embarrassed, then hurried to greet him.

Reed leaned over and rolled down the window on the passenger side. "What was that all about?" he demanded.

"What was what all about?"

"The kiss. That worm kissed you."

"It was nothing. He was having trouble with one of the kids in his class acting up, and I gave him some advice. He was just thanking me."

"Then why'd you blush just now?"

Her shoulders stiffened. "Because I knew how you'd react. Just like you're acting right now. Stuart, he's gay."

"All the more reason not to let him kiss you."

"You're behaving like a Neanderthal. You need to get some counseling, quick."

"Get in."

"Get lost."

"I see my wife kissing some guy, and I'm a Neanderthal?" Reed was shaking now.

"You're talking nonsense—have you been drinking?" Jeanne leaned forward, her eyes studying his. "What are you doing here at this hour—you get fired?"

Reed fumbled for a reply.

"Don't bother answering. I know when you've been drinking. Your nose is red." She walked away, her long hair flying.

Reed honked the horn again, leaned on it. She ignored him and stormed back into the school.

Reed couldn't face the thought of returning to an empty apartment and waiting for Jeanne to cool off. Who knew what hour she'd finally traipse in? He walked to the corner and dialed the newsroom's eight-hundred number. "Milt Roberts, please."

"He's in photo. I'll transfer you."

Reed was told that Milt was in the darkroom. A good sign. Meant he wasn't out on some assignment. When the photographer finally came to the phone, Reed said he had to talk to him.

"I thought you were sick. Claire Green was looking for you all morning, from what I hear."

"I'm better now, and I need somebody to talk to, a hunter."

"I'm almost done. Want to meet me at my place in an hour or so? I live right here in Riverton. Lafayette Street, three doors in from Richards. Blue clapboard house on the right. Can't miss it."

"Great. I'll bring the beer."

# Chapter Twenty-nine

By the time that Stuart Reed returned to Riverton the western sky glowed red with the last traces of sunlight. Feeling like a kid playing hookey, he avoided driving past the Transcript Building, lest anybody happen to see him at a traffic light. He knew that he must be in deep trouble at work—even Jeanne had sensed it this afternoon. He'd been too cocky with Claire Green after he'd caught the error in the autopsy report, and she was out to nail him. He'd made her task easier by not telling her about the interview with Jenkins, not calling in all morning, then finally calling in sick. Could she tell he was phoning from a bar? He bit his lip. He was getting neurotic.

He turned his thoughts elsewhere, to Jenkins, but thinking about Jenkins and the murder made his head pound. The investigation was turning into one of those upscale jigsaw puzzles without a photo of the puzzle on the box. He'd managed to get the pieces around the edges to fit, but he had no idea what the big picture looked like, or even if Culp Jenkins was in it. Maybe Milt Roberts could help fill in some of the holes.

Milt had been a strange choice to call, Reed knew, but Milt had seen the body, too, and would understand what Reed was going through. He didn't know Roberts all that well, but enjoyed his company when they went on an assignment together. A little rough around the edges perhaps, and the only guy he'd met who wore a gold chain with a flannel shirt, but he was so unself-conscious about it that he managed to pull it off.

Roberts lived in a two-family house on the north end of town, a few blocks from the court house, the county building, and the high-rent district. If you had to live in Riverton, this was about the only section of town you could afford and still feel safe at night.

Even so, Reed noticed that some of the houses had iron gates across the first-floor windows, just like in Manhattan, and a couple of them had metallic stickers in the front window to warn intruders of electronic security systems. The sidewalks were empty, save for the clumps of trash cans awaiting pickup in the morning.

Bearing a case of Michelob and several bags of chips, Reed knocked on the door and greeted Milt as a long-lost friend.

"What's up, pal?" Milt said in typical *Transcript* photographer fashion. The turnover rate for reporters was so high that the photographers seldom bothered to remember names. Women reporters, much to their chagrin, were addressed as "babe."

"I hope I'm not interrupting your dinner," Reed said apologetically. "I didn't even ask if you were married."

"Hell, no. I got all night. Come on into the kitchen. We can ice down the beers, and it's the warmest room in the house."

The place was strictly bachelor digs—sofa covered with a sheet, a stereo, and a TV in the living room, cheap dinette in the kitchen. Reed had been in dozens of places like it over the years, even lived in a few, and he felt right at home.

Roberts stocked the fridge, and left out four beers for them to start with. In a half hour, they'd run through the four cans and the usual *Transcript* gossip—Pritchard Majors' latest cost-cutting move, the new good-looking woman in community, the most-recent departures.

Then Roberts blundered onto touchy ground. "Speaking of leaving, pal, I hear you're in the shits with Claire Green and Majors. Does it have to do with the dead girl?"

"You might say that." As Reed spoke, he fiddled with a poptop. "Early on, right after I found the body, I was cookin'—the contact lenses, the firing range stuff. I was probably too arrogant to Claire, and now that I'm spinning my wheels she's paying me back. I'm not surprised. Hell, I half expected it."

Milt said that management never knew how to treat their employees, never cut them any slack.

Reed nodded. "You know, just after I discovered the body, the county detective told me that seeing a body in that condition can really mess up your mind, and that I should take few days off. I'm thinking now that I should have."

Roberts confessed that he'd been pretty shaken up as well, had trouble concentrating on the job that whole week. But wasn't Reed onto something big? That was the scuttlebutt in the office.

Reed finished off the can of beer. "I thought I was, but I'm out of my league. I'm not a cop reporter. Truth is that Claire was right—for once—when she told me to just cover what the homicide dicks were up to and not play Sam Spade. Know what, though? I still think my hunch is right."

"And what's that?"

Reed reached into the fridge for two more beers. He hadn't eaten much all day, and he could feel the beers. "Actually, that's why I called you, Milt. I wanted to bounce my theory off you. You know the situation, and you're not involved in all the damned office politics."

Roberts told him to go right ahead, popped open his beer, and put his elbows on the Formica table separating the two men.

"I think the killer was a hunter."

"No kidding. What makes you say that?"

Reed went over the autopsy's findings, then the video. "Do many hunters make a double cut along the underbelly like that?"

"I can't really say because I don't hunt all that much. I heard about the razor-blade deal, but most guys don't like carrying blades like that. Your hands get too cold in the woods—too easy to get sloppy and cut yourself. But the technique isn't what I'd call a deep dark secret."

"Well, I've got a suspect who definitely uses the two-blade method. I know he has a pair of hunting shoes that are the same make and size as a shoe print the forensics guys found at the scene. And I know he's familiar with the area where the body was dumped. How many people in this world fit the bill like that?"

"Not a hell of a lot, I guess. But what about that serial killer stuff you wrote about two days ago?"

Reed drank for a minute, until he'd downed the entire can. Then he explained that FBI had put a kibosh on that angle, which is how he'd got headed for the doghouse in the first place.

"What do you do now?"

"I guess I go to work tomorrow morning and start acting like a model reporter—arrive early, buy Claire coffee, that kind of crap. Otherwise I guess I could be put on probation or something, which means no raise for six months and no chance of jumping to the *Times* or somewhere. Sooner or later, my guy'll slip up and the cops'll catch him. I'll write up my notes, maybe get a good story out of it yet. But for the time being it looks like all the landfill stories I can eat. You got a better idea?"

"The only idea I got right now is to call up a couple of chicks I know and invite them over for a two-on-two party. Never know where it might lead."

"I'm married, at least for now."

Roberts laughed. "Which means you're not getting any action at home. You might as well get a head start on your new bachelor-hood."

Reed declined again.

"I gotta tell you about these women. Maybe you'll change your tune. The one girl called me up and said she was a model and she needed some photos for her portfolio. She came over that night—I got a rinky-dink studio setup in the basement—and I took some head shots and the usual stuff. She was changing outfits right in front of me, and she had a dynamite body. I said to myself, Why not go for it? and asked her if she'd like to pose in the buff. She dropped her duds, I got some pillows for her to lie on, and before I knew it, I was buck naked, too."

Reed sat there, sipping his beer in amazement.

"The next day, the chick calls and says her roommate wants to pose for me, too. All I can say is that you'll do just fine with either of 'em. What d'ya say?"

"I'd say I've had enough beer for one day. I had a fight with my wife, as you probably figured out for yourself, and I want to be home tonight when she finally shows up. You got instant coffee?"

While Roberts filled a plastic coffee mug with water from the tap and put it in the microwave, Reed went to the bathroom. He knelt in front of the bowl, stuck his index finger against the back of his tongue, and heaved. Might as well get the alcohol out of his system as quickly as he could. He found a bottle of mouthwash by the sink, and it burned his throat when he gargled. He looked into the mirror and saw someone he didn't like. The man he saw was slowly losing control, drinking too much, not running anymore. He looked away, splashed cold water on his face, and returned to the kitchen.

"Coffee water's almost ready," Milt announced.

"Changed my mind. You got a Pepsi or something? I need a hit of sugar."

Roberts got him a sixteen-ounce Coke. "Offer still stands. Chicks can be here in ten minutes if we're lucky. I can show you their pictures, so you can see what you're missing."

Reed said no. He needed to get sober and get home. "If you don't mind, I'd like to drink this on the drive home—it'll keep me awake. I'll just scoot out the back door here and let you call your lady friend."

"Can't have you do that. You came in through the front. It's bad luck to leave through another door, and you look like you need all the help you can get."

# Chapter Thirty

Jeanne Reed never came home Thursday night. Stuart Reed had dozed off, waiting for her, and when he woke up along about eleven P.M., he figured as much. So he went to the deli and bought a six-pack of sixteen-ounce Miller Lites and a roast beef sandwich. He turned up the thermostat in the apartment to seventy-two degrees, brought his provisions over to the stereo, and sat on the floor with his back propped against the brick wall. He flipped through the albums until he found a Jeff Beck album called *Truth,* and put it on the turntable. He switched the receiver from CD to phono, and hit Play.

He'd had the album since high school, and for several years had assumed that Beck was the husky-voiced lead singer. Only later, when Rod Stewart released a couple of hits, had he realized that Beck was the guitarist on the earlier album. Even at that young age, Reed mused, he couldn't get the "truth" right.

As Stewart sang "Ol' Man River" with Beck's acoustic guitar in the background, Reed wolfed down the sandwich. He then attacked the six-pack the same way he attacked a ten-kilometer race. He started slowly, eased into a steady pace, and kept chugging. He didn't want to get too drunk, he didn't even want to get sleepy. He wanted to be calm enough to think, but more important, he wanted to be calm enough to focus on one thing at a time.

After fifteen minutes, the beer kicked in. He took three deep breaths just as he had always practiced, and ran a mental inventory on the two people who were tearing up his life, Jeanne Reed and Culp Jenkins.

Jeanne: Had he overreacted that afternoon? Had it been a friendly peck that he had witnessed and misinterpreted? But hadn't she re-acted badly, defensively? Why did some couples fight all the time, as if they enjoyed the fray, and forgot about it ten minutes later? Why did he and Jeanne have to act like prize fighters, slugging it out every six months or so and leaving each other permanently damaged? He couldn't take much more of it. Of that he was certain. He'd stop drinking after tonight, he swore. He'd get a clear mind. Maybe in a week, a month, he'd see things differently, more clearly. Maybe she would as well. As the saying went, time heals all wounds.

Then there was Jenkins, and Reed asked himself the same questions. Had he overreacted after he found the girl's body, misinterpreted the evidence? But hadn't Jenkins reacted poorly this morning, defensively? Yes, damnit, he had. It was time for Reed to play the hunter, Jenkins' kind of hunter, playing a waiting game until the perfect moment arrived. As the other saying went, time wounds all heels.

The first few days after Reed had discovered the corpse, he had thought of it in terms of himself, what it might do for his career. Perhaps his reaction had been a defense mechanism, a way of dealing with the atrocity he had stumbled upon. Ever since that moment, he had been half crazed, letting instincts and impulses take over. Jeanne had told him on more than one occasion that he was immature, and the way he had handled the murder was probably what she had meant by it. Now his career no longer seemed important. All he cared about was bringing Diana Diaz's killer to justice—for her sake, not his. If that was immature, then that was the way it would be.

Reed opened the third beer. It was almost room temperature, but Reed didn't mind. It only made him drink more slowly, and he had to go to work the next day. He turned the album over and gently lowered the tone arm. He stopped thinking and concentrated on Beck's guitar work. The first song was a haunting acoustic solo, a solo far removed from the blistering guitar work that Beck had become famous for. Each note resounded sweetly, then softly faded into the next, on and on, sweeter and sweeter. The song was "Greensleeves," and Stuart Reed savored every note as he faded into sleep.

An hour later, Reed had the nightmare for the first time. Reed was driving his father's fifty-eight Ford along a narrow mountain road. The road twisted as it climbed the mountain. The trees were empty of leaves, and a full moon cast spindly shadows, eerie skeletal fingers, across the road before him.

As the old Ford ascended the mountain, the turns grew sharper and sharper, yet he continued to accelerate until the tires wailed and he kicked up gravel along the shoulder. He regained control for an instant, then hurtled the car into the next corner, then the next. By the time he approached the final curve, the car was a whisker from disaster.

From out of nowhere, a white cat appeared on the ink black

macadam. Its eyes flared fire into the Ford's high beams, and it flashed wolf teeth as the old roadster bore down on it.

Reed hit the brake with both feet. At the moment of impact, the cat vanished under the front of the car. The Ford became airborne, spinning like an auger, flying higher and faster until Reed no longer knew if the road was above or below him. A stand of trees lay dead ahead. As the car was about to mangle him into the trees, Reed screamed himself awake.

He sat bolt upright on the floor, calling for Jeanne, but she wasn't there. His body shook uncontrollably for several minutes. When he could hold his hands still, he wiped the sweat from his forehead. Then he stood, went to the kitchen, and found a cold beer.

# Chapter Thirty-one

When Stuart Reed looked back on that whole sorry chapter of his life—what he came to call the eleven days that shook his world—he used to debate when the low point came—breaking up with Jeanne that terrible afternoon, the first white cat nightmare, or what happened the next morning.

In hindsight, the split with Jeanne had been inevitable, unavoidable. The dream had a beginning and eventually had an end. But the events of Black Friday, as he dubbed it, grabbed him by his Adam's apple and knocked him down so hard that it would take him almost a year to stand on his two feet again.

He got to work twenty minutes late that Friday morning. He had awakened at seven A.M., bought and read the *Times,* had a cup of coffee. Left for work a half hour early, only to sit in traffic for forty-five minutes while the PA cops rescued a would-be jumper from the upper deck of the George Washington Bridge.

Claire Green didn't want to hear a word of it, of course. She merely informed him he was in deeper shit than he could possibly imagine, and walked away.

Reed called Cippriani, who told him the same thing. "What about the shoe?" Reed demanded.

"Screw the shoe, and screw you," Cippriani shouted and slammed the phone down.

Moments later, Pritchard Majors summoned Reed into his office.

"Ever hear of *The Alton Telegraph*?" Majors inquired as he shut the door behind Reed.

Reed replied that he couldn't say as he had.

"You should have. Famous libel case."

Reed looked for a chair to sit in. Majors told him not to bother, this wouldn't take long. "You sent a memo to a county homicide detective the other day."

"Yes, I did. Wednesday, in fact. And I told him to shred it and burn it."

"Well, somehow it got filed instead—in a credit bureau office." Reed stood there, stunned, while Majors' words washed over him.

"You talked to Culp Jenkins yesterday morning—most unprofessionally from what Culp told me. He got to wondering what you were up to. He called me and asked what you were working on. I said you were investigating that murder, and his shit hit my fan."

Reed closed his eyes, wanted to close his ears, wanted to argue but knew better.

"Jenkins hung up on me," Majors continued, "then called back half an hour later. Seems he had a chat with Glenn Brenner in Violent Crimes, who had a chat with Detective Cippriano, I think the name was."

"Cippriani."

"Whatever. Some pressure was applied, and your friend the detective mentioned a memo you had written. A memo that he had misplaced.

"Jenkins called the local credit-rating agency on the off chance that it had surfaced there. Culp was worried, understandably, that your blunder had sullied his reputation. To his utter dismay, he learned your memo was in their files."

Reed's stomach tightened, and he had difficulty breathing. Finally, he shouted at Majors. "That's absurd, and you know it."

"Culp and I go back a long way, and to be blunt, I'd believe him before I'd believe you."

"OK. Let's assume it's true—which it is not. I'll call the agency and make matters right. I'll tell them it was a misunderstanding, a prank, a joke. No harm's been done. I never wrote a story. There's nothing libelous. Nothing that will stand up in court."

Majors pounded his desk. "Shut up and listen, soldier. All of this brings us to the *Alton Telegraph,* a newspaper that went under because of a story that was never written. A reporter there was investigating a building contractor and some possibly shady dealings. He wrote his suspicions in a memo to the local constabulary. The memo ended up in a credit bureau's files, and suddenly the contractor couldn't get a loan from any bank. He checked his file at the credit bureau and called a smart lawyer. The inescapable fact, the bottom line, was that something written by a *Telegraph* reporter had ruined the contractor's business. The contractor sued. It went to court. It cost the paper more than eight million dollars. Bankrupted them."

Reed shook his head in disbelief. "It's not the same. No harm has been done here. We must have been set up. And Culp Jenkins won't sue—call his bluff. That son of a bitch butchered an eighteen-year-old girl. He's not going to let us bring that up in an open court."

Majors began to pace the carpet. "You don't get it, do you? Mr. Hotshot Reporter doesn't get it. Culp won't have to face anything in court. He didn't kill anybody. You're off the wall. But you are right about one thing—this isn't going to court. He's already let us off the hook. On one condition. You're fired."

Aldo Cippriani was clearing his desk when Reed stormed into his office. "Get out of here," Cippriani muttered in disgust. "You've gotten me in enough hot water as it is."

"I won't keep you. I just want to know exactly what in hell happened." Reed had gotten himself back under control during the drive to the county building annex. At this point he already knew he was dead. He just wanted to know what the murder weapon was.

"You tangled with the wrong dude. Jenkins is incredibly well connected—with the mayor, my boss, your boss. Hell, you showed me the photo of the four of them together at the dedication ceremonies for the pistol range. You should have known then and there that you were walking into a volcano. I should have stopped you. Never trust a reporter—that's all we hear around here. You wouldn't listen to me about interviewing Jenkins. He got wind of your stupid notions, and he decided to nail you."

"And you told Brenner about the memo I faxed to you, just so you could help Jenkins along."

"Brenner blindsided me." Cippriani's voice was rising now. "Came on real casual, full of small talk. Asked how the Diaz investigation was going, whether you had come up with anything more that could help us. I mentioned the memo, and he demanded to see it. I told him I chucked it."

"And had you?"

"Yes, as far as I can be certain of anything. I'm not exactly a master of the art of paperwork, and I guess there's a remote chance I placed it in the wrong pile, but I'd swear I chucked it. Chances are that Jenkins is bluffing. Let's face it, that memo couldn't have reached the credit agency already. But the knowledge of the memo was all the ammunition that Jenkins needed to blow you out of the water. Whether the memo exists or not is moot. Your boss and my boss both believe him. He's got you dead to rights."

Reed felt nauseous again—it was almost becoming a habit—and leaned on Cippriani's desk for support. "But all three of them are in the pistol range photo. It's a cover-up."

"Nothing you can do about it."

"But you'll keep after Jenkins, won't you? We can't let him get away with this."

Cippriani spat on the floor, then told Reed that those prospects were dim at best—in lieu of a departmental disciplinary action, Cippriani had been put on clerical work for six weeks. And he wasn't about to go sticking his nose in the same buzz saw twice.

"What about the investigation then?"

"I asked Brenner that, and he said we were turning everything over to NYPD. We've never established she was murdered on this side of the Hudson—only dumped here—and she was a New York City resident. Like I told you before, nobody over here really gives a rat's ass about her."

"But the hunting shoe—you did run tests on it, didn't you, even if it was inadmissible? If only to satisfy your curiosity?"

"Reed, the shoe was worthless. It was the same size, the same brand, but the partial at the scene was the left foot. You swiped the wrong shoe. A fifty-fifty chance, and you couldn't even get that right."

# Chapter Thirty-two

At a florist shop on Main Avenue, Stuart Reed ordered one white rose.

A far-too-pleasant middle-aged man behind the counter said: "Coming right up. This'll make the little lady happy, right?"

Reed fished in his pockets for folding money, deliberately ignoring the comment. He realized he was on the verge of either crying or throttling the fat little man, and he prayed that the craziness would pass.

The man reached into a green plastic bucket and extracted a perfect rose. He placed it on tissue paper, arranged some sprigs of greenery around it, folded the paper, and stapled it shut.

Reed's eyes filled with tears as the man handed him the wrapped flower. The florist's smile wilted. "Forgive me, young man. I don't know why I thought the flower was for a happy occasion. Here, just take the rose—it's on the house. I feel terrible. I can't take your money."

Reed was too shaken to drive his car. He wanted to drink, badly, but he fought the urge. He decided to walk. It might help him get a grip on himself. He trudged over to Richards Street and headed toward the firing range. About the same time of day, eleven days earlier, he had run along this very sidewalk, past the hamburger stands and the auto dealerships, concerned that someone from the newsroom would see him. Now it didn't matter anymore.

On he walked, down the drive past the DPW garages, toward the pistol range parking lot. He turned into the lot, half cringing at the thought of seeing the thicket of weeds and brambles where Diana Diaz had been left to rot. But the thicket was gone, replaced by a dozen neatly spaced shrubs in a bed of wood chips.

For a moment Reed thought he must be dreaming again, then understood: everybody wanted to forget that Diana Diaz ever existed, that Stuart Reed had ever found the mutilated body. Just as they'd done their best to get rid of him, they'd erased the scene of the crime as well.

He unwrapped the rose and carried it to where he'd found the dead girl. He bent to place it on an imaginary grave and discovered he wasn't the first to visit the unmarked shrine. The handle of a hunting knife protruded obscenely from the ground.

Reed could have called the cops, had the forensics boys do their Mr. Science routine on the knife, but he finally understood. The prosecutor's office didn't want to hear about knives. They didn't want to hear a syllable about Diana Diaz's murder. They just wanted it to go away.

So Stuart Reed pulled the knife from the ground, wiped both sides of the blade across his trouser leg, and wrapped it in the tissue paper. He would return the knife to its owner when the right moment arrived.

# PART III

# Chapter Thirty-three

The white cat dream followed Stuart Reed to upstate New York, visited him at night. Each time he had the nightmare, he awakened at the same point, trembling uncontrollably, unable to scream.

Even during times when he managed to forget Diana Diaz, Culp Jenkins, Pritchard Majors, and Aldo Cippriani, the white cat still crept into his slumber to haunt him. Going cold turkey hadn't helped. Nor had the torturous runs up the Devil's Apron Strings.

Although Reed wouldn't admit it, one of the reasons he took the midnight to seven-thirty A.M. job at *The Clarion* was to stay up at night, just to keep the cat dream away. But the cat kept time to Reed's internal clock, and after Reed had fallen asleep for two hours, the cat came scratching at the door to Reed's subconscious.

About a week after Reed had scaled the Apron Strings, he took the first steps toward ending the nightmare. The morning was cold and rainy, and a light fog drifted along the hollow at the base of the Ramapos. Reed was jogging easily down the road toward the ski area, warming his muscles for the ascent ahead. He looked up the road and saw a white cat in the mist. When Reed reached the spot where he thought the cat had stood, the road was empty.

The next morning was clear, but he saw the cat again along the same stretch of road—no more than two hundred yards from his cabin. The cat darted into the underbrush as soon as it saw Reed approach. Reed stopped by the edge of the woods and called for the cat to come to him. He snapped his fingers, even made squishy noises like his grandmother used to when she called her kitten. The cat yowled from deep in the brush but refused to budge. Reed jogged back to the house and returned with a saucer of milk. He left it by the roadside. When he returned from his run, the milk was gone.

The morning after, he moved the plate ten yards closer to his house; the day after, another twenty yards. Each day, a little closer. On the fifth day, Reed left the saucer of milk on the front steps. On the sixth, he left the front door open a few inches and left the milk inside. As always, the milk was gone when he returned.

On the seventh morning, Reed poured the milk, opened the front

door, and waited. After fifteen minutes, the cat stuck his head
through the door, then walked to the dish. As the cat lapped up the
milk, Reed ambushed it with a pillowcase.

The cat screamed and clawed. Reed tied a knot in the pillowcase
and tossed it into the kitchen. He took the old garden hose and filled
a trash can with water. He picked up the pillowcase, cat and all, and
carried it to the waiting trash can.

He raised the pillowcase three inches above the water. The cat
started kicking, as if it sensed what was going to happen. Reed
stopped and spoke to it: "This is the end of my nightmare."

And then he set the cat free.

# Chapter Thirty-four

The cat came back the very next day, and the nightmares went away for a while. Stuart Reed named the cat Culp, so he'd serve as another reminder of what had happened.

Nonetheless, the white cat seemed to bring good luck. From late September to mid-October, Reed found a small measure of tranquility. He started to run road races again, and set a personal best time for a ten-kilometer run in Tuxedo. The first half of the course was a gradual uphill, and Reed smoked it.

He got used to nights without sleep, and days without alcohol. And to put Jeanne behind him, Reed started to see women again— or one woman, to be exact.

Caroline Tompkins, without a doubt, had been the best thing that had happened to Stuart Reed in a year. He'd met her during his second week at *The Clarion*. The publisher was having the monthly meet-the-new-employees coffee hour, and Reed had been told to miss it only at his peril.

The audiovisual room was where the sales staff made their big slide presentations to prospective advertisers ("Just wait till you see our demographics and market penetration"). As a result, it was the one spot in the entire building aside from the publisher's office that boasted any extravagances. Plush kelly green carpet covered the floor, the chairs were polished oak, and the walls sported expensively framed front pages of local significance (Mayor Meyers Wins Re-election in Landslide," "New Shopping Mall Announced").

The get-together was at eleven in the morning, Reed had been working since midnight, and he still hadn't adjusted to the lobster shift. These were all the excuses he'd dreamed of to explain his slightly bizarre behavior in the AV room that morning, but closer to the truth was that he felt awkward in situations like this.

Small talk, chitchat, whatever you called it, Reed had never been able to master it. What was strange was that when he'd been a reporter, he flourished when he had to interview people. But in those cases he knew who'd be talking, what questions he'd ask, and where he wanted the interview to head. Here, at this coffee hour, he was merely trying to hang out until he could politely excuse himself. Killing time was tough when you lacked ammunition.

As far as Reed cared, the only redeeming aspect of the coffee hour was a tall brunette who appeared to be in her late thirties or early forties. He didn't mean it as a knock on the others present, but this woman didn't fit in. Where the others in the room were dressed somewhere between second-date casual and once-a-year church, she looked almost aristocratic. Braided hair woven smartly into a knot, a sleeveless green silk dress with gold bracelets, a tan purchased at a health resort. She wore little makeup or, more likely, just wore it well. Reed's first instinct was to introduce himself, see what her story was, but he decided he'd be wasting his time. Reed knew that he wasn't in her league.

Inevitably, as Reed eased his way toward the door, he had to pass close enough to her so that it would have been rude not to acknowledge her presence, and by that point he was too weary to feel awkward.

She spoke first. "Good morning, I'm Caroline Tompkins. Are you one of our new employees?"

"Hi. My name's Stuart Reed, and yes, I'm new. Started ten days ago."

She smiled—condescendingly, Reed thought. "Let me guess what you do. Actually, it's not very difficult. I guess you realize that since you're wearing a pair of RockSports, L. L. Bean khakis, blue buttondown oxford cloth, and a Rooster tie, you're pretty much in uniform. You're a reporter, no?"

"Nope. The new overnight copy editor, ma'am. I just got dolled up for the occasion."

"Ah, yes, I should have known from your eyes."

"Thanks." Reed fumbled for a graceful way to field the unintended insult. "You know how to make a man feel good."

Reed winced to himself—he'd come up with another great conversation ender—and sure enough, she turned to leave. He tried to salvage the moment. "Wait, you haven't told me what you do."

"Well, I've already embarrassed myself. Why don't you give it a try, too? What do you think I do?"

"If I told you what I think, I think I'd be out of a job."

"How's that?"

"Because the way I figure it, you're either at the wrong coffee hour or you're Mrs. Parisi, the publisher's wife."

She laughed. "And how do you figure all that?"

"The silk dress, the gold jewelry, the fifty dollar manicure—I find it hard to believe that you work for a living. My guess is you're here to hobnob with the new employees so you won't feel totally ill informed when you see us at the Christmas party. Or maybe you want to know who's working for your husband—just in case he kicks the bucket before he can unload this rag and you have to run the shop."

Caroline Tompkins touched her hair and laughed. "Mr. Reed, all I can say is that you're in the right job here at *The Clarion,* because you make far too many assumptions to cut it as a reporter. In the meantime, I have an appointment in ten minutes, and though I'd love to converse with you further, I must be going."

She reached into her small black leather purse. "Here's my card. Perhaps we can pursue this another time."

He read the engraved card as she glided out the door.

CAROLINE TOMPKINS
Vice-President, Advertising
Clarion Publishing Company

# Chapter Thirty-five

Stuart Reed phoned Caroline Tompkins a few times in the next week, but each time when he'd asked her out, she'd said she was busy. Reed didn't understand it. She'd seemed interested at the coffee hour, and she had given him her card, hadn't she? Maybe she just liked the attention and the ego trip that went with turning men down. But Reed trusted his instincts. Women were women, no matter the cut of their skirts.

Two weeks later, she called and asked to meet him for drinks. This time he was busy—he'd told Milt Roberts that he'd drive down to watch *Monday Night Football* with him. But Reed didn't know if he'd get a second chance with Caroline, so he accepted her invitation and canceled on Milt.

Reed met Caroline at a place in Pine Grove, an old railroad station that had been converted into a tavern. She had white wine, he had Bass ale. They exchanged war stories and office gossip, and generally found themselves liking one another. After two rounds of drinks, he offered to pay the bill, and she offered him a nightcap at her place. "Don't get the wrong idea. I just think we'd be more comfortable in my living room than sitting in these straight-back chairs."

Her place was on State Street, on a steep hill in the downtown area that had come to be known as Bankers Lane. Ten stately two-story stone homes sat in a row. Reed bit his lip when she turned her Audi into one of the driveways—he'd heard that the places were going for four hundred grand or more. He'd figured her for money, but not that much.

He parked behind her in the semicircular drive, then caught up to her on the slate walkway leading to the solid walnut entrance. It had beveled glass windows in the shape of a lady's fan, and a huge brass knocker. She slid keys into two locks and swung the door open.

She took his coat and ushered him into a living room furnished in Queen Anne antiques, from a slipper-footed table by the far window to a mahogany highboy by the entrance to the dining room. Reed was confronted by a white Persian rug that made him stop short.

"Take off your shoes if the rug makes you nervous," Caroline offered. "Makes me nervous, to be honest."

"Then why own it?"

"Who said I owned anything?" Reed watched as she bent and took off one high heel, then the other. "I rent this place. Furnished. Fifteen hundred a month. It's in my contract."

Reed pushed off his RocSports, then followed her across the carpet. They sat in a pair of matching brocade wing chairs by a picture window. Reed looked into her eyes in hopes of seeing where the night was headed, but she broke off eye contact and looked blankly out the window.

Reed tried to bring her back. "You were saying something about a contract . . ."

"My contract with Parisi—he hired me for one year to get *The Clarion* in good enough shape for him to sell. My unofficial job is publishing consultant. I'm hired to come in and shape up flabby papers—boost the profits, streamline the operations, saw away the dead wood."

Reed cringed. "You mean you're a hatchet man. Boosting profits means cutting into the news hole so the ads-to-editorial ratio is lopsided in favor of the ad boys. And sawing away the dead wood is the polite term for axing longtime employees and otherwise gutting the staff, right?" He started to stand.

She nudged him back into his chair. "You editorial types are so sanctimonious, you crack me up. *The Clarion* is first and foremost a business. If it ceases to make money, it soon ceases to exist, regardless of the quality of the news. And all you high-falutin' journalists are out of jobs."

Reed leaned forward in his chair. "So what are you doing with a high-falutin' journalist?"

"I was wondering the same thing a moment ago." She looked at her gold bracelet a moment and adjusted the clasp. "To be honest, Stuart, I'm not in the market for serious relationships. I don't like mixing my business with my personal life, and most men I meet are as ambitious as I am. It's just not a good mix. You, on the other hand, offer what I'm shopping for. You seem fairly intelligent and easygoing, and you look like you're in pretty good shape. I think I could be comfortable with you. What do you see in me?"

"At the moment, I'm not sure." He leaned back, now in retreat. "Frankly, with this place and all, I think I'm not in your class. I like beer and pizza and *Monday Night Football* and an occasional night on the town. I look at you and this house and all I see are champagne and shrimp and *MacNeil/Lehrer* and the opera. I can take champagne, but the rest I'm allergic to."

Caroline smirked. "There you go again, Stuart Reed, making those

terrible assumptions. Two and two don't have to add up to four—
sometimes they're just two and two. Does that make any sense? Yes, I
like silk and high heels, but I like to dress casually, too. They aren't
mutually exclusive. Maybe I'm wrong, but I think I could let my hair
down with you. What are you looking for?"

Reed stuttered, unsure of what to say next. "I wish I knew. I guess
I'm looking not to get hurt."

"Beyond that." Now Caroline was leaning forward in her chair.
"You don't strike me as a copy editor. . . ."

"I don't want to talk about it."

"Ah, a mystery man. What would you like to talk about?"

Reed decided to gamble. He leaned forward again, until his eyes
were a foot from hers. "I'd like to talk about you and me."

She didn't blink. "What about you and me?"

"Well, since we're mutually attracted, and we're all alone in this
big old place, I thought we might save some of the talk and get to
know each other better."

She laughed. "Not tonight. But . . ."

It hadn't been that night, but it was two mornings later. And for
the next few mornings, until she had gone to the ad convention in
Manhattan four days ago. But now she was back and, Reed figured as
he drove up the brick driveway, they'd soon resume where they'd left
off.

Caroline answered the door in an apricot terrycloth robe. Apricot
was the color of the month, Reed had noticed, and surmised there
must have been an article in *Cosmo* announcing it. Reed thought that
Caroline looked good in just about anything, and looked even better
without it. . . .

Later, Caroline sat up in the brass bed and tapped Reed on the
shoulder.

"I didn't know I was sleeping with a celebrity," she announced.

"What are you talking about?"

"You. A celebrity. I ran into somebody from *The Riverton Transcript*
at the convention."

"Who?"

"Their main ad guy, Bobby Aenias."

Reed's body stiffened. "He's an idiot."

"Funny, he said the same thing about you."

"Consider the source."

"I did."

"So?" Reed demanded.

"Don't get defensive—it hasn't changed my opinion of you." She reached for his hand, but he pulled away. "Stuart, I just happened to sit next to him at a luncheon, and when I asked him if he knew you, he cringed. I asked him what that was supposed to mean, and he said that you were famous. That you were one of the only reporters in the history of American journalism to get fired for libel on a story you never wrote."

# Chapter Thirty-six

Caroline Tompkins' mention of the threatened libel suit did more than put a severe kibosh on their relationship. It drove home the fact that he'd never live down the Jenkins disaster unless he resolved it—one way or another.

As October wore on, Stuart Reed became more and more obsessed. The night before the anniversary of Diana Diaz's murder, Reed arrived at work at eleven-thirty P.M. and, as he did every night, spent the first half hour combing the New York City papers. Maybe there'd be some sort of story about the Diaz case. He was strangely relieved when he came up empty, and a little disappointed when he didn't see any items about new murders that fit the bill. There had been that false alarm several days earlier, then nothing. Reed felt certain that Jenkins would strike again, sooner or later. Maybe not in the New York metropolitan area, but somewhere. Jenkins was a hunter. Killing was his nature.

Reed sat down at his seat on the copy desk and logged on to his computer terminal. An electronic message from Bill MacDougall, the copy desk chief, awaited him. MacDougall had to leave early, the note said, and it listed the slugs of six obituaries, a dozen local stories, and six wire stories for Reed to edit, lay out, and write headlines for. The page dummies sat in the In basket at the center of the semicircular table where the copy editors toiled.

Reed checked his watch out of reflex. He had plenty of time. *The Clarion* went on press at four A.M. sharp, and Reed had to get all the copy outputted to the computerized typesetter by two-thirty, in time for the guys in the shop to slap the type into place, assemble the pages, move them over to the camera to be shot, and then put onto the presses.

Reed's job wasn't particularly demanding unless some late-breaking disaster occurred, but news usually came from people, and people who were apt to make the front page of *The Clarion* were asleep. *The Clarion* seldom ran international news out front because the news editors had made a policy decision that international news didn't affect their readers' lives. What affected their readers were board of ed. meetings and town council meetings and zoning meetings, and *The Clarion* covered them to a fare-thee-well.

There was a saying in *The Riverton Transcript* newsroom: if evil existed in the world so that man could appreciate goodness, if pain existed so man could appreciate happiness, then meetings existed so journalists could appreciate real stories.

There was a saying in the lobby of the two-story brick Clarion Building as well, a bronze plaque that read, GOVERNMENT IS THE CORNERSTONE OF DEMOCRACY, and if ol' man Parisi hadn't said it himself, he should have. What it meant was that *The Clarion* was on hand every time ten guys with Sears suits and polyester ties convened in the same meeting room at the local Holiday Inn. Which accounted for the paper's high turnover rate.

Reed despised editing the meeting stories almost as much as he hated editing the obituaries, because both were completely formula bound. You rarely saw a good quote in a meeting story because only dull people attended them. You rarely saw much of interest in an obituary because they were primarily a listing of milestones in a person's life. All that mattered was the minutiae, and that the obit be accurate. Spell a dead person's name wrong in an obit, and you lost the family as subscribers for life. In most cases, an obit was the last chapter to be written, so—as ol' man Parisi said the day Reed was hired—"You copy editors damn well better get the obits right."

The only reason that the obits interested Reed was the chance he might come across a new murder that resembled the old one. If the obit was a young woman's and the cause of death wasn't included, he began digging.

At six on Monday morning, Reed went through the daily cop checks and wire service checks. Nothing. Then, on impulse, he dialed *The Riverton Transcript* copy desk and asked for Clancy Collins.

"Hey, Clance. Stuart Reed here. Got a minute?"

A grunt came from the other end of the line. At *The Transcript,* "Got a minute" had always meant you were about to get a headache.

"You guys write anything about the anniversary of the Diaz girl's death—like whether the cops are still working on the case, whether there have been any new leads, that kind of thing?"

"Nope."

"Crap. Thought you guys might do something on it."

"Stuart, when you gonna understand? Nobody but you seems to care about the Diaz case. In fact, most people around here are still trying to forget it. So I gotta say good night, or good morning, or whatever. I'll call if I hear word one about any new developments."

Reed put the telephone receiver back in its cradle. He decided he better not call back there for a while.

# Chapter Thirty-seven

S tuart Reed took the second murder much harder than the first. He hadn't discovered the body this time. He'd been with the woman the night before.

It was on an early November Monday, Reed's day off. He hadn't seen Caroline Tompkins in two weeks, not since the time she had teased him about the Jenkins mess, and he had no plans to call her. All Sunday night he had pored over his cartons of clippings and notes, a copy of the autopsy, the transcript of his interview with Culp Jenkins—searching for that one overlooked clue that would link Jenkins, or anybody else, to the murder.

The bulletin board over Reed's work area in the living room sported two new items. First was a copy of Diana Diaz's high school yearbook photo—the hundred-watt smile, the high cheekbones, but most of all the piercing young eyes. A few inches away was the knife from the murder scene, a mass-produced Buck blade that Reed had jabbed through the cork and into the pine-paneled wall during one of his increasingly frequent rages.

Reed had been seeking a companion photo—a photo of Culp Jenkins and his buddies at the county pistol range—but had come up empty. When he had called *The Transcript* library last Friday, he was told that the original was no longer on file, and the sleeve of negatives from the job had disappeared or been misfiled. When he had called the photo department clerk concerning the matter, she ran a computer check and said that there was no record of such a photo ever being assigned or taken.

Reed then called his pal Milt Roberts at *The Transcript* to see if he could come up with anything, and it was Roberts who awoke Reed from a sound sleep on Monday morning. "Hell, your hunting pal must really be covering his tracks. The damned microfilm for the two-week time period when the photo ran is missing from both *The Transcript* library and the Main Avenue library.

"You should be aware of one other thing," Roberts added. "I went to the LekTriever and tracked down the folder with the firing range photos. The file was empty, all right, just like you said, but a label said that the photos were on reserve for staff reference only, and that

Pritchard Majors was to be notified of all requests for the file. What do you make of that?"

Reed scratched his chin. "It's a holdover from Culp Jenkins' threat to sue us for libel. But it also means that Majors can alert Jenkins that I'm looking into the Diana Diaz case again."

Reed tried to mask his concern, but Roberts picked up on it. "Stuart, this stupid photo isn't worth the aggravation. What's it going to tell you that you don't already know? You're finally back on your feet, and Jenkins is going to chop them off again if you don't cool your heels. What's the point?"

Reed sighed. "The point is that I never looked at the photo beyond the faces. Maybe there's something I missed. I want to be more thorough this time, and go over every name associated with the photo or that news brief that ran with it, and have my cop friend Raf run 'em through the FBI's National Crime Information Center's computer in Washington—see if anybody's got a criminal record. Cippriani said that Jenkins didn't have a rap sheet, but I never asked where he checked—the county, the state, New York City."

Roberts said that Reed was probably wasting his time. "I don't know how to tell you this, sport, but for what it's worth, I think you ought to stop living in the past. It's not the happiest place to be, and I'm not sure what it accomplishes."

Reed conceded that Milt might have a point, and thanked him for his trouble. Reed remembered the canceled *Monday Night Football* rendezvous, and invited Milt and a couple of other reporters along for the game that night. Giants versus the Eagles. Shoot the breeze about the old days, gripe about the new days. Reed said he'd supply the beer and munchies. Milt signed off by saying he'd get the other guys on board, and they'd be there for the opening kickoff.

Next, on a hunch, Reed called *The Transcript* library and asked for the woman who handled the microfilm requests. He asked her if there was any way to get a copy of a missing spool of microfilm that had an edition of *The Transcript* that he needed. The woman replied curtly that he was the second person to ask her that in the past few days, and that the answer was still no.

Reed had spoken to enough bureaucrats in his life to know he was spinning his wheels. He hung up and called the Riverton Public Library. He asked for the microfilm department and identified himself as a priest. He explained he needed an obituary from a back issue of *The Transcript,* but apparently the library's roll of microfilm that contained the right edition was gone, and the newspaper itself was no help. How could he get that a copy of that missing obituary?

The librarian told him to hold for a minute while she checked.

She returned with a phone number and an address for a microfilm company in Michigan, then suggested that when he heard how much it cost, he might reconsider. A copy of one page of an old forty-cent newspaper would cost him twenty-five dollars—plus handling and postage.

Reed said money was not a problem.

"If you know the day the obituary ran, and the exact page," she explained, "you can write or call the company and order a photostat from their copy."

Reed blessed her and clicked the receiver down. He checked his watch: The microfilm company was one time zone to the west, but it would be open by now.

Five minutes and a Visa Card number later, he had ordered the *Transcript* page that had the missing photograph. He had spent an extra twenty-five dollars for an expedited order. A full-size photostat of Page B-12 from the April 13 *Transcript* would arrive in four or five days. Reed had no idea what it would be able to tell him that he didn't already know—but then the only thing he knew was that someone had seen fit to make the photo disappear.

He went back to sleep and dreamed of Culp Jenkins and the deer again.

The alarm clock buzzed Reed awake at three-thirty P.M. Enough time for a run up the Devil's Apron Strings, a shower, and a quick trip into town to stock up on Coors Lights and Doritos.

The past few weeks had seen but one day of rain, and the last traces of the autumn foliage crackled underfoot as Reed jogged toward the Iron Hollow Ski Area. By the time he reached the rental shop, the blood was pumping through his muscles to the point where he could do his leg stretches without risking a muscle tear.

In front of the chalet-style shop, the grounds keeper was busy painting new prices on the sign that listed the assorted equipment rentals and lift-ticket packages. Reed waved hello and leaned against the building to stretch his calves and Achilles tendons. "You're not that close to opening day, are you?" Reed said jokingly.

The handyman introduced himself as Peter Benjamin. He was wearing the same frayed buffalo-plaid wool shirt and patched overalls Reed had seen him wear on the few other occasions that he had run across him. "Got to get the painting done before cold weather sets in," Benjamin explained. "Otherwise, the new paint'll blister. Doc Cosky says we got to be ready to open in three weeks, just in case. Never know. Two years ago, storm dumped six inches on Columbus Day."

Reed winced at the thought. With snow on the ground, how could he run up the mountain? And if he couldn't run up the mountain, how could he sweat out his frustrations? He went through the rest of his stretches, said good-bye to Benjamin, and started toward the Apron Strings.

When he ran under the chair lift, he picked up his pace so that he'd have some momentum when the mountain's pitch became severe. This time, he made it three-quarters of the way before he had to walk. A new personal record. He was sucking air by the time he skirted the boulders and reached the shoulder of Route 71A, some twenty yards beyond the top of the outcropping.

From there, he leaned slightly forward, lengthened his stride, and switched into cruise control for the four miles of two-lane highway that curled down the mountainside and eventually deposited Reed at the turnoff for Iron Hollow Road. He'd been gone forty minutes. After a shower, he fed Culp and headed for the Grand Union.

She was standing on the toes of her running shoes in the cereal aisle, trying to get a box of bran flakes from the top shelf. She wore a pair of stone-washed jeans and a Rutgers football practice jersey that bared her midriff when she stretched her arms above her head.

Reed watched her struggle for a moment, watched her long black bangs get in her eyes, especially watched her slender hips. Then he stopped his cart and fetched the cereal for her. "Anything else I can help you with?" he asked, and knew it sounded dumb even before she shook her head no, thank you and pushed her cart away.

As she rounded the corner of the aisle, Reed studied the nicely rounded seat of her jeans. He hadn't been to the beach for so long that he'd forgotten how breathtaking a young firm behind could be, and now that his memory was refreshed, he was infatuated.

Reed went about his shopping, and looked for her in the snack aisle and again in the beer aisle, with no luck. Just as he was about to give up, he spied her in the express checkout lane on the far right. He counted the items in his cart and off-loaded the toilet paper and the catsup onto the nearest shelf.

He pulled his cart directly behind her, and he noticed that his hands were sweating. She had her back to him, and after admiring her fanny and legs again, he wondered how she looked from the front.

She turned to say something, and his thoughts made his cheeks turn tomato red. In spite of it all, he noted that she looked fine from the front as well.

He forced a smile. She returned it, second nature. "I'm trying to keep my patience," she said wearily, "but this geezer in front is driving me up a wall."

Reed craned his neck to see an older man unloading a pile of items onto the conveyor belt.

"Don't bother counting," she said to Reed. "I already did. Three times. He's got fourteen effing items. In the express lane." She drew out every syllable of the last phrase for emphasis.

Reed laughed. "So, the express is a local. If you can't do anything about it, it's not a problem, right?"

Her eyes brightened. "Oh, you've been through counseling, too, huh? This guy's enough to put me back in group." With that, she turned and started to extract groceries from her cart.

For Reed, long a connoisseur of nubile women in supermarkets, the moment of truth had arrived. In Reed's world, you were what you bought, and he'd soon learn if he had a shot with her.

He called his imaginary game Supermarket Derby, in which he rated attractive women by the items they bought. Douches and *Cosmo,* for instance, rated the max—ten points each. At the other end of the scale, diapers and Preparation H resulted in instant disqualification.

He took a deep breath and examined her purchases: a six-pack of wine coolers (eight points), one gourmet frozen dinner (six points), two packs of Salems (nine points each), a box of Clairol hair treatment (five points), an issue of *Self* magazine (six points), and a large box of dry cat food (minus five).

Reed hadn't seen a more promising load of purchases in months. He concluded that she was over twenty-one (the wine coolers), she was single (one microwave dinner), she wasn't busy that evening (the hair goo), and she enjoyed sex (he had a theory that women who smoked also enjoyed getting horizontal). What's more, she had almost used the "F" word, another indication that she didn't live over at Holy Rosary.

She turned to him again and looked at him with large round eyes —Hope diamond eyes—and Reed was certain he was in love. "Do you believe George Burns here?" she asked in exasperation. "Now he's going through an envelope of coupons, trying to save two bits while the rest of the planet stands here and waits. How much do you want to bet he pays by check?"

And then a miracle happened. Stuart Reed, the original Mr. Awkward, blurted out: "Dinner. I'll bet you dinner he pays in cash."

She demurred. "I don't know . . . The question was meant to be . . . to be . . ."

"Rhetorical," Reed offered. "Look, to be blunt, I think you're a stunner, and I want to buy you dinner. I don't give a buzzard's butt if he pays with an American Express platinum card—I want to have dinner with you. Tonight."

She looked away, embarrassed at being put on the spot. The older man was reaching into his droopy trousers for his wallet. Reed bit his lip, stunned by his own forthrightness.

When the man unfolded a check, she turned toward Reed again, her blue eyes opening wider still. "I knew it! I just knew it!"

"Then I owe you dinner. I'm Stuart Reed. How's tonight sound?"

"I'm busy."

"Do your hair some other night. Please."

She blushed. He'd guessed right. "But look at me," she countered. "I'm a mess."

"I've been looking at you." Reed offered her his best smile. "Like I said, you're a stunner. And your name is?"

"Karen."

"Last name?"

Again, she paused. "No. Just Karen. Sort of like Cher or Madonna."

"Super. Two of my favorite women."

That made her laugh.

"Where'd you like to dine, Karen? I know a nice place nearby with excellent food, a fireplace."

She smirked. "Your place, right?"

Reed couldn't think of a clever reply. "I'd be happy to supply references," he offered feebly.

"But I have to feed Puddin, and put my things in the fridge."

"Let him starve a few hours. It'll do him good. Besides, I have a starving cat myself, and I forgot to get him some chow. You could save his life. And you can put the frozen stuff in my refrigerator. Bachelors always have empty refrigerators."

"But I don't know you." She was rocking on the sides of her running shoes now.

The cashier coughed loudly, and Karen turned to see that the older man had gone. She pushed her cart forward.

"I'm waiting for a reply," Reed called after her. "You can take your own car, leave whenever you want."

She kept ignoring him, fumbling through her wallet instead.

"Please."

Karen kept digging through her suede handbag. Finally, the cash-register lady spoke up. "Look, honey, we ain't got all evening. Calm yourself a second, find your wallet, and then have dinner with this sweet guy. If you don't, I will."

Reed snapped his head and looked at the woman. She wore a red smock, standard Grand Union issue, with a big red button on the breast pocket that said "Gladys." She was about fifty, stood five-foot-eight, and had a build like a hockey player with knockers. She also was utterly charming.

He played along. "Well, Gladys, what time do you get off work?"

Karen turned, all eyes and smiles. "Don't you dare."

# Chapter Thirty-eight

On the way out of the Grand Union, Karen stopped at a pay phone for a minute, then got into her little red Renault and followed Stuart Reed's Mazda out of the parking lot. Reed, a student of women's cars as well as their groceries, decided that this, too, augured well. Women in the market for men tended to opt for red cars, Reed had observed, and the Renault was absolute proof that she didn't have a boyfriend, or at least didn't have one when she bought the car. No man would sit idly by and let a woman buy a cute but unreliable car like a Renault.

Reed kept checking the rearview mirror to make sure Karen was still following him. At a red light, he waved to her in the mirror, and he smiled when she waved back. He worried that he hadn't put on enough antiperspirant, whether the bathroom was halfway presentable, whether he'd left his sweaty running clothes on the couch. He realized he was acting goofy, and liked it.

They reached Iron Hollow Road, and Reed drove slowly around the potholes so that Karen would follow suit.

At the house, he jumped from his car and rushed to open her car door for her. He couldn't remember the last time he'd done that— for Caroline or was it Jeanne? What he did know was that he felt like he was back in college, so full of anticipation and giddy emotion.

Karen climbed out with her plastic bag of groceries in one hand, and took his hand in the other.

Reed pointed toward the front walk. "I have to warn you upfront. This is a bachelor's pad, and it's not exactly as neat as the Waldorf." Thank goodness he'd cleaned up for the football game, he thought, then cursed under his breath.

"Is something wrong?" Karen wondered.

"Nothing that can't be fixed. I invited some pals over to watch *Monday Night Football,* but I still have time to call and cancel."

She brushed a loose strand of bang from her eyes. "I wouldn't want to interrupt anything."

"Believe me, you won't." He felt awkward holding her hand—too teenagelike, he feared—and put his arm around her instead as they walked up the front steps. "They're just a couple of guys I used to work with at a newspaper in Jersey. I can see them anytime."

He unlocked the door and ushered her in. It had gotten dark while he'd been gone, and he flicked on the lamp on the table inside the door. Culp rubbed up against Karen's legs, and she gushed, "Oh, my, who do we have here?" She eagerly bent to pet the now-purring cat.

"That's Culp, the resident irritant. Just ignore him. I think he's after your cat food."

Karen stood and looked around the room—studying the aquarium, the stone fireplace with the wood stove in front of it, the old copper-lined dry sink, the pumpkin pine blanket chest, his grandmother's grain-painted rocker. "A little tidying up, and it'd be perfect," she pronounced.

"Make yourself comfortable. Throw your coat anywhere. I'll put all our groceries in the fridge, feed Culp, and open us a bottle of wine. Turn on the TV if you'd like."

Reed returned shortly with two wineglasses and a bottle of champagne. Karen was leaning back on the sofa, her Saucony running shoes propped up on the blanket chest. The TV was tuned to MTV, and Aerosmith was singing about boffing on an elevator. It was the same song that had come on in the car a few weeks earlier. Then he couldn't change the station fast enough; now was different.

He poured her champagne, nervous again, and foam cascaded over the rim. She slurped at it eagerly, and he felt himself getting aroused.

"So, Stuart, you haven't told me what's for dinner."

Reed hemmed. "How about splitting a microwave turkey divan."

Karen sputtered. "You bum, that's what I bought."

Reed looked toward the aquarium. "Or I can fry up some small fish."

She shook her head.

"Or I can broil some steaks . . . maybe bake us a couple of potatoes . . ."

"You're getting warmer."

Reed passed up the chance to get cute with her comment. No sense in pressing his luck. "Before we get settled in, I gotta call the guys and cancel. Do you know how to start a fire?"

Karen passed up the chance to get cute with his comment. Instead, she said was a Girl Scout from way back, even though she had never tried to get a fire going in a wood stove before.

"Give it a try. I have to get some wood from outside. See that little cabinet door next to the fireplace? Unlock it and open it, if you would, while I go around to the side of the house and slide some dry firewood and kindling through the opening. Matches are on the end table. If you need some newspaper to prime the fire, just rip up the real estate section from yesterday's *Times.*"

A few minutes later, Reed dialed *The Transcript* photo department and asked for Milt Roberts. A clerk said that Milt was in the dark-room—was there a message?

Reed asked to have his call transferred to Clancy Collins instead. While Reed waited for Collins to answer the phone, Reed smelled smoke and heard Karen coughing. He looked around the corner and saw a gray fog billowing into the kitchen.

"The damper—you have the damper closed!" Reed shouted.

The moment that Collins answered the phone, Karen shouted something inaudible, and the smoke alarm joined the chorus.

"Clancy, it's Stuart," Reed shouted. "I gotta make this fast. Some-thing's come up, and I have to cancel out on tonight. Could you tell the other guys? And could you tell Milt that I tracked down the photo? He'll understand."

From the living room, over the smoke alarm's din, Karen shouted: "Come quick."

Collins said, "I hear a woman's voice, and I hear you loud and clear. I'll tell the others. Now go help the lady!"

Reed hung up and ran into the living room, which was now so thick with smoke that his eyes smarted. Karen had found her way to the door and was gulping fresh air. Reed opened the damper, rolled up a section of the *Times,* lit it, and crammed it up the black metal chimney. The chimney began to make a rushing sound, which meant he'd gotten a draft working. He shoved the burning newsprint under the firewood and carefully rearranged it—kindling on the bot-tom, then the one-inch sticks, then the thicker pieces of cherrywood. Karen, in the meantime, had managed to squelch the smoke alarm.

When the fire took hold and started sucking the smoke out of the room, Reed placed three decent-size chunks of dry oak on the blaze and turned to find Karen. She was standing by the open front door. Her eyes were watery.

He found the two glasses of champagne and brought them to her. "We should sip this outside until the smoke clears."

She said she was cold, and Reed brought his tweed sports jacket to her. The white cat emerged from the house and rubbed her leg again. She laughed. "Your cat survived. How about your fish?"

Reed looked inside. "They're not smoked salmon yet."

He handed her a glass. "We didn't make a toast yet," he said.

"I think that's as close to toast as I want to get," she joked.

He raised his glass. She clinked it with hers and volunteered: "To faster checkout lines?"

"No. Then I wouldn't have met you." He looked into her eyes.

She blinked. "Aside from all the smoke, you make a girl feel pretty terrific, you know that, Stuart Reed?"

"You're the one who's terrific."

"Smoke must have affected your brain." She felt embarrassed and changed the subject. She asked how he ended up in the Warfield area. He put the best spin he could on the reply. A failed marriage ("nobody's fault"), a new start in a new area. He talked about working for newspapers, about running. He poured more champagne and asked Karen to talk about herself.

She said she was twenty-five—twenty-six in five months—worked as an assistant in a local ad agency, and felt like she wasn't going anywhere. Her cousin was sending her the classified ads from the *Los Angeles Times,* so that Karen could start putting some feelers out on the coast.

Reed asked her what her long-term goals were, and she replied that he must be a lot older than he looked.

"Thirty-six, actually," he replied, and asked her to explain what she meant.

She said she was getting chilly, and that they should go inside and start dinner. She'd wanted to say that her goal was to find a nice guy who loved her, maybe settle down in a few years and start a family, but that was heavy talk to throw at someone she'd just met in the Grand Union. Nor did she want to scare him off by her lack of career ambition. But the truth was, she thought that careers were something you thought about when you were thirty—and worried about when you were thirty-five.

Reed let the subject ride, for fear she'd turn tables and ask him about his own goals. He didn't want to talk about Diana Diaz or Culp Jenkins or the threatened libel suit that had ruined his career. Didn't want to sound fanatical. Karen had taken his mind away from all of it for nearly two hours, and he decided that she was good for him.

They shut off the TV and prepared dinner together, but both had retreated to their own thoughts. The smoke had dimmed that earlier electricity.

After dinner, Karen asked if he minded if she smoked, and she could tell from his hesitation that he did. He was thinking back to the supermarket, when his only consideration was how she filled out her jeans. The cigarettes had been a good sign then, but now that he'd gotten to know her a little, he wished that she didn't smoke.

"I don't have to smoke now," she said. "I really would like to quit."

"Go ahead. It's a little too late to worry about smoking up this room."

She lit a menthol and walked over to the wood stove while he cleared the dishes. As he washed them, he stole a few glances in her direction. She still wore his tweed jacket, and he liked the way it made her look, like a little girl playing in her daddy's coat. She was sitting in front of the stove on a massive chunk of red oak that he hadn't been able to split. The doors to the stove were open. She stared blankly into the fire, occasionally flicking an ash from her cigarette into the neon pink embers. Reed couldn't tell if her expression was boredom or contentment.

He left the silverware to soak in the sink and returned to her side. "Sorry. I wasn't being a very good host."

She patted the blanket chest. "Sit next to me a while."

"I was afraid you were getting bored."

"No, just a little strange, a little lost."

"How come?"

As he sat down, she stood and walked to the front window. She fidgeted a bit, and then it all poured out. She said it didn't feel quite right to be in Reed's house. Said she still lived at home, trying to save up a nest egg so she could move out, and said her parents would shoot her if they knew she was in the house of some divorced thirty-six-year-old guy that she'd just met in the checkout line.

Reed was speechless. What she said was true, of course, but he'd never heard himself described in stark demographic profile. It wasn't pretty, but reduce anyone to their lowest common denominator, and you divide a lot of good people.

Fortunately, Karen changed the subject. "Looks like you have company."

Reed walked to the window and saw a pair of taillights headed for the ski area. "I doubt it. Every week or so, some idiot makes a wrong turn, reaches the dead end at Iron Hollow, and turns around."

Karen had a different theory. "My guess is that it's a couple of high school kids looking for a place to make out. When I was a kid, this was quite the lover's lane when ski season wasn't going on.

Reed was jealous: Karen had lived her own life, had no doubt parked with a boyfriend or two on this very road, had had her share of lovers.

Reed put another log in the stove and stoked the burning logs to get a better draft.

Culp scratched at the wood box door. "What's with your cat?" Karen asked.

Reed looked at Culp, exasperated. "You'll have to excuse Culp. He thinks that the little door over there is his private entrance." Reed unhasped the hook again and pushed the door open, and Culp departed for the evening.

There was silence, until Reed finally thought of something to get the conversation going again. "You said you felt strange being here. How can a divorced thirty-six-year-old man make you feel more at ease?"

She said it wasn't his fault that she felt strange. The champagne, the dinner—it all had turned out swell.

"But?"

She stood in front of him, an inch or two from him. She looked up at him and closed her eyes. "Just hold me."

Reed took her in his arms, felt her breasts press against the bottom of his rib cage, smelled her hair, which carried a scent he could best describe as smoked apricot. She touched the small of his back with her fingertips, and they started to sway in a soundless slow dance.

She rested her head under his chin, and he ran his fingers slowly through her thick black hair. His other hand reached under the sports jacket and caressed her back, then slowly crept under the top of her jeans. She arched her left elbow as she held him closer, diverting his hand away from her fanny.

He broke the silence first: "You know, Karen, I've been dying to caress your butt ever since I saw it in the cereal aisle."

She tried to suppress a giggle. "I've been dying to squeeze yours, too, believe it or not. Runners have great fannies. The rest is skin and bones—but great fannies. But sorry, Stuart, not tonight. It's not right." They kept dancing to their silent melody.

"It's your call, but I'd hate to think about when you're ninety and sitting on the veranda of the nursing home and looking back on your life. . . . I'd hate for you to remember tonight and say, 'Damn, I wish I'd let him squeeze my tush.'"

She squeezed him tighter. "That was the lamest line you've tried all night. Has it ever worked?"

To Reed's relief, she didn't sound annoyed. If anything, her voice sounded flirtatious, and Reed began to get aroused again.

"It wasn't entirely a line, although I can see where you'd see it that way. But the other part, about being old and looking back on your life—I meant that, too, even if it didn't sound the way I meant it. I get concerned sometimes because I'm in my mid-thirties and I feel like I'm pissing my life away. The goals I set for myself died fifty miles southeast of here, and I'm adrift now. I'd like this evening to be a nice memory for us both, and I know we'll be kicking ourselves in thirty years if we let the evening end now, on nothing but a hug."

She hugged him and gently released. "There'll be other evenings, won't there?"

He said he hoped there'd be, but . . .

"But what?"

"Your butt. I still want to caress it tonight, just once. Beyond that, I'll behave."

Her laugh felt warm against his chest. Then she reached back, clasped his right hand by the wrist, and planted it on her left buttock. He held it, rubbed it, squeezed it, then moved to the other. It was warm and firm and soft as chamois. "I'm in heaven," he whispered into her hair.

"I never thought my sorry ol' butt could make a man so happy." She laughed, reached around behind her and extracted the roving hand as it began to probe beneath the waistband of her jeans. "Time's up."

They held each other for a while, until Karen stepped back and said wistfully, "I have to go."

"But I haven't given you my killer kiss yet."

"So I have something to live for. Maybe next time," she offered.

"Definitely next time."

She pecked his lips and turned for the door. "Thanks for the most memorable trip I've ever had to the Grand Union, Stuart Reed. When I'm eighty and hanging out in some old folks home, I'll think of tonight and how nice it felt when you squeezed my fanny."

"Me, too."

He got her groceries, put his hand on her shoulder, and, almost in a trance, walked her to her car.

In a moment she was gone.

Reed leaned against his front door and exhaled deeply and slowly. He hadn't felt so good in so long.

He pictured her dancing with him, and suddenly he remembered she still wore his jacket—and he didn't have her phone number. Hell, he didn't even have her last name to find in the phonebook. He ran out to the roadside and saw her taillights disappear a hundred yards away. Then he saw another set of taillights switch on and pull onto the road behind her.

But there were no other houses on the road.

And no good reason for another car to be there.

He recalled the car that had rolled by earlier, and his face went flush. Shit. What if it hadn't been lovers, or lost? What if it had been someone casing Reed's place? What if it had been Culp Jenkins?

He ran inside and grabbed the phone. He'd call the police, get help. But he didn't know where she lived, didn't even know her last name. He hesitated. Maybe it was like Karen said, a couple of teen-agers. Maybe his mind was playing tricks . . . maybe not.

He grabbed his car keys and sprinted to the Mazda. He threw it into gear and sped off toward Route 71A, the Mazda careening from pothole to pothole. Maybe, if his luck held, he'd catch up to her while she was still on the highway—before she turned off and he'd never find her.

The econo-box's front tires spewed gravel as Reed pulled onto the main highway. He kept it in third gear, getting the tach up to five-thousand revs per minute and the speedometer pushing eighty. He crossed the double yellow line to pass a big black Ford pickup truck, and prayed her car would come into view beyond it. Empty road.

Reed threw it into fourth and floored it to ninety. The steering wheel went into seizures.

He needed to go faster, but the Mazda behaved like his legs did at mile twenty-four of a marathon. You could push all you wanted and they just weren't going to go a lick faster.

He shifted back into third, and the four-cylinder engine screamed so loud that he almost didn't hear the police siren.

In the rearview mirror, Reed saw the strobing red and blue lights. He thought about shifting back into fourth and trying to lead the cop to Karen's car, but he knew the chances of finding her were slim to zip. He backed off the gas. The pulsing colors from the cop's flashers filled the Mazda's passenger compartment like some five-bucks-a-bottle strip joint.

It was only a question of how long the cop had been tailing him, and how many tickets he'd get. Dropping the name of his old pal Raf Wilson might help a little, but as the saying went, his ass was grass.

On a residential street three miles away, Karen Pettraglia pulled into the parking lot of the apartment complex where she lived with her folks. The lot was deserted, save for her red Renault and the man in the van who had pulled in a few seconds after her.

# Chapter Thirty-nine

Stuart Reed fell asleep at four-thirty Tuesday morning, but only after finally convincing himself that he had overreacted and that Karen was OK. His ability to resolve his crisis and go to sleep without the aid of alcohol, he chalked up to a triumph of the will.

The phone rang an hour later. Reed fought through his stupor and found the phone on the fourth grope. He grunted a hello and recognized Raf Wilson's voice.

Reed's mind began to click into gear. He had a gauzy recollection of the speeding ticket, and how he'd had the trooper radio Raf in hopes that a kind word from Raf would help Reed avoid a citation for reckless driving. . . . "If it's about last night, Raf, I owe you. Lord, how I owe you."

"Stuart ol' buddy, better brace yourself. We found that woman you mentioned last night. You're not going to want to hear this. I'm real sorry."

Reed's body shook, and he leaned his ear and the phone receiver against the bed so he could hold on to it. "Go on, Raf."

"We found the body of a twenty-five-year-old woman named Karen Pettraglia in a rest stop along Route 49, about six miles from your place. A truck driver found her actually. Stopped to clean out the cab of his semi and spotted her body behind a picnic table. We're looking at a single stab wound to the heart—at least that's what we're going on until we get the coroner's report. It was fairly quick and painless as these things go." Wilson cringed at the crassness of his comment, and apologized again.

Reed had trouble breathing, and even more difficulty speaking. "What was she wearing?" He swallowed on his words, then buried his head into the mattress while he waited for the reply.

"I'm sorry, Stuart. You gotta get a grip. I can't understand what you're saying."

Reed dug his fingernails into the fleshy part of his palms, took a deep breath, and tried again.

"She had on jeans, a college football jersey . . . ." From the flatness of Raf's voice, it was clear that he was reading from someone else's notes. "And your sports coat. Or at least it had your electric bill in an inside pocket."

Reed couldn't speak.

"Stuart, I know it doesn't mean anything to you now, but if you hadn't tried to chase after her in your car—if you hadn't gotten stopped for speeding—you'd be the prime suspect and in one huge heap of trouble. I'll go straight to the chief, make sure all those citations are ripped up. You tried, buddy. You tried your best."

"Now what?"

"Hate to ask, but you'd better get your tired ass down to the police station and fill out some statements for the county boys while the trail's still fresh. Maybe we'll catch the guy. You think it's your hunter pal again?"

Reed grunted and said he was on his way. After hanging up the phone, Reed lay down on the floor and started sobbing. His body quivered uncontrollably, and he pulled the comforter off the bed and wrapped himself in it to get warm. It didn't help.

The trip to the police station took fifteen minutes, even though it was a five-minute drive. It had taken him half an hour to get himself pulled together enough to function, but even then his hands trembled so much that he had to pull over to the shoulder twice to regain some semblance of control. The car hadn't yet warmed up and his feet were numb, but his shirt was drenched through with sweat, like an addict on the second day of withdrawal.

Reed tried to collect his thoughts enough to figure out what to say to the county detectives, tried to imagine the questions they'd ask him, and how he should respond. The lead dog would probably be an investigator from the violent crimes unit, like Aldo Cippriani, and Reed would have to watch his words. These guys had a mind-set that was looking to hang the killing on somebody. And if that coincided with the truth, even better. But they couldn't really consider him a suspect, not with those moving violations, could they?

Reed decided that if they had really decided he was a suspect, they would have come out to his house after him. By having Raf ask him to drive to the station, they had given him a chance to flee if he were guilty.

Or had they? He glanced in the side view mirror and saw two dim headlights about fifty yards behind.

He wiped his forehead and exhaled slowly. Should he call a lawyer? he wondered. Not yet, not unless someone read him his rights. At that point, he'd clam up and call Caroline, have her get him the best lawyer around.

Reed thought about Karen, then about Culp Jenkins. Should he tell the cops about Jenkins? Not unless the right moment arose. Raf might have brought it up already. Reed parked the Mazda on Main Street, around the corner from the cop shop. He wanted to walk a bit to cool off before going into the inquisition. As Reed locked his Mazda, he saw the gray van that had been behind him turn off a block away. Reed saluted, as if to say, Mission accomplished. Suspect safely escorted to police headquarters.

# Chapter Forty

The Warfield police station was less grandiose than Stuart Reed had expected. Although the address was the same as the town administration building on Main Street, the station was in the cellar, and the only access was through a cheap plywood and glass door on Oak Street. Reed knocked once and walked in.

Inside was a room the size of an average bathroom, with mustard colored polyester wall-to-wall carpeting and the lowest grade plywood paneling. Reed went up to a Plexiglas window and announced himself to Raf Wilson, who sat at a table behind the partition. Wilson nodded hello and motioned for Reed to sit in the only chair in the waiting room.

Reed took a seat and looked around. Above Wilson's chair at the dispatcher's desk were several road maps—county, town, village, and of a new condo development. To the right was a map of the Appalachian Trail, which skirted across the eastern end of the hundred-square-mile township. On Reed's left was a two-foot by three-foot poster proclaiming: CRACK LIES. He was surprised to see an anti-drug poster up here in the boonies, then realized he shouldn't have been.

Directly in front of Reed was a missing persons reward poster. This one pictured an attractive nineteen-year-old woman, a brunette with thin lips, too much eye makeup, and hoop earrings. The poster said she had disappeared at one A.M. a few weeks earlier from a town just over the state line in New Jersey. The parents, the Lions, and the Rotary had raised a ten-thousand-dollar reward for information leading to her whereabouts.

Reed had always dismissed such posters. He usually figured the girl had bummed a ride to Manhattan or run off with a boyfriend or somebody, and the parents had put up the posters to save face. But now, in the cold damp waiting room, he thought of Diana Diaz, and how she could have gone missing for months before someone found her body. And now Karen, murdered and dumped by the side of the road.

Reed rubbed his jaw and wished he'd taken the time to shave. If he hadn't been sound asleep when Raf had called, he'd have washed up and put on a good white shirt and dress pants for this interview. First impressions were first impressions—on a job interview or a police interrogation. He opened his denim jacket and glanced down at his dark green work shirt. At least it was clean. He should have worn a tie. He noticed a small food stain on his jeans. He was trying to scratch it off with a fingernail when the door next to the bulletin board opened a foot.

A haggard-looking man with a receding grayish hairline stuck his head through the opening and spoke: "Mr. Reed? We'll talk to you now."

Reed walked through the door and followed the man into an office on the right. The engraved brass sign on the door to the office said CHIEF ROBERT O. PENRA, but inside the room were two investigators from the county Bureau of Criminal Investigation—the balding man, who wore a blue blazer and gray slacks, and a woman in a conservative blue business suit. Both wore their IDs on the outside of their coat pockets.

The man introduced himself as Detective Mahr and said his partner was Detective Holmgren. Neither extended their hand. Mahr told Reed to take seat across the desk from Holmgren, and Reed gave her a quick once-over as he sat on the metal chair. He guessed from the lines at the corners of her eyes that she was in her forties, or in her late thirties and very tired. She had sandy brown hair, tied tight in the back. Reed figured that she could stand to lose ten pounds, but then Reed figured that about most women.

Mahr sat next to the desk and activated a bulky reel-to-reel tape recorder. He lit a cigarette without asking if Reed minded or wanted one. Holmgren was already smoking. Reed wondered if smoking were part of the job description—made the interrogation more like the movies. Mahr spoke toward the tape recorder, giving the official who-what-where-when information before the two investigators began asking Reed questions.

Holmgren and Mahr were pros—thorough, forthright, and all business. Holmgren explained to Reed that he was considered a suspect purely because he was the last to see Karen Pettraglia alive, and that he could call a lawyer if he wanted, but they didn't see any reason to. The traffic arrest of the night before made him a highly unlikely possibility, but they made it their business not to assume or preclude or overlook anything. They also explained that they would follow procedure to the letter and run a complete check on his pedigree—from the DMV to job history to school to service record. They added that they would make note of every person that he said he had talked to on Monday and that they would check to make sure his story was true.

Reed asked how long the interview would take. Holmgren looked at her watch. "An hour, maybe two. Depends on what you did yesterday, and what you saw."

Reed sat back and let them fire away. While he answered, he looked about the room, which was decorated in the same trailer-park modern as the anteroom. He also soon figured out that there was nothing but a poured cement floor under the tacky carpeting. He felt the cold coming up through his running shoes, and after about twenty minutes of "what did you do next," the balls of his feet went numb, followed shortly thereafter by his toes. He wiggled them to get the blood pumping, but it didn't work. He only hoped that their feet were cold as well—maybe that would cut the interrogation by a few minutes.

After an hour, he had lost any feeling in his feet, and Mahr and Holmgren were just then getting around to Karen's departure from Reed's house and Reed's sighting of the vehicle pulling out onto Iron Hollow Road behind her.

Holmgren, who had leaned back in the chief's desk chair for most of the questioning, perched on the edge of the chair now, her face almost on top of the hubcap-shaped ashtray. "Did you see the driver?"

Reed exhaled. "Too far away."

"Can you tell us if it was a car, a van, a truck?"

"Too far away."

"How high off the ground were the taillights, how far apart, what shape? Tell us anything about them. You had to have seen something."

Reed closed his eyes and tried to picture the road, the two red dots in the distance. "I don't know, they could have been a van, I guess. Or a Ram Charger–type truck."

"Why do you say that?"

"You asked if the lights were high off the ground, and it hit a nerve. It's almost a hunch, but I think they were."

Holmgren crushed her cigarette, lit another, and continued the questions along those lines, until Reed could no longer move his toes at all, and the ashtray was filled with dead butts. Reed saw it as a race against the clock: which would they run out of first, questions or cigarettes?

They went over some of his answers again, about the Grand Union, Iron Hollow Road, and his futile high-speed chase. Mahr finally looked at Holmgren hesitantly, she nodded, and they both stood. Mahr said something into the tape about concluding the interview, and Holmgren told Reed that he was free to go. They'd write up a statement based on the interview, and Reed could sign it later.

Reed asked what was next, and Holmgren explained that they were coordinating a search of the rest stop with the state and local police. They'd sealed off the area from further "contamination," as she put it, then they'd process the entire area, looking for anything from footprints and tire tracks to murder weapons and fiber samples.

She said another team was doing the same in the parking lot where the murder victim's Renault was found, at the end of the row of condominiums where the victim and her parents lived. Holmgren said that she was going to call for another unit to process the spot on Iron Hollow Road where Reed thought the killer may have been lurking.

Reed asked about the autopsy. Mahr said they should have one in twenty-four hours, that New York wasn't like Jersey, with professional medical examiners. The county coroner was a layman, often a political hack, and they farmed out autopsy work to area pathologists. There was a good one locally, and the BCI was arranging for him to conduct an autopsy right away.

Mahr told Reed to stay in the area until further notice, and to be ready for follow-up interviews if need be, then showed Reed the door. Reed bit his lower lip to mask the pain he felt with every step of his frozen feet. Mahr and Holmgren must have been wearing electric socks.

Reed thought he'd be relieved to get outside, but it was still early, still cold. The sky was the color of concrete, and the threat of rain hung heavy in the air. Reed turned up the collar on his denim jacket, rounded the corner by his car, and looked in the window of the liquor store. According to the sign, it wouldn't open for another half hour. He walked another block to Finn's Tavern. It, too, was closed. He settled for the local coffee shop, a one-room affair decorated in early seventies linoleum-cum-Formica.

Reed put fifty cents on the counter by the register and took a copy of *The Clarion,* then headed for the booth farthest from the door. He slid along the wooden bench seat and propped himself against the wall. He flipped through the first few pages of the paper. No murder story, just as he had expected. The body had been found too late to make the morning editions. Now if he'd been working, he thought . . .

If he'd been working, there wouldn't have been a murder to report, because he never would have been with Karen. He looked at the newspaper again, but he couldn't get interested in any of the stories—the same old ration of trouble in the Persian Gulf, an IRA-linked bombing in Belfast, and savings and loan bailout news.

A young redheaded waitress arrived with a menu and a cup of coffee. He waved them off. "No thanks. I've been up all night. Coffee would give me the DTs."

She gave him a look that said, Who cares?

He ordered a large orange juice and pancakes. He looked at his watch. Twenty more minutes until the liquor store opened.

# Chapter Forty-one

A black-and-white was parked on Iron Hollow Road, about fifty yards from Reed's home. Reed rearranged his copy of *The Clarion* so that it covered the quart of Jack Daniels that was shoulder-harnessed into the passenger seat.

Reed saw Detective Mahr in an olive-drab trench coat walking toward him, and he pulled the Mazda onto the shoulder. Mahr signaled for Reed to roll down his window. He was wearing one of those tweed British racing caps with the narrow snap brim that balding middle-aged men must find sporty looking.

Mahr dropped his cigarette and crushed it on the macadam. "Mr. Reed, we've been waiting for you. We need you to show us where that other vehicle was parked last night—the one you said pulled out and tailed the victim. I've walked the road from Route 71A to your place, and I've found a couple of likely spots. What I want you to do is drive to your place and sight down the road from where you stood last night. Motion to me which way to go, and let me know when I'm near the spot."

Rain began to fall when Reed pulled into his drive, and he knew he had to hurry. When the rains came, they would wash away the incriminating tire tracks or footprints—if any existed. Reed cupped his right hand in a salute to keep the rain out of eyes, then looked along the road, trying to picture how it had looked the night before. He motioned Mahr, seventy-five yards away now, to walk toward the main road. Farther. "That's it, by the big black walnut tree," Reed called.

Mahr motioned to the troopers in the state police car, and they pulled up next to the tree. Reed loped to the spot as well. The rain picked up, brittle and cold, and the air smelled of wet asphalt and rotting leaves. Reed tucked his hands in his armpits for warmth. Mahr put on a pair of thin black leather gloves. He held a spiral notebook in one hand, a distinctive black and gold Waterman pen in the other. Pretty nice on cop pay, former reporter Reed thought. Must have been a present.

Beyond the black walnut was a dirt road that led to a prime trout-fishing spot along Longhouse Creek. "Definitely here," Reed said.

Mahr bent down by the dirt road and watched the heavy raindrops splatter the loose dirt. "We're not going to pull anything off here," he said to the four troopers, who had now joined him. "But process the area—cigarettes, gum, candy wrappers, beverage cans. Anything promising." He turned to Reed. "Let's walk the rest of the road, just to make sure this is the spot."

The icy rain stung Reed's face, but he enjoyed it much in the same way that when he was going through the divorce he liked to sit in the dentist's chair and have his teeth drilled—just to take his mind off his miseries.

The two men walked the shoulder of the road in silence. They reached the turn onto Route 71A, and Reed looked up at the sky and let the rain pelt his face for a solid fifteen seconds. Then he turned to Mahr and said, "The guy you're after—he's smarter than this. He didn't leave so much as a fart anywhere along this road. You're wasting your time. You know that, don't you?"

"Mr. Reed, I've found you always have to run through the whole drill, just to be sure. Sometimes you get lucky. Perhaps the killer didn't expect you to see him pulling out of the side road. Perhaps he got careless, threw away a soda can, dumped an ashtray."

Reed thought fat chance but said, "Let me know if you turn up anything." And walked away.

The house was freezing. Reed placed the bottle of Jack Daniels on the end table just beyond the door and walked to the kitchen for a glass. He found the kitchen door standing wide open, with rain soaking the wood floor. Broken glass was scattered near the door. Reed stood motionless. Was the intruder still in here? Reed opened the drawer nearest the sink and found a knife. He gripped it like an icepick. He moved gingerly toward the living room, sliding his back along the wall as he went. He looked at a framed photo along the far wall and saw the faint reflection of a man by the front door. Reed jumped into the room, knife at the ready, only to find Mahr holding the fifth of sour mash.

"Shit, Mahr, what are you doing? He's been here. He must have broken into the house while you were questioning me in town."

Mahr set the bottle down. "Run that by me again?"

"The SOB who killed Karen. He must have been here. Back door's busted open."

Mahr walked toward where Reed was pointing, started to reach for the back door, then stopped. "We'll have to process your house as well. It'll take a day. Better find somewhere to stay tonight, and let me know where it is." Mahr reached inside his trench coat and handed Reed a business card.

Reed put it in the back pocket of his jeans. "Thanks. I got a question for you. When you had the police dispatcher call me at five-thirty this morning, did you have someone follow me into town, to make sure I wouldn't try to run?"

Mahr looked at him blankly.

"Someone in a gray van followed me to the police station this morning. I thought it was you guys. It had to be the killer. He watched me park near the police station and then drove out here."

Mahr wrote something on the notepad. "If that's the case, he had to be here to get something—or leave something. When you come back here tomorrow, run an inventory on your possessions; let us know if he took anything. Who knows, maybe we'll get lucky."

# Chapter Forty-two

While the forensics team went through Stuart Reed's house, he drove to *The Clarion* and talked to the city editor, Seb Pappas, and then the cop reporter, Susan Leith. He told each in turn what had happened the night before. Then he called the cop shop and left a message for Raf Wilson to call him.

Reed took a seat at his usual spot on the copy desk. He logged on to the Atex system and called up his electronic mail—nothing but the usual global messages about overtime (no one was eligible anymore), about leaving the top of your work area neat for your colleagues to use, and about cleaning out the communal refrigerator. On an impulse, Reed composed a note of his own on the VDT, sent it to a systems specialist, and asked her to send it as a global message—everyone in the newsroom would read it when they called up their messages.

It said:

> Urgent: If you received any calls for Stuart Reed yesterday (Monday), please advise him immediately—even if the caller did not leave a message.

A minute later, a "msg pending" blinked in the header field of his VDT. He called up the message. It was the one he'd just asked the systems specialist to circulate. Good. If he'd gotten it, so had everybody else.

Two minutes later, a "msg pending" flashed again. He called up the message immediately. It was Susan Leith, the cop reporter, asking to talk more.

Reed stood, looked around the newsroom for her, and shouted: "Let's talk over here at the rim. I'm waiting for a phone call."

Leith sat across from him and asked the usual background questions about the dead woman, but Reed couldn't supply much information. While they talked, Reed kept stealing glances at the VDT, hoping for another message.

The phone at the rim rang. It was Mahr, calling to tell Reed what the tech boys had found under the bottom drawer of Reed's bedroom dresser—a black-handled Buck hunting knife with a bloody five-inch blade.

Reed said he wasn't surprised. Mahr said he wanted to hear why. They'd meet at the cop shop again. Reed's feet winced, and he suggested the greasy spoon where he'd had breakfast. They settled on Mahr's office in the county building, a ten-minute drive.

Holmgren flicked the switch on the tape recorder, and the reels turned in tandem like miniature ferris wheels. Mahr said five words and sat back. "Tell us about the knife."

Reed spoke animatedly: "It's the killer's calling card. After Diana Diaz died, he left one on the spot where he dumped the body. And now he's left another one in my house. Tell me that's just a coincidence."

Mahr was flipping through a report. The pages were floppy, and Reed figured that they had been faxed. "I don't see any record here of a Buck knife being found at the scene in the Diana Diaz case."

Reed swallowed hard. "I never told the police."

Holmgren looked incredulous. "Excuse me?"

Reed smiled an embarrassed smile. "I never told the cops in Jersey. Nobody down there wanted anything to do with that case. Said it was New York City's problem. I could tell when I was pissing into the wind, so I said to hell with 'em."

"Since you failed to report it, the other knife doesn't exist as far as we're concerned."

Reed rose from his chair. "I still have it. Call my house. Have one of your forensics guys look on the bulletin board above my desk. It's stuck in the wall next to the high school photograph of Diana Diaz."

Mahr dialed Reed's house and instructed one of the technicians where to look. Mahr, Holmgren, and Reed waited in silence for the technician to check. After two minutes, Mahr nodded into the mouthpiece and said "Thanks anyway."

He placed the receiver back on the cradle, looked up at Reed, and told him they had a problem—"No photo, no knife, no nothing."

Reed was standing again. "Don't you see? Diana Diaz's killer is trying to frame me for this murder. Takes the knife and replaces it with the murder weapon. Figures you guys will search my house and find it."

"Why?"

"Because I started looking into the Diaz case again, and I think he found out on Friday. He's afraid I'll uncover something I missed the first time, something that will incriminate him."

Mahr remained unconvinced. "What are you saying? That this guy hid in the woods until you came home with a woman, then followed her, killed her, and tried to frame you?"

"Maybe he drove by my place and saw two cars," Reed sputtered. "I admit that I don't have all the answers yet, but I bet what I got makes more sense than anything you've got."

Reed saw Holmgren throw Mahr a look that said that Reed was off the wall.

"Look, lady, I'm not crazy."

"The name is Detective Holmgren." She glared at him. "For the sake of argument, then, could you tell me why the killer didn't simply kill you instead of Miss Pettraglia?"

"Too many people knew that I was investigating the Diaz case. If I died, they'd reopen it—who else but Diana Diaz's murderer would have a reason to kill me?"

As if on cue, the two detectives reached for their cigarette packs, and Mahr handed Holmgren his lighter before using it himself. Then Mahr said that they were doing the same thing—looking at Miss Pettraglia's death and asking themselves, what was the motive? Robbery? No. There'd been forty dollars found in her wallet. Sexual assault? No. There was no evidence of that whatsoever. Some sort of passion-jealousy-revenge deal? Now they were getting warm. Very attractive young woman. Probably had many, many suitors. Lover's quarrel sort of thing . . . Mahr paused to flick an ash from his cigarette.

Holmgren picked it up from there. "You, Mr. Reed, didn't know her long enough to care enough to get into a lover's quarrel. But somebody must have. Let's suppose, for a minute, that she and a boyfriend have a spat and break up. She meets you in the Grand Union. She decides to go home with you. She calls him on the phone from the pay phone perhaps? At any rate, the jilted suitor follows. According to our interview this morning, you and she saw a car drive past your house before she left, right? Boyfriend waits for her to get home. She's wearing your jacket. They argue. Bingo. Then he figures she's got your jacket on—why not let you take the fall? He goes through the coat pocket, finds the utility bill. Hell, he didn't even have to follow her from the Grand Union. He could have just been waiting for her to get home, and got your address off the bill."

Reed was shaking his head no, but the two detectives were too caught up in their theory to hear him out. "So he dumps the body where it'll be found fairly quickly," Holmgren said. "Then waited for the cops to call you in for questioning so he could plant the bloody knife, knowing that we'd do a search of your house at some point.

And the plan probably would have worked if you hadn't been stopped for speeding about the time of her death."

Reed jumped to his feet again. "No way. Totally wrong. I was framed, but not by some jilted lover. It was absolutely, positively, definitely, no doubt about it the same guy who killed Diana Diaz. I guarantee it. And off the record, I can tell you who it is."

Mahr leaned forward and shut off the tape recorder before Reed said the name. "The police dispatcher, Wilson, mentioned that you might bring up this gentleman's name. And he gave us the history, which is, with the best possible spin, rocky as hell. But murder is involved, so we took your theories as a possibility—assume nothing, preclude nothing.

"We called Mr. Jenkins an hour ago. His answering machine in New Jersey gave us the phone number of his television production company in Manhattan. We called there. His assistant said that Mr. Jenkins is in Minneapolis on business. Took an American flight out of Newburgh at nine P.M. last night, at least two hours, by our estimate, before Karen Pettraglia died."

Reed was shaking his head again. "Don't believe it."

"We didn't," Holmgren said. "We phoned Mr. Jenkins at his hotel in Minneapolis and had him fax us a copy of his plane ticket."

"Did you check with the front desk to see when Jenkins checked in?"

"Yes," Holmgren replied, her voice becoming more irritated. "The room had been guaranteed, and apparently the night clerk didn't bother making note of the time."

"How long ago did he make the reservation?"

Mahr stood, eyes flaring. He wagged a forefinger in Reed's face. "Look, buddy, we're conducting this interview, and we'll ask the questions—got that?"

Reed replied that he was merely suggesting that Jenkins could have just been manufacturing an alibi. "How do you know for sure that it's Jenkins in Minneapolis? Did you fax the desk clerk a photo of Jenkins and get confirmation it's the right guy?"

Mahr slammed the palms of his hands on the table. "I have two words of advice for you, Reed. Back off. We checked Mr. Jenkins' alibi. His involvement would have been a long shot, but we checked. But to argue that he had an accomplice fly out early, posing as Jenkins—it doesn't wash."

Holmgren crushed her cigarette in an ashtray. "I'm sorry, Mr. Reed, but you're grasping at straws. We are not going to pursue this. Manpower is limited. We're going with the tried-and-true formula, the obvious—that the victim knew the killer. Which happens to be true in eighty percent of all murder cases."

"But what about the knives?"

"We have only your word that there was a similar knife left at the spot where the Diaz girl was found in New Jersey," Holmgren explained, sounding more and more exasperated. "But you didn't report it to the police, and you don't have the knife, so where does that leave you? And even if you did have the knife, there's nothing tying it to Mr. Jenkins."

Mahr took it from there. "Mr. Reed, take our advice. Give it a rest. Give yourself a rest. We have a better perspective. We can weigh the facts and events objectively, unemotionally. You're wrong. Jenkins was a good sport to answer our questions and even fax his plane ticket. But he said that if we persisted, he'd see his attorney, because this sounded like the same looney who was hassling him last year, and he wasn't about to have his name dragged through somebody else's mud. He identified you by name, and said if you were going to be irrational and continue to pursue this, he'd sue your ass to kingdom come."

Reed pulled out of the county parking lot and realized he had no place to go. His house was being "processed," as Mahr called it, while a state trooper was transporting the Buck knife and a blood sample from the victim to the state crime lab in Albany. By tomorrow morning, they'd be about 99 percent certain whether they had the murder weapon.

Mahr had said that Reed could return to his house sometime Wednesday, that they'd let Reed know when. Reed thought of phoning Caroline at work and asking to stay with her, but decided against it. He'd handled enough questions for one day.

He drove to the Ramada by the interstate. He checked in, then called *The Clarion* and requested a personal day. They said they understood. Then he got a water glass from the bathroom and placed it on the bedside table. Then he grabbed the bottle of Jack Daniels by the neck and set out to kill it.

# Chapter Forty-three

Stuart Reed's bout with the fifth of sour mash ended in a draw. Reed was about preparing to finish the bottle by eight P.M. when it knocked him down. He awakened, still semidrunk, at one A.M. to take a leak, and he drank the remaining inch to make sure that he slept through till morning.

He awoke six hours later, feeling as though he'd fallen off a garbage truck at sixty miles an hour. His forehead throbbed. His tongue felt like he'd sucked on poison ivy. His right thigh had a jagged pain from where he must have walked into something on his way to the bathroom in the middle of the night. He couldn't remember throwing up; his mouth told him so.

He was still wearing his clothes from the day before, had even slept in his running shoes.

Reed got himself a glass of water, drank it in a gulp, and refilled the glass. He staggered back to the bed, swearing he'd never touch another sip of alcohol, then collapsed again.

He reawoke at nine A.M. He looked at his watch and knew he had plenty of time to kill. The liquor stores didn't open till ten.

Reed scrubbed his face with a cold wet washcloth. He went to the soda machine in the stairwell and bought two cans of Pepsi. Hardcore drinkers like Pepsi in the morning—fluid to fight dehydration, corn syrup to get them out of sugar debt, and caffeine to ease the headache. He drank the Pepsi out of the can, then showered. The hot jets of water on his face made him light-headed, and he wondered if he were still drunk. He decided he wasn't but needed to be.

After he'd toweled off, he rubbed the wet bar of soap inside the armpits of his green work shirt, then got dressed. He checked out of the Ramada and ate breakfast at a McDonald's. The coffee tasted worse than he had remembered it there—bitter and scalding hot.

He drank three sips and gave up. He tried the prefab home-fried potatoes. They tasted good and greasy going down, and he knew they'd make him feel better.

The rain of the day before had ended, and a low bank of gray clouds moved rapidly across the sky, allowing an occasional spot of sunlight to peek through. Reed thought the air felt warmer, and he left his denim jacket open as he crossed the parking lot to the strip mall. He went into the liquor store and bought another bottle of J.D.

As Reed drove out of town, small rivulets of rainwater still trickled down the shoulder of Route 49. With the radio blaring "Sultans of Swing," Reed headed past the auto dealerships and trailer parks and into the hills. He saw the sign for the rest area, flicked on his turn signal, and came to a complete stop. He waited for a semi to go roaring past in the other direction, then pulled across the oncoming lane and onto the gravel.

Reed tried to recall Raf's description of the exact location where Karen's body had been found, and instinctively drove past the pay phones and the tourist-information bulletin board to the far end of the rest area. There, three redwood picnic tables and a bright orange county trash barrel stood isolated. He had to see where the killer had left her, maybe even pick up his scent. The killer had anticipated Reed's every move, had manipulated Reed's actions the way Pavlov had manipulated his dogs. Reed knew he had to do something to change that, for a reason that was gradually becoming as clear as British gin. The next target—and Reed was positive that there'd be a next target—wouldn't be a young woman. It would be him.

He stepped from the car and walked toward the orange barrel. He tried to reconstruct the killer's movements. Near the barrel, he saw a three-inch-wide strand of yellow plastic ribbon caught on a bramble of a leafless bush. The ribbon, with POLICE LINE—DO NOT CROSS in big black block letters, was the only indication that something terribly wrong had occurred here. If other telltale signs existed, they had drowned in yesterday's rain.

Reed swung around abruptly to see if he was being watched, but the woods across Route 49 yielded no signs of life. Still, Reed felt a presence that made him queasy. Although the terrain, the location, the weather were all far different from Riverton and the pistol range, Reed felt like he had been transported back there, and he felt like he was about to vomit.

Reed knew he was starting to snap again—this killing had been so different from the first. Even the way the body had been disposed of was wrong. Diana Diaz's body had been dumped in an isolated spot. Karen Pettraglia had been dumped where she'd be found right away.

Reed was drawn to the wild rosebush where the strand of police ribbon hung limp. Reed understood now. It hadn't been left behind by some careless cop. The killer had left it. For Reed. He wheeled again to see if he could spot someone lurking in the cold damp woods, but of course no one was there. The killer didn't have to be there; the killer just *knew* Reed would come here. The same way that Reed just *knew* what he would find behind the pricker bush.

Sure enough, when he pushed his hand inside the sleeve of the denim jacket and pushed aside the brambly branches, he saw it immediately. There, buried to its hilt in the leafy wet ground, was a black-handled Buck hunting knife.

The son of a bitch had returned to leave his calling card already. Reed realized that if he had been thinking straight, this time he could have been Pavlov instead of the dog. Reed could have been lying in wait for *him*.

What next? Go to the pay phone and call Mahr and Holmgren so the cops could come and dust the knife for prints? No, the knife had undoubtedly been taken from Reed's place, and the murder weapon left in its place. The only prints on the knife would be Reed's, and the detectives would think that he planted it there himself and concocted the tale about the knife at the pistol range to reinforce the fragile link between the two slayings.

Going to the cops was a dead end now. The knife was the final gauntlet thrown down by the killer. Reed bent down and extracted it from the ground. He used his sleeve to wipe off the traces of mud. He walked to his car. Again, he wondered if he was being watched, and decided he no longer gave a shit.

He sat in the Mazda and thought for a while. He thought about Karen Pettraglia: the express lane at the Grand Union, the smoky living room, their silent dance. It had been maybe forty hours since he'd seen her for the first time, maybe thirty-six since he'd seen her for the last. People would think he was nuts if they knew how devastated he was by the death of a woman he'd met in a supermarket line and had known for four hours, but he couldn't help how he felt.

He had to drive home now, see the mess that the killer and the forensic technicians had left behind. He'd follow Mahr's instructions and do a rough inventory of what the killer had stolen. When he had finished, he would call in sick again. And then he'd put Jack Daniels in the driver's seat.

Aside from the broken pane of glass and the bloody knife, it had been what the military analysts liked to call a surgical strike.

As Reed soon surmised from checking his belongings and furnishings, the killer had left the murder weapon almost as a sick afterthought. The real reason the killer had been there was to remove everything related to the Diaz case—a year's worth of notes, newspaper clips, photos, maps, documents, audiotaped interviews. Everything. The killer had been so thorough that he'd found the copies of the Diaz and Fresh Kills autopsies that Reed had wrapped in aluminum foil and left in the freezer.

All that was left now was a messy house—with fingerprint dust of various colors everywhere but on the aquarium fish. White dust on the black wood stove, black dust all over the refrigerator-freezer.

For Reed, the theft of the files was the coup de grace. The only thing he had left was his distance runner's stubbornness. This was just a bad patch, just like in a long race, Reed told himself. He would get through it with a little help from the whiskey. Then he'd get his second wind, and when he sensed that he was closing in on the finish, he'd throw in that awesome kick. . . .

Reed sat on the edge of the blanket chest, near where Karen had sat, and broke down in tears. Who was he kidding? he asked himself. He was done. He'd messed up early on the Diaz case, and now he'd messed up again for pursuing it so cavalierly. He'd gotten some sweet young woman in the middle of it, and he had gotten her killed. He thought about the advice of the investigative editor at *The Transcript*—abandon a story early if you didn't find a smoking gun right away. He thought about an old saying favored by his grandfather: "There's only two ways to deal with a mad dog. Either kill it or leave it alone."

Reed had done neither, and Lord how he had paid. He couldn't take it anymore—the guilt, the remorse, the self-pity, the enormity and finality of his defeat. He took the bottle of Jack Daniels, twisted off the cap, and prepared to take a swig. But something shiny on the mantel caught his eye, and he set the bottle down until he saw what it was. It was a bottle of some kind, in one of those silvery party wraps that liquor stores give out. It had black fingerprint dust on it, and so did the bottle of Grand Marnier inside. A little notecard was tied to the neck, by the red wax seal.

It had a message, printed with a red felt-tip pen:

CHEERS
BUCK

Reed grabbed the bottle and flung it against the hearth. Then he grabbed the Jack Daniels, replaced the cap, and heaved it so hard against the base of the fireplace that slivers of glass exploded across the room.

He dialed Mahr's office and got an answering machine. He left a message. "This is Stuart Reed. I did the household inventory. Nothing's gone." Let the know-it-all detectives go pissing after some imaginary jilted lover, Reed thought. Let them hang themselves on red tape.

Pavlov had rung one bell too many. Reed could feel the second wind kick in, and he would run the race his way from now on. He would no longer try to react to what the killer was or was not doing. Reed's rules were now in effect, and Reed's rules were that there weren't any. No cop-outs. No cops. No lawyers. No laws.

Reed wasn't sure whether he or the killer would make the next move, but he was certain of the ultimate outcome. He would unmask the killer, and there'd be a head-on collision between them. In this battle royal, only one man would emerge triumphant. The last man standing.

# Chapter Forty-four

By the time Stuart Reed left for *The Clarion* on Wednesday night, he had a list of murder suspects and as thorough an inventory of the missing Diaz material as he could think of. Some items—notably his interview with Culp Jenkins the year before and all of his notes from the pistol range—could never be replaced, but he could send away for new copies of all of the documents that had been taken, and he could rent Jenkins' videos again and take new notes on them.

Tomorrow morning, he would use whatever goodwill he had remaining at *The Transcript* and get printouts of all the pertinent articles from the newspaper's electronic library. He'd send away and buy another duplicate of Diana Diaz's yearbook photo. And the photostat of the firing-range ribbon cutting was due to arrive at *The Transcript* any day from the microfilm company in the Midwest. Reed knew he had to reassemble as much of the material as he could, and as soon as he could.

The question that Reed had kept returning to was why "Buck" had killed Karen Pettraglia instead of him. And the answer he kept coming back to was that the only motive anyone would have to kill him was to stop him from digging into the Diaz case. But Reed's death might touch off a new investigation, and maybe this time somebody would catch the killer.

For that very reason, Culp Jenkins couldn't touch Reed. But he could have tried to frame him for Karen Pettraglia's murder or mess up his mind so bad that he'd go on a bender and forget about Diana Diaz, Karen Pettraglia, or anyone besides Remy Martin or Jack Daniels or Jim Beam.

If the killer wasn't Jenkins—and Mahr's investigation into the Minneapolis alibi made that a possibility that Reed couldn't dismiss out of hand—who else could it be? Reed had composed an extremely short list of suspects, then filled in most of the names with one phone call.

At eight P.M., Reed had dialed the 800 number for *The Transcript* and asked for Milt Roberts. Milt was on assignment, the clerk said, but she would call his beeper and leave Reed's number.

Ten minutes later, Roberts was on the line. "What can I do for you, sport?"

Reed tried to sound slightly pie eyed. "Milt, buddy, you have to help me. Remember two nights ago, the *Monday Night Football* game that I canceled out on because of some chick? Well, the chick's dead. Murdered. And I think the cops think I did it. They haven't arrested me yet, but they've been questioning me pretty hard."

Milt offered his condolences and then offered to lie for Reed. "Tell them I came up for the game. I was with you the whole time."

Reed said it was a little late for that. He'd told the cops already that he'd seen her. But Reed insisted to Roberts that he didn't do it, and he was being framed—possibly by an ex-boyfriend of hers or somebody else. Reed wanted to know which reporters had planned to come up to Reed's place to watch the game—and whether anybody else knew that he had a girl there Monday evening. "I know it sounds confusing, Milt, but then *I'm* a bit confused. I messed up. I started drinking the hard stuff again. You gotta save me."

Milt paused a few seconds, then replied: "Two reporters were going to come along with me. Clancy Collins and Julio Jones. Clancy told us about the babe when he said you'd had called to cancel on us."

At Reed's end of the line, a list of six names on a yellow legal pad became a list of eight:

1. Unknown jilted suitor
2. Culp Jenkins
3. Leon Sadowski
4. Glenn Brenner
5. Pritchard Majors
6. Milt Roberts
7. Clancy Collins
8. Julio Jones

"Anybody else, Milt? I'm hurtin' bad here."

"Now that you mention it, there's one other guy. When you phoned the other evening, I was almost out the door. Clancy Collins shouted across the newsroom that you had called. Well, as soon as we had finished talking, Mr. Big cornered me and asked, 'What were you talking to Stuart Reed about?' or something to that effect. I said I was going up to your place to watch football, but you'd canceled because you had a chick over."

"Mr. Big? Who's Mr. Big?"

"That's our latest nickname for Pritch. Pritchard Majors."

Reed didn't respond, but Roberts didn't seem to notice. "By the way, you missed a helluva show. Eagles cheerleaders were stunners. And the game wasn't bad either. Giants won it on a blocked punt, seventeen–sixteen, with fifty seconds left. Taylor ran it in for a TD. Right before it happened, I said the Eagles ought to take a safety and take the free kick from their twenty."

"Who'd you see the game with, the guys from work?"

"No. They both split. I went over to my neighbor's. He's got one of those twenty-five-inch Sonys. You should have seen it."

Reed said he wished that he'd had, and got off the line. Reed put a line through Roberts' name on the list, and underlined "Pritchard Majors."

Reed reviewed the other names on the list and drew a line through Julio Jones' name as well. Jones was notorious for bumming beers off anyone he could, and he doubted whether Jones' Yugo could even make it over the mountain to Reed's place and back. He drew a line through "Unknown jilted suitor" as well. Unknown jilted suitors did not break into homes and steal files from a murder case they'd never heard of.

No, there were three names, maybe four, to deal with, and they intersected where Reed had always known they would: opening day at the pistol range. Majors and Jenkins were in the photo—the photo that had disappeared from the face of the earth. The other name, Clancy Collins, Reed hadn't connected before, but it was because of his own stupidity. Before going on rewrite, Collins had done metro general assignment, and he had filed the six-incher on the ribbon cutting. Reed decided to call Raf Wilson at the cop shop later and ask him to run the names through the FBI computers.

At 10:50 Wednesday night, the list of suspects was back to one name. Reed called up his electronic messages at *The Transcript* and found a news clerk's reply to a question that Reed had forgotten that he'd asked:

Stuart:
Around 8 P.M. Monday, a guy called and asked for you. I said you were off Mondays. I asked if he wanted to leave a name or a message, but he just hung up. I think I noticed a faint southern accent. Hope this is of some help.

Reed was wary. Did someone call and pretend to be Culp Jenkins? And the hour threw him. He'd seen that car on Iron Hollow Road around nine on Monday night, and Jenkins would hardly have had time to drive all the way from Jersey in that amount of time—unless Jenkins didn't call from New Jersey.

Hadn't Mahr said that Jenkins had flown out of Newburgh, which was thirty miles north-northeast of Reed's place and a good hour and a half north of Riverton? Why hadn't he flown out of Newark?

Maybe Mahr knew, but it was too late to call now. Then Reed had a minor brainstorm: why not take some of the electronic-library searches he'd planned to do again at *The Transcript* and try them at *The Clarion* first?

Reed logged on to the library system and typed, "find Culp and Jenkins." He waited for the system to spew out the raw numbers:

1. 891   CULP
2. 387   JENKINS
3.  11   CULP AND JENKINS

Reed hit "DI," the code for "display," and looked at the first few paragraphs of each of the eleven stories. The first was an obituary he'd written himself. So was the second—he'd forgotten about the Culp Funeral Home. He was going to get a lot of obits with that set of key words. He tried another tack: "Find Culp and Jenkins and hunt."

It took the computer two minutes to spew out everything:

4. 891   CULP
5. 387   JENKINS
6. 411   HUNT
7.   3   CULP AND JENKINS AND HUNT

He hit "DI" again. Story one was an obit. He hit "DI" again. Another obit.

One story to go. "DI." Bingo:

LOCAL SPORTSMAN FILMS
OUTDOOR SHOW IN BRADNER CO.

BRADYVILLE—Nationally famous sportsman Culp Jenkins, who has dined with presidents and hunted moose with movie stars, has begun filming segments of his nationally syndicated outdoors show in Bradner County.

"I've traveled the world over, and take it from me, Bradner County is as close to a sportsman's paradise as you'll ever get," said the fifty-year-old Jenkins.

The renowned hunter, who owns a five-room hunting lodge on the outskirts of this hamlet, has filmed a trout-fishing show on Longhouse Creek, a rabbit-hunting segment on the Wisner Flats, and a deer-hunting segment "somewhere within three miles of the lodge."

Jenkins says he can't say where that spot is, lest too many hunters flock to the area. "That stand of trees sure has been good to me," Jenkins said. "I don't want to put the whammy on myself, but I've nailed a buck on the first day of the season for five years running."

Reed routed a copy of the story from the electronic library to his personal queue, then made a printout of it. Reed felt the adrenaline kicking in now. He no longer had to worry about going through receptionists or lawyers to get to Jenkins. He'd find the hunting lodge and wait for Jenkins there. Reed tried remembering the deer-hunting videos, and the part about going out for the few weeks before the season to choose your spot and check the deer activity in that area.

Reed logged on to the library system again and a search on the words "deer" and "hunt" and "season." The answer, he soon learned, was twelve days away.

Locating the lodge would be easy enough—he'd just call the Bradyville general store and get directions. In hamlets like that, everybody knew everybody else's business. And a mini-celebrity like Jenkins? Hell, they probably took their out-of-town relatives on tours of the grounds. Reed would call the store second thing Thursday morning, just after he looked into buying himself a pistol.

# Chapter Forty-five

The pistol in question was a Llama III Special with a marbled black-brown plastic grip. It weighed just over a pound, took six .380 caliber cartridges in the magazine and another in the chamber. It had two safety mechanisms, which Stuart Reed liked, and a price tag of two hundred dollars, which Reed liked even more. He placed the pistol gently on the faded bedspread. "I'll have to think a minute or two. You sure it works, and it's clean?"

"Man, I guarantee it. It's better than new and cleaner than Snow White's snatch." The salesman was a young man with greased-back black hair and a scraggly beard that almost concealed a virulent case of acne.

The salesman had an unlit Tiparillo dangling out of the corner of his mouth, and it caused him to mumble slightly when he spoke. His accent said one of the outer boroughs, maybe Brooklyn or Queens. "Tell you what, my man. Let's make it two and a quarter, and I'll throw in a box of fifty shells and an extra clip. That'll give you thirteen rounds at a pop, which should get the job done anywhere north of a Hundred-and-eightieth Street."

Reed picked up the pistol again. He turned it over and saw where the serial number had been filed off the bottom of the stubby barrel. He depressed the small knurled button by the top of the handle and slid the oiled magazine out, then clicked it back into place.

The Llama's grip felt comfortable, almost natural, in Reed's hand, and the pistol's compactness meant that it would fit nicely in the front pouch of his hooded sweatshirt. Reed reached into his Levi's and pulled out a roll of twenties that he'd gotten from an automatic teller machine at a bank on the way to Monticello. He had a dozen twenties; Raf had said not to bring any more than that. Reed fumbled in his front jeans pockets for a five-dollar bill, until the zit man told him to forget it, today was bargain day.

The gun dealer worked out of the second floor of a flophouse on a side street in Monticello. Reed had gotten the address from Raf Wilson, who had been none too keen on setting up the rendezvous. But Reed's alternatives were waiting six months for a pistol permit, or driving clear down to Chinatown and ordering pot luck from a street vendor, and Wilson had been able to tell from the insistent tone in Reed's voice that Reed would get himself a pistol, no matter what. As an old pal, Wilson figured he had to steer him to a guy who sold reliable merchandise.

Reed handed his money to the zit man, who put it in his pocket, then reached under the bed and slid out a battered aluminum blanket chest. He flipped up the hasps, lifted the lid, and found a box of .380 caliber cartridges among a small arsenal of pistols and ammunition. He fished out an extra .380 clip, and handed it with the box of bullets to Reed. He walked to the door, undid the three locks, and turned the knob. He pulled out a Bic lighter for his Tiparillo. With his elbow, he pushed the door open and grinned through yellowing teeth. "Happy hunting, *mon frère.*"

"How's the Grand Union Romeo?"

Caroline Tompkins tried to sound good-natured, but even over the phone Stuart Reed felt the scalpel at work. He'd just returned from Monticello, all pumped up for his target practice with his new pistol, and now he had to deal with her. He wasn't sure whether he could handle the conversation, and quickly concluded that he didn't care.

"Hi, Caroline. The Grand Union Romeo is still alive, but considering the fact that the Grand Union Juliet is not, I'm not altogether sure that your levity is appropriate." Reed sat on his couch and absentmindedly began to wipe the traces of the fingerprinting dust from the side of the blanket chest, then looked for some other way to keep busy. "How about we start again? Hi, Caroline."

Caroline apologized in appropriately chastened tones, then added: "I truly am sorry, you do know that. But it *is* exciting. You're Topic A in the newsroom, and the gossip is so hot that it has spilled over into advertising and personnel. Even old man Parisi is talking about you."

"I didn't think he knew that I existed."

"I don't think he did. I mean, let's face it. Given your job and your hours . . . I wouldn't exactly call you management. But when you get caught in a lethal love triangle and live to tell the tale, that's something we normal dull people don't hear about every day."

Reed asked what she was talking about.

"The cute cop reporter, Susan Leith, is pretty well connected at the BCI. The word there is that they're looking into the victim's former boyfriends. A jealousy deal. Didn't you read today's paper?"

"To tell you the truth, I avoid reading *The Clarion.* Bad for the appetite." Reed reached for the Thursday paper. "OK, I got the paper in front of me."

Reed perused a short second-day story on page three that was noteworthy solely for its lack of hard news, aside from the funeral arrangements, which had been announced for Friday morning. Police said that they were following several promising leads, but that no immediate arrests were expected. They had not ruled out jealousy as a motive.

Reed finished the story. "They tried shoveling that pile of horse crap in my direction, and I told 'em they were loco. This case is a replay of Riverton. Same guy. But nobody wants to listen to what I have to say. I've given up on the BCI detectives. They can look for unrequited lovers until the cows shit ice cream, but they won't find a thing."

"Stuart, I'm sure they know what they're doing."

"Oh, yeah? Did you know that the killer broke into my place the next morning, while the BCI investigators were questioning me?"

Caroline interrupted. "And that the killer left a bloody hunting knife. Tell me something I don't know."

Reed held his temper. "As I was about to say, he left a knife—and stole all my research notes on the Diaz murder. Five cartons' worth. Didn't touch anything else. Does that sound like a jilted lover to you?" Reed pushed the paper aside and reached for his denim jacket. As he talked, he removed the Llama pistol and box of shells.

Caroline asked what the cops had to say about the stolen files.

"I didn't tell them," Reed replied, failing to mask his growing agitation. "They already got their pet theories. I wouldn't want the facts to get in the way."

Caroline said that he was hopeless. Reed replied that he was anything but. That he was thinking of asking the city editor, Seb Pappas, if he'd let Reed do some investigative reporting into the second killing in hopes of turning up some similarities to Diana Diaz's death.

"Stuart, that's just it. I don't see any similarities. The first girl was suffocated, stripped, and gutted. The second girl was stabbed in the heart but otherwise untouched, right?"

Reed tried to enlighten her. "Trust me, it was the same killer. He killed the women for different reasons, so he killed them differently. Karen Pettraglia was killed in a way that should have made me the prime suspect—and totally derailed my new efforts to find Diana Diaz's killer. Thank goodness the cops stopped me for speeding. As for the Diaz girl, I don't know why she was killed, or why she was cut up the way she was, but when I find out, I bet I'll know who the killer is."

Caroline's instincts told her to hang up the phone, but she knew

that Reed was so dense, so out of control about Diana Diaz and now
Karen Pettraglia that he needed to have things spelled out. "Stuart,
you pulled the pin on this grenade once, and you got your genitalia
blown off. If you pursue this—and by 'this' I assume you're talking
about Culp Jenkins—I guarantee that it will blow up again, only
twice as bad.

"*The Clarion* will go belly-up at the drop of a libel lawyer's briefcase. If I didn't know you the way I do, I'd call old man Parisi now
and have him fire you on the spot. The paper can't risk you playing
Hardy Boy while you're in any way connected with *The Clarion*. It
may not be my place to say this, but believe me. Anybody at *The
Clarion* who has the capacity to fire you would do so right now if
they knew what I know."

Reed sat there, the phone propped against his chin, while he
loaded six shells into the magazine of the Llama. He was already
tuning Caroline out.

"Stuart, I'm writing a memo to Parisi the second that we hang up,
advising him that I ordered you not to pursue this. As a favor to you,
I won't give it to him unless you ignore my advice."

Reed slid the clip back into the handle of the pistol. "Does this
mean you won't go to bed with me again?"

Caroline was flabbergasted. "You're such a jerk. . . . Why would
I want to go bed with you? Especially now. I think you ought to be
forced to wear a warning label on your lapel that reads, 'The surgeon
general advises that going home with this man could be hazardous
to your health.' I mean, from what you're saying, that girl was killed
because someone wanted to get at you, right?"

Reed swallowed hard. "I guess you could say that."

"And if I'd been at your house Monday night instead of that
Grand Union girl, I'd be the one who's dead."

"She wasn't a girl. She was twenty-five."

"Half of one, six dozen of the other. The point is, is the killing
over?"

"Ask the BCI crowd. They seem to have all the answers."

Caroline told him to get the chip off his shoulder.

"OK. You're right. I guess your cynicism's finally rubbed off. So, in
answer to your question, if this guy kills because he enjoys it, then
he'll kill again, until somebody stops him. But I don't think that's it.
The dreaded serial killer has been overblown by movies and television. I think our man killed Diana Diaz almost inadvertently, in the
heat of passion—something like that. If I could figure out the circumstances, maybe I could solve this. . . .

"At any rate, Diana Diaz dies, and he dumps her body where in all likelihood she won't be found till the following spring. Except that within hours I come across the body and get a bug up my ass about it. He short-circuits the investigation, gets me shit canned. I come up here and keep digging.

"I start to get close to something that will tie him to Diana Diaz, so he kills Karen Pettraglia to derail me, either by framing me for it or scaring me away.

"I return to my theory about the firing range and the photo—a librarian at my old newspaper had to have told my old boss about my asking for the photo, and my old boss told his buddy Culp Jenkins. So Jenkins kills Karen Pettraglia to derail me for good— either by framing me or making me spin out like I did after the first murder."

He could hear Caroline heave a sigh. "I don't know, Stuart, it just sounds so bizarre."

Reed became more insistent. "But the fact remains that the killer broke into my house and stole my research on the Diana Diaz murder—and left a knife identical to the one he left at the pistol range a few days after he killed Diana Diaz. It's the same guy."

"So, Stuart, what you're saying is, yes, he will kill again, but he'll kill only you, and then only if he has to. Will he have to?"

"Not if I kill him first." Reed picked up the pistol and aimed at an imaginary figure across the room.

# Chapter Forty-six

U nfolded on the kitchen table were three maps. The first was a Hagstrom road map of Bradner County. The second was a United States Geological Survey topographical map that included the Bradyville area. The third was an aerial map—a huge two-foot by three-foot blue photostat really—of the same area.

After getting off the phone with Caroline, Reed had called the Bradyville general store and asked for directions to Culp Jenkins' hunting lodge. Now he was retracing the directions on all three maps, trying to get a feel for the lay of land, trying to find the place where he could get the drop on Culp Jenkins if he had to.

From what the woman at the general store had said, the Jenkins lodge was a quarter mile off Bradyville Road. On the topographical map, it was the fleck the size of a piece of ground black pepper. Judging from the brown swirls emanating from it, the lodge was located on a rise at the end of an unimproved dirt road.

Reed was beginning to tire, and he had to squint at the aerial map to find what had to be the lodge—all he could tell was that it was a man-made structure and that it was surrounded by dense woodlands. Behind the house, down the rise, was a stream. Beyond the stream was farmland. Reed guessed cornfields, since the area was a prime growing spot for both sweet corn and cow corn. Beyond the narrow farmland was a steep incline.

On the topographical map, Reed traced a dotted line that skirted the top of the Iron Hollow Ski Area and then ran along the ridge of the Ramapo Mountains north toward Newburgh. The dotted line, which denoted the Appalachian Trail, ran within two inches of the hunting lodge.

Reed poured himself some instant coffee. Didn't bother to heat it, just drank it. He yawned and went back to studying the aerial photo again. As he had suspected, that portion of the trail was so heavily wooded that it couldn't be found on the photo. He thought of traveling a mile down the heavily forested mountainside to the hunting lodge, and he thought of ticks, snakes, brambles, burrs, rocks, and poison ivy. Running along the Appalachian Trail itself was challenging enough.

Reed scanned the aerial photo again and found a swath cut through the woods approximately half a mile from Jenkins' place—high-tension power lines. Reed could do his reconnoitering by taking the Appalachian Trail to where the electrical lines crossed it, then traveling down the mountain and across the cornfields to the lodge.

Something about the stream and cornfields in the aerial photo jogged something in Reed's mind, but he couldn't quite place it. He looked over the printout of the Jenkins interview that had run in *The Clarion.* He read about how Jenkins had the same favorite spot that he hunted from every opening day, and how he'd shot some videos there as well.

Reed could feel his mind fade, and he walked to the bedroom and did a nosedive onto his mattress.

Reed slept for five hours. When he awoke, the sun had set. The bedroom was a murky gray, like a bad fifties kinescope, and he couldn't think of where he was, what day it was, what time it was.

He recognized the twilight. He sat up. He recognized his dresser, the one that had been his grandmother's. The one where the knife had been found. He looked at the clock radio, a digital job in pink plastic that he'd gotten for ten bucks at a sidewalk sale. He turned on a reading lamp. The clock said five-forty. The tiny red bulb next to P.M. was lit. He hadn't slept through work.

He looked around the room, the Poconos-tacky paneling, the paint peeling on the bedroom door, the dirty green hooked rug that was on the floor when he'd moved in, the water-stained ceiling with the tarnished brass light fixture and the pull string hanging down.

Reed thought about how hard he had worked all through school, then in his newspaper jobs. He thought about his marriage to Jeanne, and her hopes for kids and a home in the suburbs. He thought about how he had planned to go to the *Times* and be a star reporter, how people would recognize his byline, even look for it. Yet here he sat in a cruddy cabin on a dead-end road in a dead-end area, working a dead-end job on the graveyard shift for a dead-end rag of a newspaper.

He wondered how he possibly could have messed up so badly. It was the Diaz case, he knew, that had put him in this tailspin, that had kept returning to haunt him, that had killed Karen Pettraglia as well. He wondered if this failure was permanent, and decided no. If the killer was still on the loose, then Reed still had a story. And if he had a story, he could turn around this dead-end life.

Reed walked into the kitchen and pored over the three maps on the table. He tried to recall what he'd been thinking several hours before when he'd gotten so drowsy. He stared at the maps again, then read the Jenkins interview, then drove to the video rental store.

# Chapter Forty-seven

Detective Rachel Holmgren phoned Reed a few minutes after he'd gotten home from work on Friday morning. She explained that it was a courtesy call, that the tests were back from the lab in Albany, that the blood on the Buck knife matched Karen Pettraglia's. The autopsy confirmed that the knife had been the murder weapon.

As for fingerprints, nothing unusual had been found. Only Pettraglia's prints and her father's had been found on or in her red Renault, and only hers and Reed's had been found in Reed's house. Fibers, zilch. In terms of physical evidence, they were looking down a dry well, she said.

Reed wondered what the BCI was working on, and Holmgren ran through a laundry list—interviewing former boyfriends, neighbors, and co-workers, and running road checks near the Pettraglias' condo and the rest stop on Route 49. They were stopping motorists to see if they had driven by about the same time on Monday night and had seen anything suspicious. They were hoping that a deliveryman who drove through every few nights or so had seen something suspicious, but had been out of the area and hadn't heard what had happened. And they'd attend the funeral, which was about to begin in an hour or so, and check the crowd.

Reed was blunt: "So you got plenty of nothing, right?"

Holmgren said brusquely that she was confident that something would turn up. She asked Reed if he'd remembered anything else about Monday night that might be of help. Reed said that he was doing his best to forget.

"One more item," she said. "One of the forensics technicians was wondering why you didn't have a battery in your smoke alarm. It's worthless without it."

Reed scrunched his lips. "The smoke alarm definitely had a battery. It went off Monday evening when Karen Pettraglia was there. We had trouble getting a fire going in the wood stove."

"Did you remove the battery then?"

"I didn't, but Karen shut off the alarm. She might have just yanked the battery out to stop the infernal noise. But I doubt it. I didn't see

the battery anywhere—unless she inadvertently took it with her.
Might check your reports, see if she had one those little rectangular
batteries in my sports coat or somewhere.''

Holmgren said she would. Reed thanked her for the call and hung
up. He sensed that looking for the battery would be a waste of time.
He knew, and Holmgren must have known, that the case would
probably never be solved. There'd soon be a new murder to work
on, maybe a domestic quarrel that ended in tragedy, and the BCI
would throw all its manpower into that one since they knew who
did it and they'd be assured of success. The Pettraglia case would
keep getting buried deeper and deeper on their desks, until they
cleaned their desks and filed it away in the Unsolved file drawer.

Reed, on the other hand, planned to do something. He took the
Llama III Special from his top dresser drawer, along with an extra
clip that he had loaded. He took off his white oxford-cloth shirt and
his L. L. Bean chinos and folded them on the bed. He got his gray
hooded sweatsuit out of the closet and put it on. He placed the pistol
and two cartridge clips in separate white athletic socks, then put
them inside the sweatshirt's stomach pouch. He slid into a pair of
Asics Strikers, his heaviest duty running shoes, and got out a pair of
cotton gloves. He looked at the three maps one last time, and tried to
picture what he'd seen last night on the hunting videos.

In the kitchen, Reed drank a sixteen-ounce bottle of red Gatorade.
He put the empty on the counter as he left. He locked the kitchen
door, with its boarded-up pane. He placed the house key next to a
spare car key under the floor mat in the Mazda, and jogged easily
toward the ski area. He saw Peter Benjamin in the distance. The old
man walked past a row of parked snow-blowing equipment and into
the small one-story building by the base of the chair lift nearest to
Reed.

When Reed reached the lowest of the thick ten-foot-high steel
towers that supported the chair lift's steel cables, he leaned against
the tower and began to go through his leg stretches. Reed heard a
metallic groan, and suddenly the chairs on the lift lurched into motion. Reed jumped back five feet to dodge a yellow double chair that
came careening toward him. It gave him such a start that he cursed it
aloud as it swung past.

Benjamin emerged from the building to see what the commotion
was. The old man wore the same flannel shirt and overalls that he'd
worn when Reed had talked to him on Monday. He saw Reed, still
frazzled.

"Sorry," Benjamin said. "Didn't know you were out here or I'd've warned you. Heard about the other night. I'm sorry about that, too. Guess your nerves are pretty shot, huh?"

Reed nodded.

"Just checking out the Borvig, getting it ready for tomorrow. Ski patrol's scheduled to do a lift evacuation practice, and I gotta make sure both lifts are up and operating. Going to be fire trucks here, the whole works. Stop by. The firemen usually bring a few barbecue grills and kegs and party pretty heavy when it's over. Wanna see how these things work?"

Reed tried to refuse gracefully, but Benjamin grabbed Reed's sweatshirt sleeve and gently tugged until Reed followed him into the oversized shed. Inside was a desk with a few ski magazines and an electric coffeemaker, two folding chairs, some thick canvas-covered water hoses, strings of brightly colored plastic pennants, and a small control panel with three dials and assorted buttons and switches.

Benjamin pointed out the window to a circuit-breaker box by the base of the chair lift. "You fire that up so you got juice, then turn this ignition switch, and—bango—you're ready to roll."

Benjamin pointed to a large winch handle to his left. "This here adjusts the speeds. We've found that the medium speed is the best. Skiers can get on and off the lift fairly easy, and it still moves people up the hill at a decent clip. Takes about eight minutes to get to the top.

"We could put the lift in third gear like this"—Benjamin pulled the winch handle toward him—"and crank the speed up to five minutes, but you'd knock the snot out of the skiers as they tried to get on the lift. Not to mention the fact that the insurance company would shit bricks over it."

Reed thanked Benjamin for the tour and edged his way toward the door. The old man began a speech about the duties of the lift operator outside at the base of the slope. When the old man turned his back for a second, Reed ducked out the door, calling good-bye as he picked up his gait.

Benjamin came to the shed door and called: "Come by on opening day. I'll give you a free lift ticket. Anyone who can run up the Apron Strings deserves to ski down it a few times for free."

Reed made quick work of the mountain. His mind was on Culp Jenkins and the scouting mission that lay ahead, and he'd passed the pile of boulders at the top of the hill without thinking about it. He reached the shoulder of Route 71A at the ninety-degree bend just above the Apron Strings, then worked his way up the road against traffic toward the Appalachian Trail. It was only a few hundred yards, but the road curved so much that the oncoming cars were on top of him quickly. He ran as far inside on the shoulder as he could, despite the broken glass and bad footing, and was thankful when he reached the trail itself.

Although the Appalachian Trail, which stretches from Maine to Georgia, is celebrated as the most famous hiking trail on the East Coast, it is often little more than a scratched-out path through the woods. The stretch that Reed found himself on was narrow, poorly marked (an occasional splash of white paint of a tree trunk), overgrown with vegetation, and littered in spots with fallen branches, soda cans, and assorted beer bottles.

Reed found the stretch along the top of the Ramapos tougher going than he had anticipated. Several rocky stretches slowed him to a walk, for fear of spraining an ankle. He had to vault several fallen tree trunks, as well as muddy patches left from Tuesday's day-long downpour.

Reed reached the clearing for the power lines at noon. The run had taken fifty minutes instead of a half hour, and Reed figured he still needed another twenty minutes to make his descent on the lodge. He decided to go slow so that he'd have his wits about him when he approached Jenkins' property. Going in during broad daylight was less than ideal, but he remembered Mahr saying that Jenkins probably wouldn't be back east till the weekend. Reed knew the basic terrain. He just needed to pick his own stand to hunt Jenkins from.

Reed worked his way through the thick weeds under the power lines, occasionally walking along a mountain brook to catch his breath. The sun was out full blast after a week in hibernation, and Reed sweated through the gray cotton warm-up clothes both front and back. He felt the Llama and the cartridge clips through the sweatshirt.

Halfway down the mountain, the slope grew too steep for Reed to negotiate straight on, and he began weaving across the opening to ease the degree of incline. A hawk appeared and hovered overhead. Reed wondered if Culp Jenkins had gotten home early and if so, whether he could see the hawk's power glide. Could a hunter like Jenkins discern from the way the hawk floated that it was watching a man? Reed thought not but wished the hawk would leave all the same.

He looked up to see where the hawk was, and the next thing he knew, he was airborne. The toes of his right shoe had caught an exposed vine root and sent him flying. He landed on his shoulder on rocky ground, went butt over teakettle, and landed on his back. Hard.

After a moment, Reed rolled onto his side and rubbed his back. He could move. Nothing seemed broken—just banged up. Reed sat up and caught his breath. He was sweating. He was aching. He was thirsty. He was tired. He reached inside the sweatshirt and felt the cold barrel of the Llama; from the way he landed, it shouldn't have suffered any damage.

He took off the hot sweatpants and scouted the terrain ahead. Maybe fifty yards of hill, then what looked to be the stream. He would wash his face there and regroup, then make his way toward the lodge. He'd already lost his appetite for this adventure. He wanted to be done with it and be gone. The wind had changed direction, and had begun to gust. It was now coming out of the north.

Reed stood behind the trunk of a maple tree on the edge of Jenkins' property. He could see the lodge—a cabin really—through a stand of maples. Ten yards away was the stream. To his right was a hundred yards of cornfields. He replayed the videotapes in his mind, trying to picture where Jenkins stood to shoot the deer. He decided that right here could be the place. He bent his knees and ran his fingers across the ground until he found what he was looking for: a spent bullet casing. He put the tarnished shell under his nose but smelled nothing. Last year's model. He set his sweatpants by the tree and placed the bullet casing on top.

He turned to see where he might safely watch the hunter hunt. He heard a dog bark in the distance but couldn't pinpoint the direction. A sixth sense told him he had to get out of there, but he lingered a few moments longer, until he saw the two big rocks a few yards into the woods by the edge of the cornfields. Perfect.

The barking grew louder, and Reed lit out for the dense underbrush. His right foot caught on something again, but this time it ripped into his leg just above the ankle as he fell. His chin caught a rock. He wanted to scream, but instinct silenced him. Instead, he just lay there, motionless as a fallen branch.

He smelled the decay on the forest floor. Tasted his blood. Felt the rough texture of a lichen-covered rock against his cheek. Saw the sun shining through the naked branches above his head. Heard the clack of shells being chambered in a shotgun a few feet away. Closed his eyes and prayed for the first time in years.

# Chapter Forty-eight

The barrel of the shotgun pinched Stuart Reed's right cheekbone. The metal was so cold that it felt wet. Someone spoke. "I don't reckon you're carrying a knife or anything, are you now?"

He placed the voice immediately: Culp Jenkins. Reed opened his eyes slowly, saw the shock of silver hair, the patrician features. Reed said nothing.

"I'll tell you, boy. You are one stupid, stubborn cuss. Stupid to run through the woods in these parts, with so much old barbed wire underfoot. Stubborn for still coming after me a year later. And a cuss because you're dead wrong about me, and you ain't got the brains to listen."

Jenkins towered over him, legs spread, shotgun pointed at Reed's stomach now. "So what brings you to my neck of the woods, Mr. Reed? You wouldn't be hunting me now, would you? You got a pistol in that sweatshirt pocket?"

Reed nodded yes.

Jenkins stepped back. He told Reed to stand slowly and remove his sweatshirt. Reed obliged and handed the sweaty gray shirt to Jenkins. The sun had disappeared behind a bank of clouds that was rolling in from the north, and Reed started to shiver. He wore nothing but sneakers and a pair of running shorts. Jenkins, by contrast, was dressed like the lord of the manor on a hunt—blue corduroy jacket with a tan rawhide shoulder patch, red Royal Stewart plaid shirt, gray herringbone wool slacks, freshly bear-greased work boots.

Jenkins pointed the barrel of the twelve gauge toward a stone fence a few steps away. "Why don't you just set a while?"

Jenkins propped the shotgun between his armpit and his left forearm, then extracted the Llama and the two shell clips from Reed's shirt pouch. "You must be cold, running around in your skivvies like that. You can get your sweatpants soon as I defang your little peashooter here."

For the first time since he'd been caught, Reed thought he might not die after all. He decided to keep his mouth shut until further notice.

Jenkins inspected the Llama, laughing. He checked the chamber to make sure there wasn't a live round in it, then tossed the pistol to Reed. He removed the shells from the clips, put the ammo in his jacket pocket, stuck the clips back in the sweatshirt and threw it to Reed. "Put it on, and go fetch your pants. I'll cut off the bottom of one of the pant legs so it won't get caught in that nasty cut. We'll go up to the house and patch it up. And then we'll work out a way to get you off my ass for good."

Reed stood there, amazed. Jenkins was having a grand old time.

Culp Jenkins said he had been expecting Reed all day—ever since Jenkins had stopped by the Bradyville general store on his way home from the airport that morning. Jenkins had a standing request with the owner to let him know if anybody called about him or came snooping around. And what with the police detectives contacting Jenkins already about a murder, he expected Reed would find out about the hunting lodge and pay him a visit.

Jenkins poured Reed a mug of Earl Grey from a silver teapot and sat across from him at the dining room table. Reed was pulling the last butterfly suture across the two-inch gash on his right leg. It had bled profusely. Reed's running shoe had turned maroon from the drying blood. Jenkins had offered to help, but Reed had declined. Jenkins said, "Suture self," and had gone off to get the tea.

At that point, Reed had begun to realize how wrong he'd been about Culp Jenkins—and for how long. Reed wondered what else he'd been wrong about, and his brain went blank from the overload.

Jenkins returned with the tea, jabbering animatedly. "I tell you, Reed, you looked like one of those Fresh-Air kids from the city when I saw you comin' down the mountain. You took a bad spill then, too, didn't you? I thought I'd just bide my time, watching and waiting to see what you were up to."

Jenkins took a sip of his tea. "Good thing you tripped and got yourself caught. Rate you were going, you could've killed yourself out there in the woods."

Reed grunted. Jenkins was enjoying this too much, and Reed couldn't do anything but listen.

"You know, Reed, you had me so pissed off last year with your ass-backward theories about me and that girl's death that I finally had to sic my lawyer on you, which, in my book, is a worse sin than leavin' a wounded deer for the turkey vultures. But it seemed like the only way to get your attention. It's too bad you got your sorry ass fired, but nobody forced you to walk into the buzz saw."

Reed wondered which was worse—getting killed by this guy or

getting lectured by him. He looked at the bleached pine table, the sterling silver, the paisley linen napkins. Jenkins' hunting lodge made Reed's home look like an outhouse.

"Look, I can't be too pissed at you, Reed. The way you went after me is human nature—or at least what's wrong with this country. It's called coverin' your butt. A corporation president was asked one time about the secret of his success, and he said that the trick wasn't making the right decisions—it was workin' your butt off to make the decisions right."

Jenkins took a sip of tea, then continued. "Sounds good at first blush, doesn't it? Until you realize that's how America works. We make the decision to support our dictator pal in Vietnam, and then we waste a decade and sixty-thousand lives trying to make the decision right. You had it lodged in your thick skull that I killed the girl and dumped her behind the pistol range, and you set out to prove it —no matter what. The more you were told you were wrong, the more convinced you became. Your intentions were good. But the road to hell, as they as say, is paved with them."

Reed wanted to defend himself, but Jenkins wouldn't let him get a word in. "You know, I could make one phone call and get your ass fired again, but I won't. Instead, I want you to tell me everything about the Diaz case—that was her name, wasn't it?—and this new murder. As my pappy liked to say, I think it's high time we put this sumbitch out of our misery."

# Chapter Forty-nine

Over tea, and then dinner, Stuart Reed and Culp Jenkins went over every detail of both cases. Jenkins mostly listened, occasionally jotting a note on a writing tablet, occasionally interrupting to tend to something in the kitchen.

When Reed had finished, he went over his list of suspects with Jenkins—starting with Jenkins himself.

Jenkins scoffed. "If I'd have done it, I'd have killed you long ago, bucko. Or I could kill you now. Save yourself some time. Cross me off your list."

Reed asked about Pritchard Majors.

"Forget him. He couldn't stab a wienie on an hors d'oeuvres tray. What is it about you reporters? Whenever you got a problem you can't solve, you blame it on the money boys like Pritch and me. Being rich doesn't make anybody better or worse than the next guy. It just makes life easier. Pritch ain't your guy."

"Don't be so cavalier."

"Pritch Majors couldn't kill a six-pack. Go on with your list."

Reed asked about the mayor and Glenn Brenner. Jenkins snorted. "Yep, and if you reporters can't pin it on a rich guy, you blame a politician. These guys may be as crooked as an alligator's ass, but they're not killers."

Reed mentioned Julio Jones. Jenkins said he never heard of him.

"Cop reporter. Wears white high-top sneakers and has been known to take notes on them at city council meetings."

"Next."

"Clancy Collins. He's a rewrite guy, but he used to be a reporter. Wrote up the ribbon cutting at the pistol range . . ."

"I don't know about any reporter at the ribbon cutting, but I do remember the photographer—now that guy didn't have all four tires on the pavement."

Reed sat bolt upright. "Remember his name?"

"No. But he wore a dry-cleaned work shirt and gold chains. Took me aside and said he'd like to go hunting with me sometime. I think he even said he'd rented all my videos. Does that description ring any bells?"

Reed winced, then balled his hands into fists and whacked the table so hard the plates rattled. "Damnit, it's the other guy on my list —Milt Roberts. I had been so caught up in the people who were in the photo at the ribbon cutting that I overlooked the guy who had taken the damned picture."

All of a sudden, all the tumblers clicked into place for Reed. "That's how Milt knew how to get to the firing range so fast after I stumbled on Diana Diaz's body. Shit, he was probably going nuts that her body had been found so soon." Reed's mind went into overdrive. "And that's how he knew to cut open the body like you do in your deer-skinning video."

Jenkins arched an eyebrow. "How do you know you're not just jumping from one bad conclusion to another?"

"I was at his place one night. We had a few beers too many. He bragged about bringing fashion models to the studio in his basement and seducing them. Diana Diaz wanted to be a model. I bet if we check *The Transcript*'s photo log for the day before I found her—I bet Milt had an assignment in the city. Ran across her near Columbia and offered to shoot some photos of her for her portfolio. Drove her to his studio in Riverton, talked her into posing nude. Or tried to. Got turned on and wanted some action, but she refused. Called her a tease and came after her, so she screamed. Maybe grabbed a pillow and tried to put it over her mouth, but she still wouldn't stop screaming. Kept the pillow there until she'd suffocated. Had to get rid of the body but didn't want to drive very far with a dead body in his van. He can't live more than a quarter mile—a half mile at the most—from the pistol range."

Reed stopped and let everything sink in. After a while, he limped to a window and watched the stream through the stand of trees. The sky was losing its light. He turned to face Jenkins. "Is it supposed to rain or something? Either it's getting ugly out there, or it's getting dark awfully early."

Jenkins said the radio was predicting rain or sleet by midnight— "But what do they know?"

Reed stretched, and felt the day's exertions catching up with his body. He fought back a yawn, and detected some soreness along the base of his rib cage from his earlier barbed-wire tumble. He realized he had to get some sleep; he had to be at work by eleven P.M., and he'd been awake now for eighteen hours. Jenkins lent him a nylon anorak for the ride home. They agreed to talk more about Milt Roberts on the way. Instead, they rode in silence, each deep in thought.

Rain began to fall as Jenkins' Jeep Cherokee pulled onto Iron

Hollow Road. Jenkins stopped the Cherokee alongside Reed's front door, but Reed didn't get out. Instead, he stared into the darkness.

Jenkins shut off the windshield wipers and asked Reed what was up.

"I got two questions bugging me," Reed answered. "First, I know that Roberts gutted Diana Diaz the way that he did because he'd swiped the idea from your video, but why gut her body at all? What was the point of going to all that work?"

Jenkins killed the engine, and the only noise other than their voices was the rain drumming against the roof of the Jeep. "I thought about that, too," Jenkins said. "At first, I thought it was to make it look like the work of a lunatic, but that seemed like too much of a stretch. I mean, you can use a razor blade to shave some of the fur from a deer's belly so the incision is easier—I'm not sure you really need the two-blade technique at all for a human victim. But if it was a diversionary tactic, give him credit—it worked. Still . . ." Jenkins hesitated, weighing his words.

"You can't stop telling me now."

"I cringe at the thought, but the only other explanation I can think of is that she had swallowed something that would have turned up at the autopsy and possibly incriminated him."

"You mean her last meal or something? What's so terrible about that?"

"Stuart, I'm not talking about a meal. You're an adult. Use your imagination."

Reed rubbed his forehead. "You lost me."

"Didn't you say there was no sign of sexual assault? Why do you think that was, if Milt was as oversexed as you say?"

Reed tried to work the new variable into his equation. His mind spun wildly, then slowly reeled in the scene at the firing range and the girl's stark body. The image made his chest constrict, and he had trouble breathing. "I know you're saying that she was assaulted somehow, but what has that got to do with why Roberts cut her open like that and cleaned out her stomach?"

"And cleaned her throat and mouth."

Reed slumped in his seat, then dug his fingernails into his palms, the way he did to cope with pain in the dentist chair when the drill struck an exposed nerve. "That son of a bitch."

The windshield was fogging up, and Jenkins rubbed it with a coat sleeve so he could see out again. "After she was dead, the guy was just being a good hunter, covering his tracks. He was afraid that if he somehow got linked to the killing, he'd get nailed by DNA testing. His semen would match samples taken from the girl."

Reed sat in silence, trying to get a grip on his rage.

Jenkins leaned over and nudged Reed on the shoulder. "We'll get that bastard. You just wait. The thing you gotta do now is get yourself under control. You're not much good to me, the shape you're in now."

Reed slowly eased his grip, and tried the deep breathing exercises that he used before his ten-kilometer foot races. Slowly, the storm clouds in his mind began to clear, and he felt the tenseness drain from his face. He took one more deep breath, and held it in his lungs. After a long exhale, Reed asked what was next.

Jenkins leaned forward, resting his elbows on the steering wheel. "When we pulled up to the house, you said you had two questions. What was the other one?"

"Something's always bothered me. About a week or so after the Diaz girl was murdered, I went to the spot where I had found her. And you know what I found? A hunting knife plunged point first into the ground where she'd been dumped. Same thing happened where Karen Pettraglia was found Tuesday morning—I saw a knife buried to the hilt in the ground. Doesn't make sense."

Jenkins asked whether Roberts was superstitious.

Reed remembered the night he'd been at Roberts' house. Reed was about to leave through the kitchen door, but Roberts wouldn't let him—made him head out through the front. Said it was bad luck to enter a house through one door and leave through another. "Why do you ask?"

"Because there's an old superstition about people who die violently. If you jab a knife into the spot where they're found, it kills their ghost."

Reed decided that they were dealing with a major-league sicko, but didn't bother to say so. He knew Jenkins was already thinking the same thing. Instead, Reed asked how they should proceed.

"I got a hunch that if this Milt Roberts is the culprit like you say, then the Diana Diaz murder wasn't an isolated incident," Jenkins replied. "I'm not saying he murdered any other woman, but I wouldn't be surprised if he had a few splotches on his record. Any way to find out?"

Reed sat up in his seat. "In fact, I was just waiting for the new copy of the firing-range photo, and then I was going to ask my cop friend Raf Wilson to run all the names through the FBI's computers. They have a crime data base down in Washington, and police can dial into it anytime."

"What can it tell us? From what I hear, in most rape cases—which represent only about a fifth of the total rapes—either the victim chickens out before the trial or the rapist's lawyer cuts a deal on a plea bargain. I don't think you'll turn up many convictions in the FBI computer."

"I think the data base lists arrests as well as convictions," Reed replied. "Even so, I don't see the homicide detectives in Jersey reopening the case on the strength of something like that."

Jenkins smiled. "But I'd bet that your photographer pal doesn't want to take that chance. If we get confirmation that Milt Roberts is our weasel, then I'd say we're all set. Weasels are always in season. We just have to bait the trap."

"With what?"

Jenkins looked Reed square in the eye. "You."

Reed trembled. "If we get anything from the FBI computers, shouldn't we notify the Jersey authorities?"

Jenkins guffawed. "What would you tell 'em?"

"Our suspicions," Reed replied weakly.

Jenkins snorted again. "Our suspicions ain't worth a squirrel's nuts."

# Chapter Fifty

For the second time in five days, Stuart Reed found himself calling Raf Wilson for a favor: Could Raf dial up the FBI's computers and see if a man by the name of Milt Roberts—current address Lafayette Street, Riverton, New Jersey—had a criminal record?

Raf grunted and muttered something about the FBI data being less than a hundred percent reliable. Reed said the information wasn't for publication—he just wanted confirmation of a hunch. Culp Jenkins stood by Reed's fireplace and nodded his approval.

It took twenty minutes for Reed's hunch to be confirmed. According to the FBI's National Crime Information Center data base, Roberts had been arrested twice in Manhattan three years earlier for sexual assault, but the charges had been dropped. Wilson said that this wasn't uncommon in cases of date rape and other sexual assaults—the victim gets cold feet and the charges are dropped, or the defendant cops a plea to a misdemeanor.

Reed thanked Wilson and told him that as far as he was concerned, this conversation never happened. Wilson laughed and replied, "You got that right."

After ending the phone conversation, Reed asked Jenkins again if they should take the new information to the homicide detectives in New Jersey.

Jenkins scoffed at the idea. "With what? Two arrests and no convictions? They never considered the Diaz case a sex crime anyway. You don't have any real evidence to make them change their minds. Legally, you ain't got jack shit."

"Milt Roberts must think it would lead to something, or he wouldn't be homicidal about it."

Jenkins said that is the reason they'd be able to set their trap. After they worked out the details, Reed called Milt Roberts. He got the photographer's answering machine.

"Milt, this is Stuart Reed, calling at seven-thirty P.M., Friday night. After the nightmare I went through last Monday evening, I figure I'm going to need some help getting through the next one. Give me a call if you can make the Monday night game. I'll buy some brews and chow."

For an instant, Reed thought of the supermarket and the checkout line, and pushed it from his mind. "I did manage to get some good news," Reed said into the mouthpiece. "The microfilm company airmailed me the photostat of the pistol range story and photo. I'm going to take a look at it when I get to work tonight, and have a cop friend run the names through the FBI computer. I have to catch some sleep before my shift starts, so do me favor and don't call me back till tomorrow. Take care."

Reed hung up and looked at Jenkins, who had the grin of a young boy about to pull a prank on his sister. "I think I'm gonna like this, Stuart Reed. I'm gonna like this a whole lot. Reminds me of the way my Uncle Dudley and his drinking buddies used to hunt deer. They'd go up to their hunting camp in the Smokeys every November a few days before deer season opened, mostly to do some hard drinking. But they'd also bring along some corn and other chow and throw it out in back of the cabin every night—just to bring any deer in the area up close.

"Well, first day of the season, Uncle Dud gets stuck doin' the breakfast dishes. His pals are out before the crap of dawn, headed to a stand of trees they'd scouted out, and Uncle Dud's left scrubbin' the fried egg off the plates. Well, he takes a cup of coffee and a hunting magazine and goes to sit on the john for a spell. He takes a few sips, looks out the window, and spots this huge buck no more than twenty yards away. Scrambles for his shotgun, opens the window gingerly, sits back down on the throne, and blasts the deer with both barrels. *Kaboom.* Only one of the whole gang to nail a deer that whole trip, and he hardly had to leave the crapper."

Reed forced a laugh. So much for the honor of the hunt.

"Don't give me that look, Stuart Reed. I don't condone that kind of huntin'. I'm just tellin' you what huntin' for Roberts'll be like. That photostat'll have him come running, and we'll nail him easy." Jenkins looked around the room. "You say the sumbitch was here, huh?"

Jenkins took a deep breath, then wiggled his nose for effect. "Thought I smelled a trace of weasel." He cocked his head to one side and sniffed again. "Tell me what our weasel friend did while he was here."

Reed took a deep breath. He still felt weary. His leg wound started burning again, and he thirsted for a heavy hit of Jack Daniels. He felt a chill, like he did sometimes after a long run.

Reed put his hands under his armpits. "Tell you what, Culp. If you could get a pot of coffee started over there in the kitchen, I'll change into some warmer clothes, splash some water on my face, and try to think about what all Roberts was up to while he was here. I'm just too tired to remember just now."

Ten minutes later, they were seated on the couch, and sipping black coffee. Reed had run out of milk and had thrown out the sugar after the forensics boys were done. The caffeine did shake Reed's brain out of neutral, and he talked about the documents that had been taken, and the bloody knife.

Jenkins shook his head no. "We're missing something here. It's bothering me. I think I was too smug about this weasel. He's too cunning to come in here, steal the files, and leave the knife just to do a mind tap on you. That's what your average wise-ass weirdo would do. This guy's shrewder than that. He wouldn't leave that knife just to show off. It's not his style."

Reed cradled his mug of coffee and put it to his lips, but the coffee's warmth felt better than it smelled. He decided against drinking any more of it and put it back down on the blanket chest. He asked Jenkins what he meant by Roberts' "style."

"This guy's always three steps ahead of you, right?" Jenkins said. He took a flat wooden toothpick from his shirt pocket and started to chew on one end. "So something else is going on here. He set a trap for you Tuesday morning, but it wasn't nothin' as blunt as that knife. Think. What else did the detectives say?"

Reed stood, limped over to the thermostat, and thumbed the dial clockwise until it read sixty degrees. He could hear the furnace huff on as he hobbled back to the sofa. He thought about the price of heating oil, and thought about lighting a fire. That's when he remembered the smoke alarm.

Jenkins listened closely, leaning more and more forward as Reed explained about the missing battery. "That's it, my friend. Our weasel plans to do some cooking here. Probably in the middle of the night one of these nights. Now, with your message, maybe we're talking this evening."

"Assuming he got the message."

"In this case, you have to assume. And be ready." Jenkins chewed on the toothpick again. "To level with you, I don't know what the weasel's up to. I'm not sure he's not outside watching us right this minute or listening with some hidden mike the cops couldn't find."

Reed began to stand, but Jenkins waved him off. "Don't bother. If the cops couldn't find any mikes, you won't either. I don't think it's his style anyway. But the smoke alarm. That's his style. You better try to get some of that coffee down your gullet. Because it's goin' to be this evening. I can sense it. I'm betting he makes his move a half hour or an hour after you turn out your lights."

Favoring his bad leg, Reed walked slowly to the window. "If he's out there already, fine. Let him freeze." Reed pushed back the curtain and pushed his face against the dull cold pane. "Our weasel better have thick fur. I think it's snowing. Big thick flakes. Now what do we do?"

Jenkins stood and looked for his jacket. "I leave in the Cherokee, go home, and get dressed for some winter hunting. Then I drive back here and come in the last half mile on foot till I get to a spot where I can watch the house. It'll take forty-five minutes. No, make that an hour, to be safe. If you get your lights out in forty-five minutes, that means I'll have to hang loose out there for at least fifteen minutes, probably more. But it'll be worth the wait. I don't reckon I ever bagged a weasel that big before."

The two men then ran through the particulars of the plan and the contingencies. The details were unimportant. What was important was that they agreed on three things:

1. If Milt Roberts came after Reed tonight, then Roberts had to be their man. 2. But even if Roberts did come after Reed, there was still no iron-clad and conclusive evidence connecting Roberts to the murders of the two women. Even if Jenkins and Reed were convinced of Roberts' guilt, he could never be brought to trial. 3. Given No. 1 and No. 2, they agreed that given the opportunity, they'd have to kill a weasel tonight.

# Chapter Fifty-one

After Culp Jenkins departed, Stuart Reed spent the next half hour readying himself for the worst. Jenkins had returned the ammo, and the first thing Reed did was reload the two clips and slide one back into the handle of the Llama.

Next Reed prepared himself for the possibility that Roberts might get to Reed's place before Jenkins got Roberts. In that event, there was a good chance that the house would be torched, and Reed would be flushed outside, where he'd become an easy and freezing target.

Reed slid into his black Lycra running tights, wincing as he nursed the satiny fabric over the cut at the base of his right leg. He put on his long-sleeved polypropylene turtleneck, then his insulated long underwear, then jeans and a flannel shirt. The cut on his leg felt like it was on fire, and Reed worried that it was getting infected.

When Culp the cat rubbed up against Reed's jeans, Reed went to the kitchen and treated the cat to canned food. Then he tried to push the cat out the back door. If Roberts did manage to attack, Reed didn't want to have to worry about a stray cat. But Culp balked and dashed for the living room. Reed sighed, it would be every cat for himself.

Reed slugged down the dregs in his coffee mug, then looked at the clock. He needed to talk to someone, talk away his fears. He called Caroline, but she had company. He cringed and hoped it wasn't that jerk Bobby Aenias. He begged for a minute of her time, and blurted that he'd found a way to bring the killer out in the open.

She told him not to do anything stupid.

He said he missed her.

She said good-bye.

He'd run out of reasons to procrastinate. It was show time. He put a new battery in the smoke alarm, turned the lights out in the kitchen and living room, then went into the bedroom and pulled the blinds shut. A pair of olive-drab polypropylene gloves, the Llama, and the extra bullet clip sat in a neat row on the dresser.

Reed pulled the chord on the ceiling light, then fumbled through the darkness for the flashlight on the bedside table. He flicked it on, trained it at the small case by the bed, found the book he wanted, and climbed under the covers to read while he waited for the witching hour. Fifty minutes, maybe more, he guessed.

He fell asleep with the flashlight shining on a volume of the encyclopedia that lay open on his chest. Culp Jenkins had uttered the word "weasel" with such contempt that Reed, ever the reporter, decided to look it up.

"Weasels are slim, swift, and very bloodthirsty," the old *World Book* said. "They have keen sight and smell and are good hunters. . . . At times they seem to kill merely for fun."

The snowstorm was gathering strength, and Culp Jenkins slid his ski goggles down over his eyes so he could see enough to pick his way along the old fishing camp road, which was now two faint tire tracks and heavy underbrush.

Jenkins stopped and listened. A faint rumble of traffic on 71A, then an eerie quiet. Jenkins wished he could use his flashlight but knew it would be suicidal; the flashlight's beam would provide a perfect spotlight for a sniper's bullet.

Jenkins heard a twig snap just to his right. He started to bring his shotgun into firing position when his peripheral vision picked up a blur to his right. As he wheeled, the blur came thundering into Jenkins' skull just above the ear. Jenkins fell to his knees. The second swing of the aluminum softball bat caught the base of Jenkins' skull, and the ball game was over.

# Chapter Fifty-two

The pulsing electronic wail of the smoke alarm pulled Stuart Reed out of a bad dream. He coughed smoke and realized that hell had arrived. He rolled onto the floor. What had happened to Jenkins? And where was Roberts? Reed concluded that neither question mattered. All he could think about was staying alive.

He crawled to the dresser and groped his hand around on the top for his pistol, the extra clip, then his gloves. He pulled on the gloves, then crawled through the darkness toward the kitchen. He could see the brilliant orange glow in the living room and feel its heat as smoke engulfed the upper portions of the room. He had a three-foot crawl space below the black smoke, but his eyes still burned. When he reached the back of the kitchen, he reached up, grabbed the doorknob, and leaned into the door. It wouldn't budge.

He scrambled toward the living room, and felt the rush of heat. Gunfire erupted in the middle of the room, and Reed dropped flat.

Reed lay motionless, waiting for more gunfire, until he realized that the fire must have reached the blanket chest and the box of ammunition. His throat and nostrils burned now. He had trouble breathing, and he knew he had to find a way out—fast—before the smoke killed him. The front door was out of the question. Roberts, somebody, must be waiting. But the back door had been barricaded so that Reed would be forced to go out through the front.

Reed thought about smashing a window and climbing to safety, but Roberts would hear the breaking glass and be waiting. Then Reed heard Culp the cat yowling by the wood box door. It was time to do some winter running.

Reed rolled across the floor into the bedroom, opened his closet door, and found his cross-country spikes. He threw them on, laced them, and then scrabbled on all fours toward the wood box door. He found his white cat cowering in a corner of the fireplace. Reed unhasped the hook on the two-foot-square door and shoved. The freezing air poured in, and Culp the cat dived out. Reed grabbed the top of the door sill and swung himself through the opening. He skidded onto inch-thick wet snow.

Rolling into a crouching position, Reed could see the headlights of a van pointing toward the house. Roberts—if it was Roberts—must be lurking in the darkness just beyond. Reed broke into a sprint for the shed behind the house. The spikes dug in, and Reed dashed along his side yard until a bullet grazed the outside of his left thigh. He fell forward, more out of survival instinct than pain. He rolled behind a tree, released the safeties on the pistol, and came up shooting.

Four slugs, two seconds apart—*blam, blam, blam, blam.*

Three disappeared into the night. The other shattered the headlight on the driver's side of the van. Reed had no way of knowing if any of the other shots had hit Roberts. The odds were against it, but at least now Roberts knew that Reed wielded some firepower of his own. Maybe he'd back off, pull the plug on the assault. Somebody had to smell the smoke, see the flames, and call in an alarm. When was Culp Jenkins going to arrive? Reed knew he couldn't afford to wait.

Reed rolled to his right, taking cover behind a blue spruce. He peered past the trunk and saw a silhouette approaching. A shotgun blast pulped the bark by his knees. He wanted to run again, but his left thigh was screaming. He said to hell with it and ran anyway.

Ahead stood the old shed, with the roof he'd never finished fixing. To the shed's right was the massive wild rosebush he'd never gotten around to trimming. The tangle of branches and thorns stood five feet high and ran from within a few feet of the shed clear to the rocky banks of the stream.

Reed took ten steps and tumbled toward the shed. He landed hard and rolled under the ladder that ran from the base of the wild rosebush up against the shed roof. In the process, he had lost hold of the pistol. He looked frantically for it, and spotted its blackness on the snow, just out of reach. Then he saw the silhouette closing in. Reed scrambled around the corner of the shed and prayed.

In a fetal position, Reed lay shivering, bleeding, waiting to die. Inexplicably, his mind flashed back to Culp Jenkins' hunting video, when Jenkins had shot the deer and then moved in to make sure of his kill. That was what this was like. One more shotgun burst, and then the blackness.

Reed heard a cough, maybe ten feet away. It was Roberts, at the ladder, struggling to get through the brambles of the rosebush, and Reed finally realized what had happened. The ladder had forced the superstitious Roberts to pull up short.

Reed reached out and groped for a rock, then shouted: "Come on, asshole. Walk under the ladder. Test your luck."

# Chapter Fifty-three

Stuart Reed had started to pass out when the distant drone of a fire siren brought him back. A dream? No. Real. He took a chance and looked around the corner of the shed. In the distance, a single headlight swung wildly as the van pulled onto Iron Hollow Road. The rear wheels fishtailed as it retreated.

Moments before, Reed thought he was going to die. Now he raged because Roberts was getting away—and because if Roberts made it over the mountain, the son of a bitch would be home free.

In the next instant, Reed retrieved his wayward pistol, then was on his feet, running through the pain in his legs, running toward the Devil's Apron Strings. If the snow were bad here in the hollow, then Route 71A on the mountain would be treacherous. And Reed figured that if he could make it on foot to the top of the Strings soon enough, he might still have a shot at Roberts.

Reed hit the base of the mountain on the fly, took ten steps and stumbled. The spikes weren't gripping the hill right. He clambered onto his feet and pushed onward, only to stumble again. This time he slid and tumbled down the slope. Tried to stand. Felt his thigh and tumbled again. A phone. If he could get to a phone, call the cops. Where was there a phone in the ski area? The shed.

Like a first-time marathoner at mile 25, Reed half ran and half hobbled to the shed. Then he lay on his back and kicked with both legs. The door ripped from its hinges. Reed rushed inside. He couldn't see a phone.

But he did see the control panel for the lifts, and remembered what Peter Benjamin had said.

Reed went outside and threw the circuit breaker, then fired up the Borvig. Then he yanked the winch to set the speed at full tilt. The room exploded in mechanical grunts and screeches, and Reed was out the door.

He jammed the Llama into his pocket and bear-hugged a lift chair as it swung wildly around the base tower. It dragged him several yards before he could pull himself aboard. No matter. He was headed up the mountain.

Reed sat huddled on the metal chair, trying to gather his strength, but now that he had stopped running, the bitter cold set in again, and Reed began to fade again.

As the chair lift screamed up the Devil's Apron Strings, the weather seemed to grow nastier. Reed wondered if he would even be able to see the van on the road—let alone be able to pull the trigger with his numb fingers.

Fifty yards from the top, he realized that chair lifts were designed for people wearing skis to dismount, not gimpy-legged runners in spikes. He moved onto the outside edge of the seat, and as the chair lift swung around the top stanchion, Reed pushed off. He tried to land on his feet, but his legs gave out. He kept scrambling on his knees, then willed himself to run again.

He was past the stone outcropping that formed the Devil's Apron Strings now, coming up onto Route 71A. Dropping to one knee, he pulled the Llama from his pocket and lined up the sights on the mirrorlike surface of up-bound lane. Nothing was moving.

From the other direction, near the crest of the mountain, came the rumble of a truck and the metalic clatter of snow chains on its tires: a county road crew, spewing salt and cinders on the slick asphalt. Reed looked up the road and saw the truck's high beams slicing through the snow in the distance. He turned the other way and saw one headlight storming up the roadway.

The county truck was barreling down the mountain toward Reed. He had no time to think. The one-eyed van had to be Roberts', and Reed had to stop it. He fired his last shots.

Suddenly, the van lurched to the left into the cinder truck's path. The truck driver swerved a few feet, but too late. The corner of his snowplow blade rammed the van's windshield and sent the van spinning wildly back across the highway toward Reed. He dived behind a boulder as the van hurtled past. It caught a boulder sideways, bounced, and finally thudded to rest on its passenger side. A flat tire on the driver's side, still spinning, was the only sign of life.

# Chapter Fifty-four

Somehow, Stuart Reed managed to stumble and slide back down the mountain. He stopped only to throw the pistol into the deepest woods. At the base of the hill, he shut off the ski lift. Ten minutes later, a fireman saw him wandering dazed along Iron Hollow Road.

Before Reed knew it, he was wrapped in several wool blankets in the backseat of a big American car. A burly red-faced man in a rain slicker climbed in the driver's side door and announced that he was a fire captain, and that an ambulance was on the way. The car's heater was cranked full blast, and Reed felt the heat returning to his body. All he wanted to do was pass out.

When Reed closed his eyes, he heard snippets of a report over the police scanner on the dashboard, and his mind snapped back. He asked the fire chief to turn up the volume. The chief locked the scanner into a police report from the top of the mountain. There'd been a bad two-vehicle accident.

"Van ate a snowplow," the cop on the radio said. The dispatcher was phoning in a computer search on the van's Jersey plates now.

A paramedic cut in, and said her MICU was on Route 71A, about two miles away but making poor progress on the icy roads. She wanted to know if were there were any survivors.

"Snowplow driver's fine, but the driver of the van is a goner."

The paramedic asked the cop how long ago he'd lost the driver's pulse.

The cop hesitated. "I don't think you get the picture, lady. I haven't tried to find the driver's pulse. Hell, I haven't even found his head yet."

# PART IV

# Chapter Fifty-five

Indian summer returned to Bradner County the next day. The temperature, pushing seventy degrees, reduced Friday night's snow squall to puddles but could do little to resuscitate the area's skeletal trees and fading lawns.

Through his hospital window, Stuart Reed heard the sounds of teenagers laughing. He peered out to see three boys in T-shirts, shorts, and shades. They were tossing a football around on their way home from a ball field down the block. He envied them. They were everything that he was not—young, free, happy.

Reed knew that he couldn't be young again, and that happiness would somehow remain beyond his grasp. A shot at freedom, and redemption, was all that remained. He needed to finish what he had started a year earlier, if he only knew how.

On Friday night, the fire chief had rushed Reed to the hospital moments after Reed had lost consciousness. He was out cold for fifteen hours. While he was under, the doctors had patched up his legs, given him two pints of blood, and put him on an IV.

He had his first visitors at one-fifteen on Saturday. The two investigators from BCI, Mahr and Holmgren, had waited four hours to talk with him. After a quick show of concern for his well-being, they cut to the chase. What exactly had happened Friday night?

Reed hadn't had time to sort it out. Suddenly, scattershot images —cascading smoke, snow, gunfire, a van crashing toward him—tore through his mind. Had it really been Milt out there trying to kill him? Had the cops figured out that Reed had shot out the tire? He tried to remember what had happened to Culp Jenkins, and came up blank.

He realized that he couldn't find out anything if he were answering questions instead of asking them. So he fell back on his old reportorial trick. He played dumb.

"Sorry, officers, but I'm afraid I don't remember much. I woke up dazed in the middle of a terrible fire. I know I got out of the house somehow, but I couldn't tell you how. I think I stumbled around outside for a while—maybe went to the ski area in search of a phone. I must have been wandering up Iron Hollow Road when a fireman found me."

Holmgren took a pad from her briefcase. She read over some handwritten notes on the top page, then asked: "I understand you were wearing track shoes when they found you?"

"No kidding. I guess I really was dazed."

Holmgren glanced at her pad. "And you know about Culp Jenkins?"

"You lost me."

"Culp Jenkins—the guy that you claimed was responsible for the murder of the two young women—what happened?"

Reed didn't have to feign ignorance. "I don't know what you mean."

Holmgren said that Jenkins' body had been found in the rubble of Reed's house fire.

When Reed reacted with surprise, Holmgren explained her theory on what had happened.

"Remember when I said that the battery in the smoke alarm was missing?" she asked.

Reed nodded.

"Well, we figure that was part of the plan—to set fire to your house while you were asleep. And when he was starting the fire, he must have somehow gotten gasoline on himself. We found his remains under a fallen roof beam on the back porch this morning—after finding his Jeep Cherokee along an old fishing road about half a mile from your place. What was left of a gas can was a foot away from his body. You get the picture. . . ."

Reed didn't get the picture. Had Jenkins been part of the scheme with Milt? It didn't make sense.

"Don't look so confused, Mr. Reed. Don't you understand? You were right all along. We did a search of Jenkins' Jeep and found a photo of Diana Diaz, and a bra that matched the description of the one that Diana Diaz's mother said her daughter wore the day she disappeared. It's headed to the city now for ID. Plus we found all kinds of other goodies. A Buck knife in the glove compartment—a Buck knife just like the murder weapon in the Pettraglia killing. And a little nine-volt battery like the one that was taken from your smoke detector."

Reed wondered why they didn't realize that their luck was too good to be true, but said nothing. Milt Roberts must have gotten Jenkins somehow. Reed sensed that the incriminating evidence had been intended for his Mazda, and that Roberts must have improvised. Why hadn't they asked about Roberts yet?

Mahr patted Holmgren on the leg and stood to leave. "Sorry to hit you with all this, Reed. You're still too stunned by everything to respond."

"What about my house?" Reed said, although he wasn't sure he wanted to know.

Mahr and Holmgren looked at each other to see who'd have to answer. Mahr sighed, then gazed out the door as he spoke.

"Your house is gone, Mr. Reed. The firemen did what they could, but it was an old wood frame house, primed with gasoline. You won't find much there. The firemen did manage to push your car out of harm's way. I guess that's small consolation. And you were insured, right?"

Reed's eyes were welling up.

Holmgren spoke next. "I guess that's small consolation as well. But if you want to put all of this behind you, you're going to have to put the best spin on this that you can."

Reed grunted. "And what might that be?"

"You're alive, and Culp Jenkins is dead."

Caroline Tompkins stopped by next, looking stunning wherever Reed's eyes roamed. Her hair was coiffed salon perfect. Her eyes had the look of a professional tune-up—eyeliner and her full lashes coated with a blue mascara that picked up the light blue in her eyes. She looked tanner than the last time Reed had seen her. She wore a pink cotton turtleneck that accentuated her breasts.

But if her appearance had been intended to perk Reed up, it had the opposite effect. He still felt whupped, both mentally and physically, and he struggled to be cordial.

She had called earlier, asking him what she could bring, and he'd said Levi's, a denim work shirt, and a hundred-dollar loan. Now, as she handed them to him, he thanked her and said that he had heard that she'd signed for him in the emergency room the night before.

She shrugged. "Something like that."

"I appreciate it."

"You asked for me. It was the least I could do."

Reed didn't remember doing any such thing, but took her word for it. Truth was, he couldn't recall much, period. He pictured himself escaping from the fire, taking the ski lift up the Strings, and shooting at the van, but now wondered if he had dreamed it.

Caroline sat at the foot of the bed. She moved her arm to pat him on the leg, but he bristled like a spooked cat. "Sorry," he said. "My legs are banged up pretty bad."

She apologized and tried to make small talk about large matters.

She said that Reed had missed enough news to last a month—the freak blizzard, the fact that his house fire had been arson, the fact that the arsonist had been Culp Jenkins. And on top of all that, there'd been several motor vehicle fatalities. Reed sat up.

"I don't know if you heard, but one of your cronies at *The Transcript* died a few miles from your place last night. Milt Roberts. I think you mentioned him once."

Reed said that they'd had a few beers together, then added: "Good photographer. He took the crime scene shots of Diana Diaz."

"And he ends up dying a couple of miles away from your place the same night that Culp Jenkins tries to torch you. Ironic, no?"

Reed agreed that it was, and felt his stomach muscles tighten.

"His van apparently blew a tire or something during the storm while he was going up Route 71A," Caroline continued. "DOA. I'll spare you the gruesome details, but they got his name from his driver's license and then confirmed the ID through his fingerprints this morning. Neighbors said he'd come up here to get ready for the opening day of hunting season."

Reed asked Caroline whether she knew how much longer he had to stay in the hospital.

She replied that he'd probably be released Sunday, but could probably stay another day if he wanted. She added that the extra day was a good idea, since he'd need to rest up for the media blitz.

"What media blitz?"

"When everybody hears about what a hero you are. About how you solved the murder of that Diaz girl a year ago—but no one would listen to you. About how you insisted, through thick and thin, that the killer was Mr. Sportsman, Culp Jenkins. About how he died trying to burn you to death. . . ."

Caroline was so excited with the prospects that she was oblivious of the hurt in Reed's eyes. "Don't you see, Stuart? It's so exciting. We'll buy you some good clothes for the interviews when you get out. You can stay at my place until we find you someplace new."

"No."

Reed's reply brought her up short. "It's not a bother", she said.

"No. I mean no to everything. No new clothes, no interviews. It's not right. The whole story hasn't come out yet."

"Saving it for a book?"

"I'm not going to write a book—at least not the one you expect."

She looked annoyed.

He tried to explain. "Remember a while ago when you kidded me about how I was the only reporter to ever get fired for a story he never wrote? I'm still that guy—the guy you then proceeded to ignore. I'm not who you think I am, or who you're looking for."

Susan Leith, *The Clarion* cop reporter, arrived last. Reed had told the duty nurse that he was too fatigued to talk to anyone else, but Leith had barged in anyway.

As Leith asked her questions, Reed began to feel better, or at least well enough to get pissed off. Like too many reporters—like Reed himself—she already knew what she would write. She was interviewing Reed solely to cover all the bases in case an editor thought to ask.

From Leith's questions and comments, Reed surmised that she had been talking to Mahr or Holmgren again. Leith said she was working on a story for the Sunday paper on the death of Culp Jenkins, and how it brought two unsolved murder cases to an end. She wanted to know how Reed felt, to be vindicated after all the abuse and ridicule.

Reed wanted to tell her the truth, off the record. But he knew he couldn't trust any reporter with a story this hot—she wouldn't think twice about implicating him in Milt Roberts' death.

Instead, Reed said that from what he understood, the evidence against Jenkins was totally circumstantial. And since Jenkins had never been charged with anything, let alone found guilty, it would be irresponsible to accuse him of murder.

She disagreed. "How's Jenkins going to stop me? Corpses can't sue for libel."

Reed left the hospital by a side door twenty minutes after Susan Leith. He used ten of the hundred dollars that Caroline had floated him to take a cab to his place.

The house was what he expected, a burned-out shell. He made his way to where the living room had been, but nothing was left to salvage. All he could recognize was the twisted metal outline of the fish tank, sitting atop of a pile of smoldering rubble.

Reed stood there and thought about what mattered, and how it all had gone up in smoke—Jeanne, Karen Pettraglia, Culp Jenkins. When his eyes began to smart, he walked away.

The spare key to the Mazda was where he always left it, under the floor mat. He started the engine, revved it a few times, then put it in neutral, and got out of the car.

Reed walked to the edge of the woods across the road and shouted. In his own good time, Culp the cat emerged, yowling at Reed for abandoning him.

Reed planned on heading south to New Jersey. In fact, his Mazda was two miles from Mahwah when he hung the U-turn.

Reed arrived at *The Clarion* at eight P.M. The guard in the lobby said that cats weren't allowed in the newsroom. Reed said that he'd take full responsibility and walked on by.

Two copy editors were at the rim, preparing the last wire stories for typesetting. They stood to shake Reed's hand, but he brushed them off as politely as he could. He set Culp on the floor, and the cat headed under the nearest desk to get some sleep.

Reed asked if Seb Pappas had told them that Reed would be stopping by to fact check Susan Leith's page one story on Culp Jenkins. The copy editors looked at each other uneasily, and said they'd shipped the story. Reed said no problem. He'd read it in CMPDON-NWS, the computer queue where electronic files were sent after typesetting.

Reed logged on to the computer and ignored the blinking "msg pending" in the command field. He called up the Sunday news budget on his VDT, got the computer slug for Leith's story, then called it up on read access.

The story read exactly as Leith had bounced it off Reed. The late Culp Jenkins, the well-known host of a syndicated hunting TV show, had been implicated in two murders of young women. . . .

One of the copy editors stood to leave, and Reed told the other that she was free to go as well. Reed would work the night shift to fill in for the shift that he had missed the night before.

As soon as the copy editors had gone, he called the composing room and told the foreman to hold the start of the press run—he had two new paragraphs coming for the end of the jump of the Jenkins story.

Reed tapped out the two new paragraphs, then wrote a note in longhand and slid it under old man Parisi's door.

Stuart Reed was back on the road when the computerized typesetting machine spewed out the new ending. It would be substituted for Leith's copy without a hitch. The Saturday night composing-room crew rarely read what they pasted up. All they cared about was going home.

As Reed drove south again toward New York City, he allowed himself a wisp of a smile. He rubbed the underside of Culp's neck, and Culp purred.

It had cost a year, a marriage, three more deaths, and untold misery, but with the addition of those two new final paragraphs, he had finally gotten the story right.

   . . . Stuart Reed, a *Clarion* copy editor who resigned last night in protest over the thrust of this story, said that the evidence against Jenkins was totally circumstantial, and that the late TV sportsman would someday be vindicated.

   Reed said that a thorough new investigation into the murders of Diaz and Pettraglia would implicate New Jersey newspaper photographer Milt Roberts, who died in a motor vehicle accident near Reed's house shortly after the fire broke out.